Mixed Blessings

Other Five Star Titles
by Diane Amos:

Getting Personal

Mixed Blessings

Diane Amos

Five Star • Waterville, Maine

First Edition
First Printing: May 2004

Set in 11 pt. Plantin by Liana M. Walker.

Printed in the United States on permanent paper.

Library of Congress Cataloging-in-Publication Data

Amos, Diane.
    Mixed blessings / Diane Amos.—1st ed.
      p. cm.
    ISBN 1-59414-117-7 (hc : alk. paper)
    1. Erotic stories—Authorship—Fiction. 2. Mothers and daughters—Fiction. 3. Women novelists—Fiction. I. Title.
PS3601.M67M59 2004
    813′.6—dc22
                                                2003064708

To my sister,
Linda Blanchard,
with love

Acknowledgments

Thanks to my art students and fellow travelers who've read my chapters, helped me plot out my books, and offered their advice: Mary Gannon, Mary Lou Spencer, Clarinda Andrews, Shirley Hatch, Carol LePage, Sonia Woodrum, Sharon Williams, Dick Grant, Dee St. Pierre, Nat Pilsbury, Gloria Pottle, and Jan Cote. Special thanks to Lucille Bauer and Shirley Beaule for inciting a lively discussion about one particular book and encouraging everyone else to read it.

Thank you, Sue Pelletier, for laughing when you should, Penny Bubier, for keeping me on my guard, and Carole Hodgkins, Gary Price, Nancy Stanley, Vicki Hartford, Lorraine Daigneault, Diana Carrigan, Carol Dulac, Joanne Gastonguay, Mary Dycio, Gale Hasenfus, Sandy Sawyer, and Pat Collins for offering your support.

Chapter One

"Freedom!" I swung my arms triumphantly and smiled at my best friend, Jeannine Lessard.

Jeannine adjusted the wreath of carnations on my head. "I bet you'll miss your mother."

"Never, nada, no way, not on your life."

"Three months is a long time."

"Not long enough." I stole a peek at myself in the mirror. My lacquered curls were subdued with enough hair spray to withstand gale-force winds. Strands of fuchsia beads hung around my neck over a lacy white peasant blouse. My pink toenails peeked from open-toed leather sandals, beneath the hem of a crimson, floral sarong.

The door to my bedroom burst open, and in rushed my mother in a matching lime-green outfit. "I wasn't this nervous when I married your father." She paced the length of the room, nodded at Jeannine, and regarded me. "Monique, you're beautiful. That color does wonders for your pale complexion. While I'm in Europe, I'll keep my eyes open for clothing that'll add pizzazz to your wardrobe."

"Thanks." I somehow refrained from rolling my eyes.

She wrenched her hands. "I'm a wreck. I should have eloped."

"It's a little late to think of that now. Our relatives and friends are waiting at the church." I was pleased with my reply. No one would say Monique St. Cyr, maid of honor and devoted daughter, had ruined her mother's wedding.

When I glanced at my reflection in the mirror, my resolve weakened. I was ready to rip the idiotic-looking flowers from my hair.

My years of parochial schooling surfaced. *Angelic nudge on my right shoulder. It won't kill you to go along with your mother's wishes.*

The familiar stronger tap on my left shoulder. *But enough's enough.*

"The wreath has to go," I said, loosening a hairpin.

My mother issued a long-suffering sigh. "If you feel you must, then go ahead and take it off, but it'll ruin the effect."

Guilt-ridden, I dropped my hands to my sides and nodded in agreement.

She tucked a stray curl behind my ear. "Close your eyes, dear, you could use a little more hair spray."

A thick scented cloud formed over my head.

"I'll worry about you while I'm gone," she said with a sniff.

Through a perfumed haze, I squinted at my mother. "Have a good time. I'll be fine." I frowned so she wouldn't guess how happy I was she was going. I loved her dearly, but some distance would do wonders for our relationship.

No more listening to her advice for my own good.

No more tips on makeup and clothing.

Ninety glorious days!

"I'll miss you, Mom, but I want you to have the time of your life." *I certainly will.*

She fidgeted with a folded piece of paper. "This is our itinerary in case you need to reach me. Also, I've written a few important things I'd like you to do for me while I'm gone." She slipped the paper under the jewelry box on my bureau.

"I won't need to reach you, and I'll take care of every detail on your list."

"I feel better, dear," she said with a wobbly smile.

"Do you want me to read what you've written in case I have any questions?"

"We don't have time now, dear. The limousine will be here any minute."

I hugged my mother in a heartfelt embrace.

"E-mail, I'm taking along my laptop. Of course, I'll be busy with Frank so don't expect me to reply right away. A bride has to take care of her new husband."

"Mother!"

As we stood in the church vestibule, Matthew and Mark, my five- and six-year-old nephews, tugged at my skirt.

Mark stretched the elastic band of his bow tie and let it snap against the collar of his white dress shirt. "You know what, Auntie Monique, we're wearing monkey suits."

My brother, Thomas, chuckled under his breath.

I shot Thomas a you-should-be-ashamed look and patted Mark's head. "Your father might look like a baboon, but you're handsome in that tuxedo."

"Me, too." Matthew pulled the bow tie like a slingshot.

"Yes," I said, kissing his cheek. "You're a good-looking dude."

My mother peeked outside. Cold January air filtered into the room. "Your grandfather and your Aunt Lilly should have been here hours ago."

"I was surprised they decided to drive all the way from Texas instead of flying," I said, shutting the door so we wouldn't freeze.

"They wanted a chance to see the sights, and your aunt wanted to practice her driving."

"Did Aunt Lilly finally get her license?"

"No, the examiner walked behind the car and instructed her to switch on the lights. While squeezing her rabbit's foot, she twisted the key and tried to put the car in drive. She mistook the gas pedal for the brake and slammed her foot down. Your grandfather's '55 Oldsmobile bolted in reverse. Thankfully, the examiner dove onto the trunk or who knows what might have happened." My mother sighed. "Poor Lilly might never get her license."

"It's probably for the best."

"Your aunt says just sitting behind the wheel of any car gives her a bad case of the vapors."

I shook my head. "Vapors?"

"Dizzy, fainthearted."

"No one talks that way."

"Your aunt does," my mother pointed out. "Anyway, she's a lot less self-reliant than us. Though Lilly is younger than I am, she's always acted older, maybe because she spent so much time taking care of our mother. I don't want you to give her a hard time while she's here. And remember, Lilly has very tender feelings."

"Sheesh, I'm not a kid. I know how to act." Dealing with my aunt would require all the patience I could muster.

Perpetual blush on her pale cheeks, Aunt Lilly didn't laugh, but instead uttered a high-pitched tee hee hee that grated on my nerves. She fluttered gloved hands nervously about her face whenever men were present. An odd duck, I thought, but I kept my opinion to myself. "Between you and me, I've never met anyone as superstitious. It's hard to believe the two of you are sisters."

"Your aunt has a few idiosyncrasies."

Clearly, an understatement.

"We should have brought along the hair spray." My

mother toyed with a curl along the side of my face. "Lilly's a dear, and there's nothing she wouldn't do for you. I only wish you two had an opportunity to get to know each other better."

"That is too bad," I said, frowning convincingly.

"You mean it?" my mother asked.

"Of course."

Angelic tap on my right shoulder. *Sin alert—telling lies in church!*

Tiny white lies, I countered to myself, and expected a bolt of lightning to pierce my heart as I continued, "Anyway, I'll make the most of our short time together, but it's too bad Aunt Lilly and Gramps live so far away." I said a fervent prayer of thanks for small favors.

My mother smiled with satisfaction. "This marriage is truly a mixed blessing." She ticked off on her fingers: "A husband for me, a stepfather for you, and as a bonus, you get to visit with your aunt and your grandfather."

Spending time with my aunt was small peanuts compared to being with my grandfather. Partially deaf, with an eye for the ladies, Gramps whispered inappropriate comments in loud tones while my aunt tried to quiet him, tee hee heed, and fluttered her hands. The two together for prolonged periods would send me to the loony farm. But I could put up with my relatives for a short while.

"Thomas, maybe you should call the state police and ask whether there are reports of an accident on the turnpike," my mother said, nodding toward my brother.

Matthew dipped his fingers in the holy water font and sent a spray of water over his brother. Thomas settled a firm hand on his youngest son's shoulder and dabbed Mark's face with a white handkerchief he pulled from his pocket. "I already checked. There've been no accidents."

"Gramps is a careful driver," I reminded my mother so she'd stop worrying. Truth was, Gramps was a threat to everyone on the road. When conditions were optimum, he revved up the Olds to a whopping thirty-five miles per hour. I pictured a line of traffic from Kittery to Portland as he straddled both lanes and crawled along, oblivious to the blaring horns and arm gestures behind him. And God help us all if Aunt Lilly was behind the wheel.

The organ resonated with the first chords of "Here Comes the Bride."

My mother yanked the door open for one last look. "I'll just feel better when they arrive."

"Stop worrying," I said.

She dashed a tear from the corner of her eye. "I'll miss you while I'm gone."

"Same here," I said.

Mark and Matthew started down the aisle, holding satin pillows with fake rings attached to crimson and green bows. I came next on wobbly legs, my fingers wrapped around a bouquet of pink carnations.

When I reached the front of the church, I turned. Though my brother would never hear it from me, he looked gorgeous in his black tuxedo as he escorted my mother down the aisle.

Truly a radiant bride, my mother walked toward her future husband. The instant their eyes met, their faces glowed with love. My mother brushed past me and reached for Frank's extended hand.

Sometime later everyone hushed as the bride and groom exchanged vows. Even my nephews were silent. My emotions churned as I watched the happy couple. I could be next. A ripple of anxiety shot through me.

Jake Dube, the love of my life, had proposed. And I'd said yes. I still wanted to get married, but not within a year as I'd promised. I needed more time to build my career as an investigative reporter. Somehow, I had to make Jake understand.

I also had mixed feelings about my mother getting married. She could be a real pain in the neck, but she was *my* pain in the neck. We'd grown close over the years, and until now, I hadn't had to share her with anyone. Our relationship would drastically change. She'd always be my mother, but a big part of her would now belong to Frank.

I dabbed a tear from the corner of my eye.

Our pastor, Father Willingham, smiled down at my mother and Frank. "I now pronounce you husband and wife."

The door to the vestibule opened and shut. "Hot damn, Lilly, did you take a gander at that little filly!"

"Shussssh, tee hee hee."

My mother looked visibly relieved.

You can do this, you can do this, you can do this, I chanted to myself. I was a grown woman. I could deal with Gramps and Aunt Lilly for a few days.

A week at the most!

At the reception Aunt Lilly sat ramrod-straight, her back against the chair, and her feet flat on the floor. She wore a dove-gray cotton dress with a high collar and long sleeves buttoned at her wrists; the familiar bottle of smelling salts wrapped in a clean hankie bulged beneath her cuff.

Gramps wore a white ten-gallon Stetson, rope tie, a Western shirt, and black dress pants. The heel of one snakeskin boot was hooked over the chair rung. Though no one would guess by his appearance, he's never ridden a horse and until ten years ago had resided in Boston, Massachusetts.

Aunt Lilly whispered. "It breaks my heart to see you pining away while your mother fights off suitors."

I laughed. "I'm not pining for anyone."

"Two marriages in one lifetime doesn't seem fair when some of us can't manage to snag one man."

"Snag a man!" I downed my flute of champagne and refilled my glass. *You can do this, you can do this, you can do this.* A few days. A week at the most!

The sound of silverware clinking glasses rang throughout the banquet room. Frank stood, pulled my mother to her feet, and kissed her soundly. The guests cheered.

The pinging intensified.

Frank bent my mother backwards. She wrapped her arms around his neck, encouraging the embrace.

Aunt Lilly tapped her forehead with a lace handkerchief and gasped for breath. "Goodness gracious, at this rate, those two will be doing the dastardly deed right before our eyes."

Frank and my mother came up for air.

Gramps thumbed his hat back. His gaze traveled over a shapely woman wearing a polka-dotted skirt. "Son of a gun, Lilly, reminds me of that Appaloosa we had a few years back."

"Shussh, tee hee hee." Lilly waved her hand in front of her face.

"Dad, speak softly," my mother warned.

"Huh! What'd ya say?"

I wanted to crawl under the table and hide. When I swung around to see who was staring at us, I knocked a fork and spoon on the floor with my elbow.

Lilly leaned toward me. "You know what that means, don't you?"

"Yes, that I'm clumsy."

"You'll be getting some company. A spoon means a female will drop in, a fork means a male. You'll have a full house unless you throw that knife down."

I stared at her incredulously.

"The knife," she said with certainty, "will cancel your company. Go ahead and heave it onto the floor."

Restraining myself from doing bodily harm, I curled my fingers around the plastic knife handle. "I don't believe in this dribble."

"It never hurts to be safe," Lilly replied with conviction.

Under the table, my mother's foot connected with my ankle.

You can do this, you can do this, you can do this. "I like company."

"I'm glad to hear that."

My mother turned to her sister. "Monique was saying it's such a shame you two haven't had the chance to really get acquainted."

"That's so sweet." Lilly traced a gloved finger over the condensation on her glass of champagne. "I feel very close to you even though we live far apart. We have so much in common."

"You're absolutely right." From what I could see, we had nothing in common.

My mother sent me an approving nod.

I smiled at my aunt. "From now on, we'll call each other every week and e-mail often."

"The art of letter writing has almost become extinct," Lilly said with a shrug.

"A computer can be lots of fun," I added enthusiastically.

"Love computers," Gramps said. Heads turned as he continued in a booming voice. "Bought myself a Pentium 4 from Radio Shack a few months ago and got hooked up to a cable modem. Hot damn, I can download pictures of fine-looking cowgals in seconds."

"Shussh, Papa, tee hee hee." Lilly reached over me to tap his arm.

I swore under my breath.

Mother gave me the hairy eyeball.

I took the hint and smiled demurely at Gramps. "I'll e-mail you often so we can keep in touch."

"You're a darlin' granddaughter," he said, in a tone heard across the room.

My mother managed a strained smile. I knew she doubted my ability to deal with my relatives. Well, I'd show her! This was my mother's special day. Under no circumstances would I ruin it. No way, nohow. No! I'd sit here and bide my time, my manners intact and my mouth shut.

First Frank and my mother danced. The DJ then played a waltz while the bride danced with her father. My mother looked happy; Gramps looked happy. Everyone looked happy except for Aunt Lilly.

"Too bad," Lilly whispered. "I know what you're going through."

Since I'd decided to ignore her bantering, I nodded in agreement and lifted the glass to my lips. Champagne dulled my senses and lessened my irritation toward my aunt. After two glasses, she seemed quite nice. A few more ounces and her dress no longer looked dowdy. "Great outfit," I said.

"Thanks. A woman should dress modestly, I always say."

"Absolutely." I lifted my glass. "Here's to modesty."

She toasted with her water glass.

"You don't drink?"

"I don't imbibe."

"Here's to imbibing or not imbibing," I toasted.

"Alcoholic spirits can lower a woman's guard. I won't allow the devil to dance in my shoes."

Here's to dancing devils. I swung my glass. "Here's to my fa-

16

vorite aunt. May we keep in touch with lots of phone calls and daily e-mails."

"I'll drink to that," Aunt Lilly said, sipping ice water.

The DJ played "The Twist," and I stood to join the group forming on the dance floor. "Let's go, it'll be fun."

"I'd rather not," she replied, glancing at her feet.

"Then I'll stay here, too."

Aunt Lilly stood and sidled up next to me. "It's a shame your mother beat you to the altar."

"You make it sound like a race," I said, sounding a little annoyed. I reined in my irritation and smiled.

Wringing her gloved hands and looking pathetically shy, Aunt Lilly exhaled a shaky breath. "I understand how you must feel. It's tough on me, too."

"In what way?"

"Well . . ." Aunt Lilly shuffled her no-nonsense black shoe along the hardwood floor. "Weddings are embarrassing. I notice the pitiful glances aimed at me." She rested her hand on my wrist. "Poor Lilly, the relatives are whispering. What a shame she can't find herself a man."

"I doubt anyone thinks that."

"I know they do, and they say plenty more. They refer to me as *the poor dear*. *The poor dear* can't even get her driver's license."

Lilly heaved a frustrated sigh. "But I don't mind. I've accepted my situation. In fact, I'm quite satisfied with my life just the way it is."

"And you should be happy. Nowadays, a woman doesn't need a man to feel complete. Being a career woman is nothing to be ashamed of," I said, sending her a fortifying smile.

She bit the inside of her right cheek. "Back in my day, a career woman was called an old maid. Career woman sounds a lot better, but it still means the same darn thing."

The hair at my nape stirred. "I am not an old maid. Neither are you," I added, again expecting a bolt of lightning to strike me.

"Don't mollycoddle me," Lilly said, her eyes tearing.

"I have a man in my life," I added, doing my damnedest to prove I was not and never would be an old maid, and instantly regretted I felt it necessary to defend myself.

Aunt Lilly glanced at me timidly. "I've accepted the fact I'm an old maid, but I see you're still fighting the obvious."

I counted slowly to ten, reached over the table, and sipped more champagne.

"Your mother mentioned you had a beau, but since he's not here, I assumed he'd already skedaddled."

"Jake hasn't gone anywhere." Excitement bubbled in my chest as I remembered our lovemaking earlier that morning. Memories of Jake's tongue sliding over my breasts sent a tingle up my spine. Poor Aunt Lilly would need her smelling salts if she could read my mind. "Jake's working, but he should be here soon."

"I don't see a ring on your finger." Lilly craned her neck to check out my left hand.

"I plan to concentrate on my career before I settle down. The world has changed since you were my age. Women have more options."

My aunt glanced at me with doubt-filled eyes. "You don't have to try to save face with me. We're both old maids, career women if you prefer."

"Jake wants me to marry him."

"If that were true, he'd give you a ring."

A losing battle, I decided, giving up the fight gracefully.

Several minutes later Jake came up behind me and kissed my neck. Leaning into him, I inhaled his masculine scent. "I was just telling my aunt about you."

He beamed a charming grin at Lilly. "Glad to meet you."

Aunt Lilly's lips thinned as she shook his hand and peered at him with distrust.

Jake had to be the best-looking man at the reception. Tall, wide shoulders, smothering brown eyes directed at me. Wowza!

"I'm going to get myself a drink. Would you ladies like anything?" he asked.

"None for me," my aunt answered, covering her mouth with her glove.

"The bottle of champagne at our table is running low," I mentioned. "Please hurry back."

When Jake left, Aunt Lilly fanned herself with her lace hankie. "What does he do for employment?"

"He's a policeman."

"Ohhhh," she stretched out, worry streaking across her face. "Policemen have a very high divorce rate."

"So I've heard."

"He has that look about him."

"What look?"

"A devilish glint in his eyes."

"Yes, isn't it great?"

"I'd be mighty wary if I were you."

I nodded because it was easier than arguing.

The master of ceremonies picked up the microphone and waved his arm in an arc. "All you single ladies meet me in the center of the room and stand in a half-circle around the bride."

I pulled Lilly along.

"Goodness gracious." Aunt Lilly skidded to a stop. "Go on without me."

"What's wrong?"

"I don't want to catch the flowers."

"Why not?"

I grabbed my aunt's arm and ushered her into the middle of the dance floor where my mother stood, spearing me with a warning look.

My aunt fled, but I caught up with her several feet away.

Her pupils narrowed to pinpricks. "I'll not budge one more inch. I'm not taking part in this depravity."

Maybe the champagne had numbed my brain, or maybe I'd simply lost my mind, but for reasons I didn't fully comprehend, I tugged at Aunt Lilly, unwilling to take no for an answer.

"Catching the bouquet will be fun."

She slapped my hands away.

"You need to loosen up."

"You're loose enough for the both of us."

"Come on, we're heads taller than those other women. We stand a good chance of winning. That's it, the missing link! We do have lots in common," I said to my aunt, who seemed pleased at my discovery. "We look alike. We have the same unruly hair." *We're both big-busted and wide through the hips.* Fortunately, I hadn't consumed enough champagne to broadcast that fact.

"I'm glad you finally see the light, but I'd rather not catch the bouquet."

"Let's go!" I insisted.

I heard a drumroll.

I pulled at Lilly.

The bouquet bounced off my head and landed in Lilly's extended arms.

"Goodness gracious," my aunt mumbled.

My friend Jeannine and another woman held Lilly's arms as she half-walked, half-stumbled to a chair in the center of the room where the single men gathered around Frank, waiting for him to throw the garter.

Jake came up behind me.

"How come you're here instead of there?" I asked with a nod.

He pulled out a scrap of lace from his pocket and wrapped his arm around my waist. "There's no need. Frank slipped me a spare garter. I figured I'd put it on you later tonight."

"Maybe," I said, angling my head and kissing him.

He grinned. "There's no maybe about it."

Gooseflesh peppered my arms as I met his heated gaze. I flashed a saucy smile.

I heard another drumroll and watched grown men fall over themselves. One fist closed around the garter.

I didn't recognize the man until he turned, the garter dangling from his little finger like a trophy.

My boss, editor of the Portland Enquirer, *Mr. Winters!*

Fortunately, Mr. Winters was a gentleman, a man who conducted himself with decorum.

My aunt had nothing to worry about.

Aunt Lilly stared at the garter in Mr. Winters's hand and crossed her legs.

My boss dropped to one knee, fondled her ankle, and wiggled his gray eyebrows. "Sweetheart, before I'm through, you and I will no longer be strangers."

The men hooted and cheered.

"You, sir, are an uncouth barbarian. A despicable savage!" Aunt Lilly fluttered gloved hands in front of her face and fainted dead away.

Chapter Two

Filled with guilt, I elbowed my way to my aunt's side. "Should I call a doctor?"

"No, Lilly will be fine." My mother flicked the bottle of smelling salts under her sister's nose.

"How can you be sure she'll be all right?"

My mother peeked under Lilly's eyelid. "She'll come to any second, she always does."

I sighed with relief.

"Monique, while Lilly's in Maine, I expect you to shelter her from stressful situations."

I nodded and knelt on the floor. "Aunt Lilly, can you hear me? I'm a horrible niece. I should have never insisted you try to catch the bouquet."

I studied my aunt, sitting there, head cocked slightly to one side, her hands crossed on her lap. Even unconscious, she looked ladylike and dignified. If I fainted, I'd be sprawled on the floor, skirt up to my waist, drool in the corner of my mouth.

My mother's accusing gaze cut through me. "Your aunt has a delicate nature. You should have respected her wishes."

"She's my flesh and blood!" I said, my voice ringing with champagne-induced euphoria. "Give her credit for having some guts."

Aunt Lilly's eyelids fluttered. Her lips pursed, and she

wrapped her gloved fingers around my wrist. "Thank you, Monique, that's the nicest thing anyone has ever said about me."

Our blue eyes met. I felt a strong bond with the stranger who called herself my aunt. I wanted to help Lilly escape her boring existence. I wanted her to eat, drink, be merry, and maybe dance naked in the rain.

But I couldn't do much for Aunt Lilly because she'd be leaving in a few days, a week at the most. I issued a silent cheer.

Soon, everyone would be gone. No doubt, my life would go to pot, but I'd have a great time reaching my destination.

"I don't approve of that look on your face," my mother said as we helped Aunt Lilly to her feet and escorted her to our table.

I smiled innocently and lifted my glass of champagne in the air. "Here's to my favorite aunt, Lilly. Here's to a life filled with stamina and adventure."

Lilly lowered herself onto a chair. "A life of stamina and adventure," she repeated softly, a look of awe in her eyes. "If only that were true."

"Is your luggage in the Olds?" my mother asked Gramps sometime later.

"Darn tooting," he replied, eyeing a voluptuous female.

"Good, you can stay at my duplex."

Gramps swung his gaze toward my mother. "Lilly and I figured we'd rent a couple rooms at the Holiday Inn."

"You most certainly will not! There's no reason to throw away good money while my duplex is sitting empty."

Trepidation streaked down my spine.

"I won't hear of it," my mother insisted.

Frank reached for my mother's hand. "Let's show your father your duplex now. Before we leave, we'll say our final good-byes."

"Great idea," my mother said, smiling approvingly at her husband.

"Would you like to dance?" Jake asked me, nibbling on my earlobe.

"I can't abandon Aunt Lilly."

"Then let me find someone to dance with her."

Jake disappeared before I could object.

"How do you feel about waltzing with a handsome gentleman?" I asked my aunt.

"I don't dance."

"Oh." I refilled my glass. "Here, take a sip of this."

"I already told you I don't drink."

"I know, but champagne at a wedding is not really drinking. Anyway you'll like the way the bubbles tickle your nose."

"But I shouldn't."

I pushed a champagne flute into her hands. "It'll take a few swallows for you to feel the bubbles."

Her eyes clouded with indecision. "I wouldn't want to imbibe and make a fool of myself."

"Don't worry, I'll keep an eye on you."

My mother wrapped tight fingers around my arm. "Monique, I need to speak with you for a moment."

"About what?"

"Privately," she said out of the corner of her mouth, pulling me to my feet.

I stepped away from the table.

My mother inhaled a deep breath. "What do you think you're doing?"

I shrugged. "What do you mean?"

"Lilly is like a fragile butterfly. You need to honor her

wishes. She's told you she doesn't drink, so accept it."

"I want her to have some fun."

"She is having fun."

"How can you tell?"

"She's a mellow kind of person."

"You mean boring." I cast a glance at my aunt, skeptically eyeing the champagne in her glass.

"She likes her life so don't go trying to change it. Promise me you'll behave yourself while I'm gone."

"Of course, I'll behave."

"Under no circumstances do I want to get reports of you corrupting my sister."

"There's not a chance of that. Lilly won't even drink one sip of champagne."

"Good, see that she doesn't." My mother's eyes misted. "I'll keep in touch. I love you." We hugged and kissed.

I blamed the alcohol for the tears in my eyes. "Don't worry about a thing."

"I'm a mother. Worrying is what I do best."

A few minutes later I sat down next to Aunt Lilly and watched my grandfather leave the reception with my mother and Frank.

Lilly stared into the glass of champagne.

"It won't bite," I said, laughing at my wit and nudging my aunt's hand and the glass toward her mouth.

She took a small swallow and puckered her lips. "It's kind of like ginger ale, but different."

"Different good or different bad?"

"I'm not sure."

"Drink a little more so you can decide."

She lifted the glass to her mouth, swallowed, and sat deep in thought for a few seconds. "It's not half-bad. Tee hee hee, you're right about the bubbles tickling my nose."

Jake leaned over and kissed me, his hand on my knee under the table. "I'm horny as hell," he whispered, his eyes blazing with lust.

"Wowza," I said in a throaty voice.

"Would you care to dance?" Mr. Winters asked Aunt Lilly, his voice startling me.

Lilly turned, her face blazing with indignation. "You, sir, are a loathsome hooligan!"

Mr. Winters uttered a hearty laugh. "I've been called lots of names, but never a hooligan."

Aunt Lilly fluttered gloved hands about her face.

"He's my boss," I whispered to her. "Dance with him as a favor to me."

She threw him a haughty look. "I'd rather dance with Satan himself."

Wiggling his eyebrows, Mr. Winters reached for Aunt Lilly's hand. "I fancy myself a devil of sorts."

"The man is a lunatic," my aunt whispered in my ear.

"Remember, he's my boss."

"I need to defend my virtue."

"He only wants to dance."

"He's no gentleman. I saw the glint in his eyes when he held the garter. The words from his mouth were abominable."

Mr. Winters planted a kiss on Lilly's upturned palm. "Mysterious lady, you've piqued my curiosity. Honor me with this dance."

After a prolonged moment of silence, Mr. Winters cupped his hand under her elbow and escorted a protesting Aunt Lilly to the dance floor.

"Have you lost your mind coming back here with Mr. Winters? It'll be your fault if Aunt Lilly faints again," I said to Jake, who wrapped a possessive arm around my waist and pulled me to my feet.

"Your boss was the only man willing to dance with your aunt. Besides, I have a feeling the old gal is stronger than she seems."

"It's sad, don't you think, the way she's going through life without experiencing it? I wouldn't want that for myself."

Jake's intent gaze raked the embers in my stomach. "You have nothing to worry about. Just wait until I get you alone tonight."

"Copper, you're a hot-blooded hooligan."

"Is that a complaint?"

"No, definitely a compliment," I murmured, leaning my head against his shoulders and swaying to the slow beat of the music.

I awoke the next morning with a pounding head, a furred tongue, and gritty eyeballs. I threw an arm over my face and groaned.

"Wake up, sleepyhead," Jake said, his cheerful voice drilling into my skull.

"Go away."

"That's not what you were saying last night."

A memory of our lovemaking flicked through my brain. "Mmmm," I murmured, basking in the warmth that spread through my belly.

"I need to go to work. Will you be all right?"

"As long as I don't move my head, I'll be fine."

Jake frowned. "I warned you about drinking too much champagne."

I blinked an eye open. "It's not every day a daughter attends her mother's wedding."

"So you said several times last night. Your grandfather came over earlier to borrow some coffee. I let him take your parrot, Long John, next door to their duplex."

"The last thing that bird needs is time alone with Gramps."

Jake bent down and kissed me. "You might want to check on your aunt."

"Why, is something wrong?" I managed to sit up, pushed my legs over the side of the bed, and steadied myself with both hands.

"She's probably hungover, too."

"Aunt Lilly doesn't drink."

"She did last night, thanks to you. Fortunately, she only had a few glasses of champagne."

I focused on the last hour of the wedding reception. "I remember doing the bunny hop."

"Think a little harder."

I squeezed my eyes shut and concentrated. "Oh, no! Aunt Lilly was hopping right alongside me!"

I dragged myself off the bed and pulled the remains of my leather belt from the mouth of my bulldog, Cobbler. Keeping my head stiff, I made it to the bathroom, washed my face, combed my hair, slipped on a loose-fitting sweatshirt and sweatpants, and left my duplex.

Gramps answered the door. "Darlin', isn't this nice, starting the day off by seeing my granddaughter. I was just going to cook myself some bacon and eggs. Care to join me?"

My stomach convulsed. "I'll pass, thank you."

"Or maybe you'd prefer one of my specialty omelets. I toss in everything, including sardines."

Gagging, I covered my mouth with my hand. "Please don't talk about food."

"I see," he said, opening the refrigerator. "Have you tried tomato juice? It works every time."

"I'll keep that in mind." I glanced into my mother's bedroom and saw my aunt under the covers with a towel over her face. "How's Aunt Lilly doing?"

"Either she's hungover or we should be calling the undertaker." Gramps threw bacon into the frying pan.

The smell gagged me; the sizzling punctured my eardrums.

"Great knockers," Long John squawked, bobbing his head in front of his mirror.

"That's the smartest bird I've ever seen. Learns quick, too. Listen to this." Gramps slapped his backside and said, "Nice butt."

Long John eyed my grandfather and tipped his head to one side. "Nice butt, nice butt, nice butt."

With a groan, I tiptoed into the bedroom and shut the door to dull Gramps's raucous laughter and the nauseous breakfast smells. I crossed the room. "Aunt Lilly," I whispered, running my hand along the sleeve of her flannel nightgown. Her fingers were like mine, I noticed—long with blunt nails.

"I feel terrible," I said, remorse gnawing at my conscience.

She moaned. "Me, too."

"It's my fault you drank the champagne."

"No one held a pistol to my skull."

"I hope you'll forgive me."

She slid the towel from her face and squinted. Her bloodshot eyes stood out in her green-tinged complexion. "My hair follicles throb."

"By tomorrow you'll be back to your old self."

"That's nothing to get excited about."

"You're saying that now because you're too weak to think positively. You're an attractive older woman," I said, eyeing her drab gray hair.

"I'm boring."

"No, you're not. We had one devil of a time last night."

Aunt Lilly groaned. "I remember very little about last night."

"My memory's also a bit foggy."

"Maybe it's for the best."

I managed to smile. "Your visit in Maine is too short to be worrying about the past. Let's concentrate on the time we have left together."

"Monique, I wish I were more like you."

I rested the palm of my hand over her forehead to check her temperature. "You're in worse shape than I thought."

"I mean it. You may be an old maid like me, but it doesn't seem to bother you. You are the most confident woman I know."

The words "old maid" drummed inside my head like a tom-tom. "I work at that image. Inside I'm a mass of insecurity." I couldn't believe I'd confided that to my aunt.

"You're a dear, dear niece. I love you more than words can ever explain."

Mushy feelings coursed through my body, due either to residual alcohol in my bloodstream or a temporary lapse of sanity. "You're my favorite aunt, and I'm really looking forward to spending time with you."

"I'm glad to hear you say that."

"I only regret we have just a few short days together."

"Me, too."

"We bonded last night. We're a pair of single women on the prowl."

Aunt Lilly propped herself onto one elbow, her gaze searching my face. "You aren't just saying this to be nice?"

Maybe I was, but I owed her. No matter how much she denied it, I was at fault for her hangover. "If it were possible, I'd love nothing better than to live next door to you all year long."

My aunt dropped back onto the pillow, her face glowing from my praise. Contrary to my parochial school training, I sincerely believed white lies were not a sin when told for a person's own good. Clearly, my small untruth had given Aunt Lilly much happiness.

My guardian angel's familiar nudge to my right shoulder interrupted my thoughts. *You never learn. Your lies always come back to haunt you.*

White lies, I countered smugly.

My aunt reached for my hand. "Before going to bed last night, a brilliant idea struck me."

I nodded approvingly. "Some of my best inspiration comes right before I fall asleep."

"Until this very minute, I wasn't so sure, but I've decided to make some changes in my life." Her red-rimmed eyes widened with excitement.

"I'm proud of you."

"I've decided to live here until your mother returns from her honeymoon."

Surely, my ears had deceived me. "That's three months."

"Precisely."

"What about Gramps?"

"He's looking forward to seeing a nor'easter."

Chapter Three

Jeannine shook her head. "Tough break."

"I don't know why I can't keep my big mouth shut."

"You're like the Energizer Bunny. You never stop."

My cat, Taffy, stretched her neck appreciatively as I rubbed between her ears. "This time I've learned my lesson. And I'll be paying for three long months. Ninety excruciating days!"

"What are you going to do?"

"Who in their right mind would want to spend the winter in Maine?"

"Snow is exciting to someone who hasn't seen it in a while."

"I guess so."

Jeannine tapped a pencil on the tablet I kept by the phone. "Maybe they'll change their minds and leave after the first blizzard."

"It's my only hope. Meanwhile, according to my aunt, we girls are going to have ourselves a rollicking good time. She even expects me to give her driving lessons."

"Your aunt is rather . . . old-fashioned."

"She'll cramp my style. I'd looked forward to my mother leaving. Now I have two people living next door. I'm in worse shape than before!"

"Chances are everything will work out better than you think."

"This is a disaster."

"You need to get your mind on something else. Maybe we should go to the mall."

"Or maybe we should go to the shooting range. I'll be the target."

Jeannine laughed. "See, you're feeling better already."

"No, I'm not."

"You're joking around."

"I was being serious."

She pulled me off the couch. "Let's get some fresh air and go for a ride."

"If you insist." I rose and entered my bedroom in search of my jacket and hat.

Jeannine followed me.

"I can kiss my freedom good-bye."

"Maybe you and your aunt will be good for each other."

I grabbed my jacket from the chair and slipped my arms into the sleeves. "I don't see how. We're so different."

"That's just it. She seems so cautious and ladylike. You on the other hand . . . well . . . I think you could learn a lot from each other. Look at it as an experiment."

"I'd rather conduct the experiment via e-mail." When I pulled my hat off the bureau, a slip of paper floated to the floor.

Jeannine bent down and handed it to me.

"This is my mother's itinerary and list of what she wants me to do while she's gone. I'm not up to reading whatever she wrote."

"Aren't you curious?"

"I've already had my quota of bad news for one day."

Jeannine tugged the paper from my hand.

Before I could stop her, she'd unfolded my mother's note. As she read, her mouth turned up. Small lines crinkled from the corners of her eyes. She then threw back her head and laughed. "You better not look at this for at least a month."

Too curious to wait any longer, I grabbed the paper and scanned down the list of phone numbers and hotels where my mother and Frank would be staying. In italics at the bottom of the page were these words: *I need an itty-bitty favor.*

I gritted my teeth.

Monique, I know you said never again, but I'm counting on you to do the research for my next erotic fiction. Now stop frowning. It's very unbecoming. In time, those creases will become permanent.

My hero is a live-on-the-edge kind of guy, a retired para-trooper, looking for excitement and adventure. My heroine will provide him with plenty of both. Anyway, when I return, my deadline will be looming. I couldn't very well have Frank go on our honeymoon alone. But if you can't help me out, I'll understand. Just call the number on this list, and I'll return home on the next flight.

P.S. I've signed you up for a few classes. Jot down some notes as you leap from the plane! Oh, one more thing, ask the instructor whether it's possible for two people to have sex while dangling from parachutes.

"I should call her bluff and tell her to come home," I said to Jeannine.

"So what are you going to do?"

"I couldn't live with myself if I ruined my mother's honey-moon."

When Jake arrived later that afternoon, I was lying on the couch, staring blankly at the television screen.

I groaned. "As I see it, it's either them or me. Ninety days with Aunt Lilly and Gramps will drive me crazy. You might as well help me dig a hole in the backyard because I'm going to need it to hide the bodies."

Jake kissed me. "So they've decided to stay."

I sighed. "Yup. You better put me in a straitjacket before you leave, or I won't be responsible for my actions."

"Get up. I have something special to show you."

"What?"

"It's a surprise," he said with a wink. "I hope when you return, you'll be too happy to worry about your next-door neighbors."

"Sounds very interesting. Can you give me a hint?"

He grinned. "Nope."

I ran into the bedroom to change into wool slacks and a turtleneck. I threw on my jacket, wrapped a scarf around my neck, grabbed my purse, and taking Jake's hand, rushed out the door.

"Such enthusiasm," he said, claiming my mouth in a long kiss that under other circumstances would have had us dashing back inside and postponing our departure.

"All day I've tried to chase away the blahs. I can't wait to see what you have in mind." I hopped into his pickup and fastened my seat belt. "I feel better already. Who knows, maybe Jeannine is right, maybe the ninety days will fly by." Who was I trying to kid? Fortunately, I'd have Jake to keep my mind off my troubles.

Jake hopped in and slammed the door shut. "I love you," he said, squeezing my hand and putting his truck in gear.

"Me, too."

"You have trouble saying the words," he pointed out.

Jake was right. I'd been hurt too often to take the small phrase lightly. "I love you," I said, because it was true, and he expected me to say it.

"The day you agreed to marry me, you made me the happiest man on earth."

Apprehension tightened the muscles between my shoulders. Last month I'd been promoted to rookie investigative reporter at the *Portland Enquirer*. I needed more time to focus on my career. I needed to postpone our wedding. I figured in a year we'd become engaged. In two years, we'd get married. I prayed Jake would understand, but I feared he wouldn't.

"I can see our children running and playing in our fenced-in backyard, little Monique, mud-streaked face, leading little Jake through a puddle." Our smiling gazes met in the rear-view mirror.

I playfully punched his arm. "Maybe our children will all be boys."

"I'm not giving up until we have ourselves a little girl even if it takes a dozen tries."

"Ouch!" I forced a laugh.

He was kidding, but that didn't ease the trepidation stirring the small hairs at the base of my skull. I loved babies, but they required lots of attention, more time than I was willing to give, at least until I'd established my career. In a couple of years, I'd be ready to settle down.

"According the December issue of *Vogue* magazine, lots of women have babies well into their thirties and even their forties," I pointed out.

"If we have our children while we're young, we'll be able to enjoy them more as they grow up." He stole a glance in the rearview mirror. "We're going to have a wonderful life together," he said with warmth in his voice.

Because I didn't want to ruin the evening, I postponed telling Jake what was in my heart. Very soon, we'd have a serious talk.

But tonight, I wasn't up to a confrontation.

He pulled his truck into a space in the mall parking lot. "I thought we'd grab a bite to eat in the food court. But first, I have to show you what I'm buying for you."

"Give me a tiny hint."

"Not on your life," he replied, enjoying himself.

I ran my hand up his knee. "Copper, do you take bribes?"

"You're shameless. Get out of the truck before I decide to spend a little time in the backseat."

"Just one hint?"

He opened the driver's door. "If you get your fanny out of my truck, you'll know soon enough."

I looped my arm through his and we walked into the mall.

Smiling, we strolled the mall corridor glancing into shops. Since Jake had complained about watching television on my nineteen-inch, I envisioned a wide-screen TV in my living room. Or maybe he'd bought a king-size bed because he liked to sprawl while he slept.

I placed my bets on the television and was mentally re-arranging the living room furniture when he turned into a jewelry store and led me to a lit counter with sparkling diamond rings.

I wasn't ready for this.

A salesman hurried toward us. "I'm glad you made it back before the store closed," he said, smiling at Jake and removing a lovely marquise solitaire from the display case.

Face beaming with happiness, Jake picked up the ring and held it a few inches from my nose. "What do you think?"

Tears clogged my throat.

"It's stunning," I replied, biting back a sob.

"Would you prefer a different cut?"

I'd never seen a more beautiful ring. "No, it's perfect." Bad timing. Much too soon.

"Let me size your finger," the salesman said, taking my hand and slipping a cold band over my knuckle.

I felt trapped. Sweat beaded my forehead. I wanted to

faint like Aunt Lilly. Needing to escape, I glanced into Jake's startled face and ran from the store.

Jake barely spoke to me on the way home. He pulled his truck into my yard and escorted me to my door.

"Aren't you going to come inside?" I asked, tugging at his hand.

"I can't. I need some time to think."

"Why can't you understand how I feel? I'm only asking you to delay our wedding for one more year."

"That's what you say, but I've been there before. Elaine kept postponing our wedding day, too. I thought you loved me enough to wear my ring."

"I will, next year. I promise. Please believe me. I won't do this again. But Mr. Winters said I might get the chance to travel a little and write about breaking events. I need to concentrate on my career."

"And I want to marry you," he said, resting his hands on my shoulders, the pain in his voice weakening my resolve.

"I've put off my career too long already. If you love me, you'll be willing to wait a bit longer."

He kissed me, his lips crushing mine. "I want you to be my wife."

"What's the rush? We're happy. You can stay over anytime you choose. We're as good as married."

"No, we're not." He shook his head. "I have to go. I'll call you tomorrow."

An icy chill settled in my heart as I watched Jake climb into his truck and drive away.

I went into the kitchen, threw my coat over a chair, and grabbed a dish. After cutting a banana in fourths, I scooped out a large serving of double chocolate chip ice cream, squirted lots of whipped cream, and sprinkled my creation with nuts and colored jimmies. I then plopped down on the couch and spooned a large bite into my mouth.

After I polished off the banana split, I started on a bag of potato chips. Jake would come around. I was sure he'd give me some slack. But I'd hurt him, and that bothered me.

I reached for the phone and punched in his number. He answered on the second ring.

"I'm sorry. I love you with all my heart," I blurted out.

"I know. I shouldn't have rushed off the way I did."

"Then you understand?"

"No." A few seconds of silence ensued. "Because you mean so much to me, I'm willing to wait a little longer. Hey, there's someone knocking at my door. Hold on a minute."

I heard some mumbling in the background. A woman's voice and hushed whispers.

"Monique, I'll have to call you back."

"Who's there?"

"An old friend," he replied, sounding evasive.

"Bye," I said, wanting to ask more questions.

"Bye."

After Jake hung up, I realized he hadn't ended the call by saying he loved me, followed by a smacking sound—he never hung up before sending me a kiss. A shiver ran down my spine. Feeling edgy, I set the receiver down and waited for him to call me back.

An hour later, I heard a vehicle pull into my driveway. Thinking Jake had arrived, I hurriedly swung open the door and watched a slim blonde woman slide out from behind the wheel of a silver Porsche.

She was short, petite, everything I wasn't. Grace and femininity radiated from every inch of the delicate creature. An eerie feeling settled in the pit of my stomach.

"Can I help you?" I asked when she stepped in front of me.

"Are you Monique St. Cyr?"

"Yes," I replied, my voice catching in my throat.

"I'm Elaine Morgan. Jake used to be my fiancé."

The information wedged in my chest like a sharp stone. I stared at her incredulously. "So?"

"I intend to marry him."

Chapter Four

"Thanks for coming," I said to Jeannine as she walked through the door, clad in flannel pajamas, fuzzy slippers, and a hooded jacket.

She threw her coat and mittens over my computer chair, stepped around Cobbler, and sat on the couch beside me. "I wish I could help you."

"I just need someone to talk to," I said, realizing I'd dug my own hole and would probably have to figure the way out.

"What's she look like?" Jeannine asked.

"Elaine Morgan's thin and too damn pretty, with a trim waist and tiny hips. She looks smart, rich, and successful."

I pasted a foolish grin on my face. "What Jake ever saw in her is a mystery to me." My forced lightheartedness vanished as I pounded my fist against the stuffed arm of the couch. "There's not a man alive who wouldn't lust after the woman."

"Except for Jake," Jeannine said, patting my hand and yawning.

"They were engaged. And she wants him back."

"I will say this, I've seen Jake and you together. The man is head over heels in love with you."

"He's not happy with me at the moment."

"From what you told me on the phone, I don't blame him, but he'll come around."

"Do you really think so?"

"Have you considered changing your mind and getting married sooner?"

"Of course not. I'm surprised you'd ask me that question. You know how I feel about being able to support myself."

"I thought maybe under these circumstances, you might bend your principles."

"No, I won't. Life is too short to spend wondering *what if*. I've put off my career three other times for men. Jake knows all this. If he can't wait an extra year for me to be his wife, then he doesn't love me enough."

"Maybe you should at least become engaged. Seal the deal, so to speak, especially since *you know who* has showed up on the scene."

"How would it look if I called Jake and said, guess what, you aren't going to believe this, but I've changed my mind about the ring."

"He'd probably be very happy."

"But I haven't changed my mind. Besides, he'd see right through me. I'd look insecure. Don't say a word." I raised my hand to ward off Jeannine's next comment. "It'll take more than a diamond ring to send Elaine flying back into her bat cave. She's on a mission. I saw it on her face. The woman isn't giving up until she has Jake or until he sends her away."

"If we're going to pull an all-nighter, let me get us something to drink." Jeannine rose, disappeared into the kitchen, and returned a moment later with a glass of ginger ale and a glass of Merlot.

"Here, drink up," she said, handing me the wine.

"You're not having any wine?"

"Not tonight." She hesitated a moment before asking, "Are you planning to confront Jake?"

"No, I figured I'll let him tell me about Elaine. I think she went to his apartment tonight. She's not the type of woman to sit back and wait for things to happen."

"That same thing could be said about you," Jeannine pointed out. "I hope you know she came over here hoping to intimidate you."

"She succeeded." I took a few swallows. The wine slid past my throat into my stomach where it created a warm glow. I tossed back the contents of the glass and closed my eyes. "The nerve of the woman strutting her stuff over here."

Jeannine refilled our glasses. "She's got a lot of gall."

"More like balls of steel," I added with a strained laugh.

"And small breasts?"

"Boobs like mosquito bites." Though I laughed like a hyena, deep down inside, I was crying.

Would Jake choose Elaine over me?

I tried to tell myself I had nothing to worry about. He loved me and had said he always would.

"Besides, Jake told you he prefers his women with a little extra padding," Jeannine reminded me.

"Elaine does a remarkable job of hiding her excess weight beneath her size-five designer clothes."

The statement issued with a grin held no humor. Like a barnacle clinging firmly to a submerged ocean pier, a horrible thought wedged itself in my brain—maybe Jake had fallen in love with me on the rebound.

Maybe he would run back to Elaine.

Shortly after Jeannine left the next morning, Aunt Lilly showed up at my door. What little sleep I'd managed was spent dreaming of Elaine throwing herself at Jake. Damn the man for not turning away, for looking at her the way he did me. Anyway, I wasn't in the right frame of mind to put up with my aunt. I decided to be polite and get rid of her as quickly as possible.

"Come in. I was about to make some coffee. Would you like a cup?"

"Sure. I had to get away for a little while. Father and that parrot will drive me to drink."

"Before you turn to the bottle, remember how you felt the morning after Mom's wedding."

"Tee hee hee, how can I forget? My stomach is still a bit queasy."

She followed me into the kitchen and sat at the table while I poured hot water over the instant coffee in two cups. "You don't look too chipper this morning." My aunt eyed me with a strange look on her face. "Wild party, huh?"

"No, I didn't sleep well."

"Oh," she said, sounding disappointed. "I was hoping you had some scandalous gossip to share with me."

I pulled out the chair opposite hers and sat down. "My life is probably dull compared to yours."

"Lord have mercy! I sure hope not. I'm counting on you to add spice to my existence."

I usually drank my coffee with lots of milk, but this morning I needed a quick wake-up call so I drank it black.

Aunt Lilly dropped two teaspoons of sugar into her cup and turned bright eyes toward me. "What are our plans for today?"

Our plans! I groaned. "I don't have any plans, except maybe to take a little nap and do some wash."

"Not on your life," Aunt Lilly said, sounding like a general in charge of her troops, all of a sudden reminding me of my mother. "We gals are going to the beauty parlor and on a shopping trip. My treat."

"Gee, that's nice, but . . ."

"It's the least I can do for my favorite niece. Besides, it's time I dusted the moths off some of my hard-earned money."

"If you want to go shopping, I'll take you later."

She shook her head vehemently. "I figured I'd drive."

Suddenly, I was wide-awake.

I stood outside on the stoop for a few minutes planning what I'd say to Aunt Lilly. I'd come up with a good argument. She should wait until she knew the area before trying to navigate Portland's crowded streets. Besides, the traffic was congested. The roads were icy, definitely too dangerous for an unlicensed driver.

As I entered the duplex, I felt confident I could persuade her to change her mind. "Where's Aunt Lilly?" I asked Gramps, in a loud tone so I'd be heard above the Western movie playing on the small television on the kitchen counter. "She was supposed to meet me outside fifteen minutes ago."

"Lilly has a migraine." Gramps stuck a carrot wedge between the bars of Long John's cage. "How's my buddy this morning?"

The parrot chewed the end of the carrot before tipping his head to one side. He whistled "Nice butt."

Gramps laughed. "Monique, you've done a great job teaching Long John to speak."

I rolled my eyes. "I can't take the credit. His owner was an old sea captain."

"Well, the man was a genius. I had a parakeet once, and I couldn't get the damn bird to say one word."

I should be so lucky.

I peeked into my mother's bedroom and spotted Aunt Lilly covered to her chin with a quilt, a washcloth over her face.

Long John bobbed his head. "Stick 'em up."

"That a boy," Gramps said in an encouraging tone. "I hope to teach him a lot while I'm in Maine. I can't get over how smart he is."

"Tell Aunt Lilly I'll check on her later."

Gramps pulled me into my mother's office. "Lilly's scared to death of getting behind the wheel of a car. She wants to get her license, but her nerves are shot."

"You think she's faking a headache?"

"The pain's real enough."

I tiptoed back into the kitchen and studied my aunt's still form beneath the heavy blankets. *Don't even think it,* I warned myself as I edged into the bedroom.

"Aunt Lilly," I whispered, taking her hand and sliding the towel off her face.

"I'm sorry, dear, but we're going to have to postpone our trip to the mall."

"Maybe we can go later, but I'll drive. The traffic is a bitch in the morning. It would be better to wait for mid-afternoon for me to give you a lesson."

"A bitch," she said, her cheeks turning rosy. "Hand me the pad and pencil by the lamp so I can add that word to my list."

"What list?"

She pushed herself up in bed. "My, my, I'm starting to feel so much better. I may be up to our shopping trip after all." I watched her scribble in her notepad. "I've decided to add some color to my vocabulary. Bitch is a good start, don't you think?"

Carrying a large black handbag, an hour later Aunt Lilly climbed onto the passenger seat of my Explorer. She wore sensible black shoes, black gloves, a long fur coat, and an ancient-looking gray hat with netting that fell over a face devoid of makeup. Her wavy gray hair was subdued in a tight bun at her nape.

She inhaled a shaky breath and cast a timid smile in my direction. "Here's to a rootin' tootin' good time."

I swallowed a yawn and tried to look excited.

"And a new beginning," she said. Like a drowning person gripping a life ring, she wrapped tight fingers around my forearm. "Do you have any suggestions?"

Yikes! Big responsibility. Besides, if I made poor choices, my mother would kill me when she returned from her honeymoon. She loved her sister and had warned me repeatedly not to meddle in Lilly's life. I saw my aunt as a fragile fledgling clinging precariously to a branch, never daring to fly.

Did I dare give her a tiny shove?

As I backed the vehicle onto the street and steered around a moving van, I imagined myself a potter about to mold a lump of clay into dazzling artwork. A surge of power drummed through my body.

"Well . . ." How does a thoughtful niece tell her aunt she needs a complete makeover? Not a small task. When I spotted the familiar bulge at her wrist where she'd tucked her smelling salts, I figured the odds of success were slim to none.

Instead of letting my words fly, I exercised some self-control. "What did you have in mind?"

"A trip to the beauty parlor always makes me feel like a new woman."

"The Harem's Boutique at the mall takes walk-ins. But you might have to wait a while."

Aunt Lilly pulled a blue spiral tablet from her purse.

"What are you writing down?" I asked.

"Boutique, I love that word."

I nodded and turned onto Congress Street.

47

"If we have extra time, we can meander around the shopping mall and purchase a few essentials," my aunt said, tucking her tablet into her purse.

"Is there anything in particular you'd like to buy?"

A blush crept up her neck and tinted her face scarlet. "I need to buy some unmentionables."

I translated that to mean underwear. "I'm sure you'll find whatever you need at Victoria's Secret."

"Tee hee hee." She covered her mouth with her glove. "I'm thinking of throwing out my cotton underpants and . . . you know . . . get some of them highfalutin fancy ones you see on television."

"Oh," I said, doing my damnedest to erase from my mind the image of Aunt Lilly in a thong.

We arrived at the mall twenty minutes later and after circling the parking lot a few times, I found a space.

Aunt Lilly clasped her purse to her chest. "I hope to learn a lot from you." Her eyes glowed with adoration.

My head swelled.

She hopped out of the Explorer and like a woman on a mission walked hurriedly toward the Maine Mall entrance.

I picked up my pace and caught up with her at the door.

Her eyes sparkled, and her mouth curved into a soft smile. For the first time, I realized Aunt Lilly looked younger than my mother. I knew very little about the woman. "If you don't mind my asking, how old are you?"

"Almost forty-one." She gestured impatiently. "Point the way to the boutique."

I nodded right, and we took off at a trot. Aunt Lilly had the stamina of a marathon runner. Trailing my aunt by several yards, sometime later I arrived at the boutique out of breath.

"Can I help you?" Jillian, a hair stylist with spiked orange hair, stood poised with a pen.

"Yes," my aunt said, turning to me for advice.

My chest puffed with pride. "A cut and a style," I said, gauging my aunt's reaction.

Lilly nodded approvingly.

"Maybe a color rinse?"

For a moment indecision streaked across Lilly's face. "Whatever you think is best," she said, fluttering her hands nervously.

"Did you want your nails done, too?" Jillian cocked a hip, crossed her legs at the ankles, and lifted painted acrylic fingernails for Lilly to inspect.

My aunt gazed down in wonder. "I've never seen anything quite like these." She raised bright eyes and proclaimed, "I'll have the works!"

Because I was broke, had nothing better to do, and *the works* would take a while, I left the mall and decided to go for a leisurely ride. A moment later I found my Explorer crawling past Jake's apartment. My vehicle had made this journey so often I wasn't surprised to discover it knew the route by memory. I assured myself my destination was not deliberate but simply another of life's coincidences as I eyed every car in sight, searching for a silver Porsche. Finding none, I breathed a sigh of relief.

Shame slammed into me.

Was I checking up on Jake? I trusted him, did so with my entire being. However, it couldn't hurt to be cautious. I definitely didn't trust Elaine Morgan. The more I thought about the woman, the more I disliked her. A less generous person might even hate her. *But not me.*

Since her ugly Porsche, more a dull gray than silver, was nowhere in sight, my feelings stabilized near or slightly above dislike. Nothing could be gained by hating a woman I didn't know. In fact, I felt pity for the slim, delicate creature whose voice sounded like honey, overly sweet and sticky. *Yuck!*

A more vicious person might even compare Elaine Morgan's brown eyes to odorous cesspools, her lips to blood sausages, and her cute, turned-up nose to a sow's. Granted, such a person would derive much joy from such shallow sport. *But not me.*

My kind attitude faltered when I spotted a silver sports car that stopped within inches of my car.

Elaine rolled down her window. "Jake's not here," she said, her voice grating on my nerves. "I just left him. I met him for his break."

A lesser person would have told the bitch off.

For a moment our gazes met and held.

Her eyes did resemble odorous cesspools. Blood sausage was too kind a comparison for her mouth which curled into a despicable grin, above which hung a pig's snout.

She was within reach. A lesser woman might have pulled her hair or called her names.

But not me.

I waved a one-finger salute and drove away with my dignity intact.

Chapter Five

I was still stewing sometime later when I entered the mall and walked past a stranger with fire-engine red hair and a netted hat tucked under her arm.

"Monique, what do you think?" The woman sounded like my aunt, waved her hand around her face like my aunt, and held her purse like a shield in front of her chest like my aunt.

My jaw dropped. "Aunt Lilly?" I eyed her heavy makeup, hair like a rooster tail, stiff strands over her forehead and the sides of her face. She looked years younger but resembled a punk rocker.

"At first, I asked Jillian to style my hair in a bun at my nape, but she said this was more . . ." She withdrew a small spiral notepad from her pocket and flipped through pages. "Rad," she said, her eyes glowing. She tapped manicured fingers over her hair. "So, do you think it's too much?"

Too much!

The color, red with neon-orange and fuchsia highlights, was blinding. Were I in the same room with Lilly for prolonged periods, I'd wear sunglasses to protect my vision. "I wonder whether your hair glows in the dark?"

"Tee hee hee. I only regret Anne Marie isn't here to see my transformation. I'm tired of blending into the background."

"Trust me, your new hair color boosts your visibility big time."

Lilly looked pleased. "Thanks."

My mother would kill me!

Fortunately, in three months the color would fade. With luck, once the novelty wore off, Lilly would go back to being her sweet, dull self.

As we strolled past a large trash bin, Lilly plucked her hat from under her arm and heaved it away. "I have you to thank for all this. When Anne Marie calls, I'll tell her how you've helped me escape from my dreary cocoon."

I cringed. "A cocoon can be a cozy, safe place. You don't want to change too much too fast."

"Nonsense," Lilly said in a take-charge tone. "I want to be just like you. A vibrant woman on the loose. With your help I'm going to shed my inhibitions the way a snake sheds its skin."

That said, she curled long painted claws around my forearm and pulled a Visa from her pocket. "Let's do some serious damage. I want an entire new wardrobe. While we're at it, let's buy you one too. Later tonight, we'll have ourselves a bonfire, roast marshmallows, and burn my old clothes."

My mother's unhappy face flashed through my thoughts. When she returned and discovered I'd corrupted her sister, I wouldn't have a moment's peace and quiet until the day I went deaf or died. Hoping to save myself, I grabbed my aunt's hat from the trash can. "There's still plenty of wear left."

She tore the hat from my hand and tossed it away. "Hogwash, there's no need to be thrifty. I've had that old thing for years. I've never gone on a real shopping spree. And I bet you have." Raising her arm like a gladiator ready for battle, she said, "Onward, lead the way!"

I forgot about the promise to my mother not to interfere with my aunt's life. Instead I was swept away by the excitement.

"You've come to the right person. If shopping were an Olympic sport, I'd be weighted down with gold medals," I said, taking Aunt Lilly's elbow. "I can max out most credit cards in less than an hour."

After helping Lilly carry in her purchases, I went to my duplex, hoping to relax. I'd no sooner slammed the door shut and picked up a partially chewed leather belt from the floor than I heard a knock on the door. "Bad dog," I said to Cobbler, who blinked up at me with sad eyes. Heaving a weary sigh, I gave his head an affectionate pat.

The door bounced open and in walked Jeannine covered from head to toe with a knitted hat, scarf, long woolen coat and knee-high boots. She threw her gloves on my computer table and glanced at me critically. "You look like hell."

"What do you expect! I couldn't sleep last night, and this morning Aunt Lilly dragged me to the mall for a full day of fun and games. My aunt could run the Boston Marathon without breaking a sweat. We covered more ground today than I do in a month. I'm exhausted, and I ache all over."

Especially my heart. I tried to console myself. Deep inside, I knew Jake loved me. He'd told me often enough, but insecurity chewed at my self-confidence which wasn't stable even on a good day.

Jeannine shed her coat and dropped down next to me on the couch. "Let me guess, you haven't been able to get Elaine Morgan off your mind."

"I saw her this morning, driving past Jake's apartment, looking like she had a right to be there. She's lucky I didn't pull her out of her drab gray car by her ugly, shiny hair."

"I'm sure that would have impressed Jake when he showed up in his squad car moments later to find his old girlfriend bald and battered."

"That flat-footed, donut-eating pig spent his break with Elaine," I said, getting little satisfaction from the playful name-calling.

"I'm sure there's a perfectly good explanation."

I nodded. "He's still loves her, that's what."

"You're overreacting again. You need to trust Jake. Just last night he was ready to give you a ring."

"I refused it, remember? That makes him free for the picking."

"Not necessarily. Is Jake working tonight?"

"He said he was."

"Hey, don't go letting your mind run amok."

I sighed. "You're right, but each time I close my eyes, I see Elaine swooping down like a vulture to sink her talons into Jake."

"Then fight. Show him how much he means to you. Show him how much fun you are to be with. Don't allow one dull moment to pass."

Hmmm . . . I'd been called lots of names, but dull wasn't one of them. "I do have a good imagination."

"Too good," Jeannine said, rolling her eyes. "But then that's one of the things I like about you. I never know what's going to happen next."

"I'm sure if I give this some thought, I can wow Jake off his feet."

"You've already wowed him. I tell you he's head over heels for you."

"But it couldn't hurt to nudge his memory a little." *Or a lot!*

After thinking for a while, my brain outdid itself. "The last time I was in the Old Port I walked past a small shop named Condom Mania. It had some very interesting paraphernalia in the window display. With your help, I'll find an outfit guaranteed to etch my image into Jake's mind and insure he thinks of me every waking minute of every day."

Looking unsure, Jeannine tugged at her lower lip.

Before she could refuse, I added, "We'll go after dark. Anyway, I'm sure perfectly normal people frequent the shop."

"Define normal," Jeannine said, standing and walking into the kitchen. "Do you have any ginger ale? My stomach feels a bit queasy."

"In the fridge. If you're saying that to get out of going to Condom Mania with me, it's not going to work."

Ice cubes plunked into a glass. "Can I get you something?"

"Naw, I'm on a diet."

"Not again."

"I need to shed a few pounds. It won't do for Jake to see the exciting new me probably covered in sparkles with rolls of flab around my waist and thighs."

"You don't need to go to that extreme. Just keep him on his toes."

"When I'm through with Jake, he'll be so shell-shocked, he won't remember Elaine Morgan's name."

Jeannine walked into the room. "Instead of driving yourself crazy imagining the worst, talk to Jake, tell him you're concerned about Elaine. Ask him how he feels about her."

"Have you gone mad! If I do that, he might tell me what I don't want to hear. I'm going to wait for him to bring up the subject. If he doesn't, I'll put my battle plan into gear. I'll stock up on artillery and ammo at Condom Mania and wage a war unlike any seen in our history. Before I'm through *Elaine 'The Bitch' Morgan* will slither back under her rock." I derived great pleasure thinking of Elaine in a nest of vipers. In fact I almost smiled. "Now that I have a plan, I'm feeling much better."

"It would be a lot simpler to just talk to Jake, but you've never taken the easy path, so why start now?" Jeannine's complexion turned a bit green.

"You do look sick."

"Once I drink a little ginger ale, I'll be good as new." She set her glass down, covered her mouth, rose quickly, and dashed into the bathroom. I hurried after her to make sure she was all right.

Sometime later she entered the living room, looking pale and shaky.

"Maybe you should lie down for a while."

She sat on the chair by the window and closed her eyes. "I'll be fine in a minute."

I handed her the ginger ale and rested my palm over her forehead, which felt clammy. "Call in sick tomorrow."

"I might." Jeannine set her glass down.

Hoping to get her mind off her upset stomach, I decided to change the subject. "How's Ted?"

"All right," she said, looking evasive.

My curiosity was piqued. "You're hiding something."

Jeannine took several breaths, and her color returned to normal. With a sly smile, she said, "Things are great between us, couldn't be better. I think he's going to propose."

I jumped up and down, pulled her to her feet, and temporarily forgetting she was sick, I swung her around and shouted. Jeannine joined in. Soon we were laughing with tears running down our faces.

"When were you going to tell me? Isn't this a bit quick?" I asked, trying not to sound apprehensive. "After all, this is a big step."

A rosy glow tinted Jeannine's cheek. "I want to marry Ted."

"For the rest of your life, you'll wake up next to the same man."

"Yes, that's what I want."

"Aren't you afraid of making a mistake?"

Jeannine sat back down and took another sip from her glass. "No."

"What about your job?"

"Unlike you, I'd love nothing better than to be a stay-at-home wife and mother."

"Before I accept a ring from Jake, I'm going to have a career I can depend on. I don't want to dampen your good mood, but Ted's a policeman, too. What if something happens . . ." I allowed the comment to trail off, barely able to make eye contact with my friend. My insides clenched with fear for myself and for Jeannine.

"I'll worry about it then. Your mother did fine for herself."

"It was rough on her after Dad died," I said, a familiar ache settling in my chest.

Jeannine ran a finger along the condensation of the glass. "I'm not going to allow 'what ifs' to rule my life. I'm going to grab all the happiness I can now and worry about the future when it arrives."

Jeannine looked so happy I couldn't continue. Besides, our views about marriage were different. "If it's what you want, then I'm pleased for you."

"I was hoping you'd say that."

"Who are you having for your maid of honor?"

"You, of course."

"It's a good thing you said that because I used up all my self-restraint on Elaine." I glanced at the calendar over my computer. "I'll help you plan the wedding. June's a nice month, but it might already be too late to reserve a hall. You might have to wait until July or August. Then, too, autumn's

57

a nice time of year for weddings. And I look better in fall colors than pastels."

Jeannine rose and looked out the window. "I want an intimate ceremony with a few of my close friends."

"You have to allow me some time to give you a shower and a proper send-off. I'll organize a bachelorette party, complete with a naked man jumping out of a cake."

Jeannine laughed. "That'll be some cake."

"And you get to lick the frosting off his body. Of course, I'll be by your side in case you need any help."

"I knew coming over here would make me feel better. I've been so tired lately. It's all I can do to crawl out of bed in the morning."

"Spend the night. We'll drink wine, talk, and start planning your shower." I dropped down on the couch, and after reaching for a pen and tablet, jotted down several names. "Of course, we'll invite everyone from work, even Doris, though I hate the thought of spending an evening with our witchy copy editor. But looking at the bright side, if I can get her drunk, I may have a chance to take pictures of her with our naked male guest, which might come in handy the next time she complains about my work."

"That's called blackmail," Jeannine said with a giggle.

"No, it's self-defense. Most likely, she won't accept my invitation, which is just as well." I drew a grumpy face next to Doris's name. "We'll plan the get-together for after my mother returns from her honeymoon. I'll tell her to keep an eye out in Europe for raunchy door prizes."

Jeannine turned, and shaking her head, walked toward me and sat on the couch. "I love Ted so much I hurt inside," she said, placing her hand over her heart.

"I know, I feel the same way about Jake."

"Don't you want to have Jake's children?"

"Yes, in the distant future."

"Not me, I want a baby right away."

"There's plenty of time to have babies."

Jeannine's face sobered for a brief moment.

I waved away her concerns. "You should enjoy being a wife before you start scraping doo-doo from diapers. The smell alone would curb anyone's romantic mood."

"I suppose so."

"There's no maybe about it. Babies are cute, but they can be little stinkers, both literally and figuratively. Just think, you're snuggled next to Ted, and your hand connects with a certain vital body part that springs to action. You're both primed and ready to go when over the intercom comes a piercing cry. So instead of making love to your husband, you drag yourself out of bed and go change a poopy diaper."

Jeannine laughed again. "You paint such a glamorous picture of motherhood."

"I'm merely stating facts."

A dreamy look washed over her face. "I get goose bumps just thinking about holding our infant in my arms. Before going to sleep at night, I close my eyes and imagine running a finger over my baby's downy hair. I can almost smell the talcum powder and feel him nursing."

I examined Jeannine, sitting next to me, her eyes radiating warmth. "You'll be a great mother . . . someday."

"I'll do my best."

"Meanwhile, we need to get back to more pressing matters. Besides the stud who leaps from the cake, do we need additional strippers?"

I waited a moment, but since Jeannine didn't answer, I voiced my opinion. "Personally, I vote for the strippers. A party can never have too many good-looking, naked men sauntering around."

Gazing at me, Jeannine settled her hand over mine. "I want a small intimate ceremony with a few close friends. Instead of summer, I was thinking of getting married in January."

"That's this month. That's not enough time for me to give you a send-off you'll never forget."

"Then you'd better speed up your plans."

"My mother would never forgive me if she missed the party of the century. Anyway, what's the big rush?"

"I'm two months' pregnant."

Chapter Six

Air whooshed from my lungs. Like a computer, my over-loaded brain cells crashed. Seconds ticked by as I tried to think of appropriate words to convey this momentous occasion.

My best friend Jeannine was pregnant.

In seven months she would hold her precious infant in her arms. I dug deep for the right expression, something profound, something Jeannine would remember in future years with fondness, and something worthy of an investigative journalist.

Looking concerned, Jeannine shook my shoulder. "Of course, you'll be the godmother."

"Holy shit," I said, unable to stop myself. "A baby. I can't believe it." Tears of joy sprang to my eyes. "A baby! You sly devil, why didn't you tell me last night or earlier today when you first arrived?"

"I felt I should tell Ted first."

"So Ted already knows?" I asked, ready to call the bum several choice names.

"Yes, I told him last night. At first he seemed a little upset. He'd planned to make detective before starting a family."

The jerk! "Just like a man, always thinking of himself first."

"Once he had a chance to calm down, he seemed fine with the news."

Seemed—a weak word if ever I'd heard one. "How did you get pregnant?"

Jeannine chuckled. "Ask Jake to explain."

"Maybe I'll have him demonstrate," I said, building on my battle plan. "I thought you were on the pill."

"My doctor thinks the antibiotic I took a couple months ago diminished the pill's effectiveness."

"I'm swearing off that drug. There should be a warning on the label—CAUTION, this medication can cause nausea, a distended belly, and *contractions*."

"I think the brochure that comes with the prescription warns about having unprotected sex while on antibiotics, but I never bothered to read the fine print."

Mental note—buy a magnifying glass to read *even the tiniest print*. "But you're happy?"

"Yes."

I knew by looking at her she was telling the truth. "Good, once I'm through planning your bachelorette party, I'll throw you a combination wedding and baby shower. A pregnant bride isn't a big deal nowadays," I said for Jeannine's sake, hoping to erase the worry from her eyes.

"I'm so happy I don't care who knows about the baby."

"Good, you've done nothing to be ashamed of. Having a baby is a wonderful experience. Although I'm a little disappointed because I always thought we'd have our children around the same time so they'd play together."

"If you hurry, that can still happen."

"No, thanks, but maybe my first child will be closer in age to your second. They'll grow up together and be best friends like us."

"I'd like that," Jeannine said, her eyes tearing. She tapped a tissue in the corner of her eyes. "My emotions are a mess."

"That's to be expected." I inhaled a deep breath. "This is

so exciting. I can't wait to buy my godchild clothes and toys. Plus, I'll be by your side every step of the way, gleaning information for when I get pregnant. If I do my research, I'll be better prepared for the grand event. I may even write a story about childbirth. First thing tomorrow I'll break into my bank account and buy the best camcorder on the market to record every step of your pregnancy for posterity."

"I'm glad you didn't have the camera tonight when I was puking up my guts."

"Just think, whenever my mother wants something from me, she mentions her long labor and rough delivery. You'll have the proof. Instead of *Sesame Street,* your child can watch Mommy suffering to bring him into this world. Guilt alone will insure he toes the mark until he leaves home. Your child will have the cleanest room and the best grades. Your only responsibility will be driving him to his weekly appointments with his shrink."

"I don't know where you get your ideas," Jeannine said, laughing.

"They just pop into my head, and I blurt them out before they spontaneously combust and are never heard from again."

"You should have allowed this idea to disintegrate."

"You may feel that way now, but when Ted Junior is mouthing off, giving you a tough time, you'll call and beg me for the tape. Just for spite, I won't give it to you."

A short while later I went into the kitchen and poured myself a healthy dose of Merlot before hurrying back into the living room. "Have you thought of names? Will you and Ted live in your apartment or his?"

"We haven't discussed names. I didn't want to overwhelm Ted with details. I wanted to give him a chance to get used to the idea of having a baby before bombarding him with questions."

"Oh." So far, I wasn't impressed with Ted. "How did he react when you told him?"

"I had my head on his shoulder, and I was so nervous, I felt sick to my stomach. All day I'd practiced how to slowly break the news to him, but when the time came, I simply blurted it out: 'Ted, we're going to have a baby.' His arm stiffened and he rose. I caught a glimpse of his shocked expression before he turned and stared out the window with his back to me. He said nothing for a while, but when he looked at me again, I saw acceptance on his face. I'm sure he'll be just as happy as I am once he gets used to the idea."

That dirty, good-for-nothing, lower than the belly of a snake . . . I wanted to punch Ted in the nose for his less than stellar performance. "Is that when you discussed getting married?"

"Ted didn't come right out and say the words, but he did mention providing a stable life for our child."

"Is he working tonight?" I asked, wondering why he wasn't down on his knee this instant with a ring in his hand.

"No, he's gone out of town. He called earlier today to say his father had had a stroke. Ted took a leave from work and plans to be gone for a week or more. He said he'd call if he could and that I shouldn't worry because we'll work out everything when he returns."

Mighty big of him. Sipping Merlot, I kept my opinion to myself and smiled. "I'm sure he'll propose the instant he comes back. Meanwhile, to get your mind off your delicate condition, you can help me pick out a few necessities at Condom Mania."

I pulled the hood of my black sweatshirt over my head and tightened the tie under my chin. Only a narrow sliver of my face remained visible.

"You look like you're about to rob the store instead of make a purchase," Jeannine said. "I hope no one sees me here."

"We're adults, for goodness sakes, there's no reason why we can't indulge in a little frivolity with our loved ones." Once the last customer left Condom Mania, I grabbed hold of Jeannine's hand so she wouldn't abandon me, and hurried inside.

"What can I do for you two ladies?" the clerk asked, casting a knowing smile.

I didn't bother to question his cheesy grin. "We just want to look around." I eyed key chains, ice cube trays, straws, and pasta shaped like male body parts. "I think we've found the theme for your bachelorette party," I said, nudging Jeannine who stood frozen by my side. I wrapped my arm around her waist and forced her to walk beside me.

"The section you want is across the room," the clerk said, stocking a shelf with decks of playing cards. I yanked Jeannine toward the display and found myself in front of an assortment of lesbian books.

"He thinks we're . . ." Jeannine said, not finishing her sentence.

I picked up a tin of Booby Mints, small pink nipples guaranteed to melt in your mouth. "Six bucks is kind of high, but won't Jake be surprised when he spots this candy in a bowl in the living room."

"Don't you think that's kind of tacky?" Jeannine asked.

"After I see the surprise on his face, I might offer to have him sample the real thing."

"Look at that," Jeannine said, eyeing cellophane-wrapped tassels with tiny lights that, according to the sign, twinkled like stars when you moved.

"I've always wondered how strippers can swing their breasts in opposite directions. It probably takes practice, like crocheting or dancing."

"According to this package, the secret is inside the box," Jeannine pointed out. "Plus there's a fake jewel for the dancer's navel, along with . . ."

I heard a familiar voice and clamped my hand over Jeannine's mouth. Pulling her next to me in the narrow space behind the bookshelf, I heard Jake say, "Just checking in."

"Everything's fine, Officer," the clerk said.

If Jake saw me here, that would ruin my surprise. A bead of perspiration rolled between my breasts. My heart drumming in my ears, I held my breath until I heard the bell over the door jingle. Had Jake left or had another customer arrived? I was still pondering that question when I heard the clerk clearing his throat and saw him eyeing us suspiciously.

"Control yourselves, I don't allow any hanky-panky in this shop."

I didn't know what he meant until I noticed my arm slung over Jeannine's shoulder. Once I got his meaning, I looked guilty as hell. "This isn't what you think. We were hiding back here for a reason . . ." I stopped talking because I could see my words weren't connecting.

"I'm sure you have your reasons. But I cater to respectable customers, and I won't put up with any monkey business behind the bookcase."

When confronted with a stressful situation, I sometimes react irrationally and do the first thing that comes to mind. So, with the clerk looking on, I pressed my mouth to Jeannine's cheek.

"Let's go, sweetheart, we'll take our business elsewhere."

I wanted Jeannine to spend the night with me, but she insisted on going home in case Ted called. I pulled my Ford Explorer into the driveway and was surprised to see my aunt with her ear against the door to my duplex.

"What are you doing?" I asked. Her red hair really did glow in the dark.

"I thought I heard a noise."

"It's probably just one of my animals."

"Of course Gramps didn't hear a thing, but then he never does, and I didn't want to make a fool of myself by calling the authorities."

I stuck my key in the lock, opened the door, and flicked on the lights. Shredded paper covered everything, the couch, the computer, and the rug. Several damp pages of one of my mother's books lay beneath Cobbler's chin. "Dammit," I shouted at the animal. "When will you ever learn?"

"I'll help you pick up the mess," Aunt Lilly said.

"You don't have to do that."

"I want to."

I nodded toward the closet. "In that case, the broom and trash bags are over there."

Lilly swept up the small pieces of paper. "Is the furnace on the fritz? It's cold as the dickens in here."

Until now I hadn't noticed, but I could almost see my breath. "I always turn down the thermostat when I leave. Maybe I set the dial too low, but I'll check it in a sec." I picked up a book cover and loose pages. Since I was certain I had only one copy, I was surprised to find two *Thrust or Bust* book covers, my mother's book.

"This sure looks like a lot of pages," Lilly said, mirroring my thoughts.

When I glanced at my shelf, I saw my autographed copy of my mother's book intact. "That's strange."

"What's strange?"

"I must be mistaken because I don't remember having extra copies."

Assuming my overactive imagination was again wreaking havoc with me, I tried to brush aside thoughts of an insane creature, a hulk of a man, his eyes red and glowing as he ripped the bindings from my mother's books. My common sense blamed Cobbler for the destruction. It wasn't the first time he'd ripped one of my books, but when had he developed an appetite for erotic fiction? Shivers raced up and down my spine as I tried to erase the crazed being I'd conjured from my mind and sent the dog a threatening look.

Cobbler approached me, and I wrapped my arms around his neck and scratched behind his ears. "You need to behave," I said to the animal as he issued an appreciative moan.

"I never had a dog," Lilly said, looking sad. "Mother was allergic."

"You can have this one," I said, joking, figuring no one in their right mind would take me seriously.

"I couldn't accept such a generous offer. Besides, he's yours."

"He's not mine. I offered to take care of him for a little old lady who later moved to Florida."

"Are you sure?"

I couldn't believe my ears or my good luck. "Absolutely."

Tears sprang to Aunt Lilly's eyes. "This is turning out to be one of the best weeks of my life. First I get my new hairdo and color at the beauty parlor . . . ."

"Boutique," I corrected.

"Boutique . . . and now I own a wonderful dog."

"I should warn you his favorite treat is leather." *Shoes, belts, purses.*

"I'll take him to obedience school." She swept the last of the shredded paper into a black trash bag.

My heart jumped for joy. I'd never expected to find someone who'd willingly adopt Cobbler. The dog had cost me a fortune, the most expensive venture when he'd eaten the backseat of Jeannine's Mustang.

"I'd hate for you to change your mind after I've grown fond of the animal. I want you to be one hundred percent sure about this."

"I'm certain. If it'll make you feel better, I'll draw up a sales slip insuring neither of us can back out of the deal." I quickly jotted down the terms of our agreement where both parties solemnly swore to uphold their end of the bargain. We both signed our names.

"I should give you some money to seal the contract." Aunt Lilly reached into her pocket and slapped a dollar bill in my hand. "It's too late to back out now."

As if I would.

She dropped to her knees and stroked the animal's head. "Cobbler, we're going to be great pals."

I silently sang the "Hallelujah Chorus."

For the last couple months I'd gotten in the habit of hiding my purse on the top closet shelf. My cats spend most of the day perched on the refrigerator out of reach. My life would be simpler. I could leave my shoes on the floor without fear of finding them pulverized and covered with slime.

"I won't allow you to back out of our deal," Lilly said, folding the piece of paper and tucking it into her pocket.

"That goes both ways. You can't give him back to me."

"Cobbler's mine now." Aunt Lilly looked genuinely happy.

I was feeling quite happy myself until I heard a noise in the kitchen. Gooseflesh peppered my arms.

"What was that?" Lilly asked, her voice edgy, her eyes wide.

The hackles on Cobbler's back rose. A growl rumbled from his throat.

"I'm sure it's just one of the cats." But I wasn't sure. Cobbler had never reacted this way to my other animals. The clumsy dog emitted a deep bark, and snarling, took off at a gallop, tipping over an end table. A lamp crashed to the floor. In the other room, he slammed into a chair that hit the table. Dishes shattered and silverware clanged.

With Aunt Lilly at my heels, I ran into the room and found Cobbler standing on his hind legs, his front feet anchored against the countertop, barking at the open kitchen window.

There was a footprint on my sink.

Before I could digest the information, I heard a loud crash in the living room and splintering glass. When I entered the room, I saw the broken picture window and one of my mother's books bound with a red ribbon, surrounded by shards of broken glass.

Taped to the cover was a note with a warning:
Stop, or you'll be sorry.

Chapter Seven

When Jake arrived a few minutes later along with another policeman, Officer Williams, Aunt Lilly fled next door for her coat, her smelling salts, and her spiral notepad.

I clamped my arms around Jake's neck and wouldn't let go.

"Are you all right?" he asked.

"Of course I'm fine. We reporter types don't frighten easily." I felt safe as I tucked my head into his neck, filled my lungs with his masculine scent, and tried to still my pounding heart.

Fortunately, my mind clicked into gear. I needed to remain calm and stay alert. This could be another opportunity for a whopper of a story. *Front page* if all went well. The investigative reporter in me sprang to attention as I released my death grip and leaned nonchalantly against the computer cabinet—not easy with my feet shaking in my boots.

"Did you see anyone?" Officer Williams asked.

"No, but I'm certain the perpetrator is a big brute."

"What makes you say that?"

"Intuition. Every reporter is born with it." I sent Jake's partner a confident look.

Aunt Lilly arrived, the bottle of smelling salts bulging at her cuff, her blue eyes sparkling in her otherwise pale complexion.

"Ma'am, do you remember seeing or hearing anything suspicious?" Officer Williams asked.

"I was next door when I heard some noise. My heart pitter-pattered so loud I couldn't hear myself think. But I'm turning over a new leaf. See," she said, pointing to her red hair, "and I'm through hiding from my petty fears and missing all life has to offer. So I gathered what little courage I could muster, hurried outside, and leaned my ear against the door. That's where Monique found me a minute later. Had the hoodlums confronted me, I was prepared to throw myself at them. That's if I didn't faint first." Her cheeks glowed pink and she fluttered her hand about her face. "Tee hee hee."

"So you heard more than one person inside the duplex?" The officer jotted notes on a tablet.

"I'm not sure . . . what are you writing?" Aunt Lilly craned her neck and glanced at his notes.

He snapped his book shut. "Just keeping track of the facts, ma'am."

I slipped my jacket over my shoulders and faced him. "As I see it, the scumbag was in here when we arrived, I bet with an accomplice. It just occurred to me maybe they were interested in my computer files, fearing my knowledge of the crime world might implicate them in drug trafficking or worse." I tapped my temple. "Little did they know I'd outsmarted them because I keep all pertinent facts tucked away on a disc hidden where no one would ever think to look."

I'd intended to put my files, which included research for my stories and some of my favorite computer games, in a safety deposit box but had never gotten around to it. Instead I taped the disc under my underwear drawer. Clever, if I did say so myself. "An investigative reporter can never be too cautious."

"If someone was interested in your files, they'd have taken

your computer," Jake pointed out.

Damn the man for his rational mind. Never one to give up easily, I added, "But Lilly and I cut their visit short. So who knows what might have happened if we hadn't arrived when we did."

"We're not ruling out any possibilities. But if your theory is correct, why bother ripping up books?"

"Maybe to throw us off track. Plus, anyone who watches television knows that's the perfect place to hide receipts, the numbers to safety deposit boxes, a travel log, or a list of names."

Aunt Lilly seemed impressed with my vast knowledge of the devious criminal mind. I cocked an eyebrow and smiled at her.

An amused grin flicked across Jake's face.

I folded my arms over my chest. "I did that piece last fall about drugs smuggled inside fish. And for all you know, there's lots of confidential material on my computer."

"Sweetheart, take it easy. I just don't want you to make more of this than you should. Nothing valuable was taken. This could be no more than some teenager's idea of a prank." The dark look on his face worried me. Was he hiding something?

The stress of the last two days culminated. A person could take only so much. First Elaine, then Jeannine's pregnancy, and now this break-in. "My mother's books *are* valuable." I emphasized each word so both men would get the message. No way in hell would I allow the male gender to look down their noses at women's contemporary fiction.

"Sorry, hon, your mother's a great author."

"You better not be saying that just to pacify me."

"Never." His damnable grin said otherwise.

Were we alone, I'd have reminded him that he'd benefited

from my mother's prose. No living, breathing man could read my mother's love scenes without getting hot and bothered.

Jake, I'd discovered, was no exception.

As Jake hunched over to dust a bookshelf for prints, I took the time to admire the man I loved. He had the goods—all six feet, three inches of him a mass of sculptured muscles. He looked almost as handsome in his uniform as he did buck-naked. Although given the choice, I preferred his birthday suit. *Hmmm.* Despite the cold air in my apartment, my insides simmered.

Aunt Lilly grabbed the plastic bag of shredded paper. "I'll put this out by the Dumpster."

"That's evidence," the officer said. "We'll have to check its contents for prints."

"Oh, on television most criminals wear rubber gloves so as not to leave behind evidence."

"That doesn't always work, ma'am. If the gloves are thin and the hands have pronounced friction ridges, it's possible to leave behind a print."

"Bet the hooligans are shocked when they're arrested for a crime they say they didn't commit, and all the time you have the proof to throw them in jail." Aunt Lilly wrote furiously on her pad.

"It does my heart good when that happens. Also, I'll have to fingerprint both of you so we'll know which prints are yours."

"That's grand," Lilly said, looking pleased as she turned toward me. "I'm glad I showed up when I did. I'd hate to miss out on all this excitement. Thank goodness you didn't arrive earlier and scare off the culprit."

Aunt Lilly's words jolted me.

What would have happened if I'd startled the person ransacking my duplex? I envisioned an armed man with menacing eyes and a machine gun pointed at my chest. To steady myself, I clasped my hands together.

A person does not almost stare death in the face without reevaluating their life. I considered throwing myself at Jake, telling him I'd made a big mistake and that I wanted to get married and have his children. I blamed my temporary lapse of sanity on my emotions, stretched thin under the circumstances.

I'd eventually marry Jake, but not now. Of course, if Elaine had her way, that would never happen. As thoughts of that despicable woman sprang into my mind and held fast like an undetected leech, I considered the possibility she might be involved in the destruction of my property. The longer I thought about her, the more convinced I became.

Why would she go to these lengths?

Puny Elaine blew away my big brute theory. Had my reporter's intuition again led me astray? I quickly dismissed the notion. Elaine had hired someone, an accomplice to help do her dirty work.

Motive?

Simple.

If she threw me off balance, I might spend too much time consumed with fear or on the trail of my next newspaper story, thereby ignoring Jake. Then she'd swoop in and claim her prize. That really irked me.

Stop, or you'll be sorry.

As I reread the note, I fully understood its meaning. Stop seeing Jake, or I'd pay the price. How low would Elaine stoop to win Jake back? Would she resort to violence? I had at least twenty pounds on her—all right, make that thirty—so if push came to shove, I could easily defend myself.

One piece of the puzzle eluded me. Why would Elaine rip only my mother's books? Possibly, in a moment of sexual frustration, she'd taken out her rage on my mother's erotic fiction.

Did I dare tell Jake my suspicions?

No, I wouldn't mention Elaine until he did, or at the very least until after we'd celebrated our twenty-fifth wedding anniversary.

If need be, I'd conduct my own investigation. When Elaine finally confessed, I'd press charges. I pictured her wearing stripes and standing beside her new best friend, a husky gal with short hair, nicknamed Bubba.

I almost laughed out loud.

"I haven't had this much fun since I don't know when," Aunt Lilly said, duct taping cardboard to my front window. "First thing tomorrow I'll jog down to the store and get Cobbler, bless his precious heart, a special treat. He's our hero."

I swept up the rest of the broken glass. "How do you figure that?"

"If my dog hadn't caused a ruckus, who knows what dastardly deed might have occurred."

"If Cobbler hadn't let the jerk into my duplex to begin with, none of this would have happened."

Lilly smiled down at her new pet. "Officer Williams found a large soup bone on the rug. He thinks the dog was bribed."

"That's hardly a hero," I pointed out.

"He came through when it mattered most." Lilly toyed with a spiked strand of her red hair. "Two attractive unmarried ladies like us could easily drive a deranged male into a sex-crazed frenzy. I can almost see his feral eyes, a scar across his mean chin, and if I close my eyes, I can easily hear his sandpaper voice."

I decided I'd inherited my vivid imagination from my aunt.

"I'd better stop, or I'll be needing a whiff of my smelling salts. Hell's bells, I'll be lucky if I get any sleep tonight."

I hadn't intended to tell anyone about my suspicions, but I couldn't allow Aunt Lilly to worry needlessly. "I think I know who trashed my duplex."

"Goodness gracious, why didn't you tell the police?"

"Because Elaine Morgan is Jake's former girlfriend, and she's determined to win him back. The last thing I want to do is give him reason to defend her."

"How can you be sure she's responsible?"

"Because the little slut knows where I live, and she's out to cause me grief."

Aunt Lilly's face clouded with confusion. "I still don't understand how you can be so sure."

Until now I'd been charitable but no more. I was no longer willing to simply dislike Elaine Morgan. "Because I hate her, that's why. Maybe she didn't rip up my mother's books, but if she did, I'm going to find out."

"How will you do that?"

"Let's just say I have connections."

Aunt Lilly's eyes widened. "What kind of connections?"

"I know a private eye," I said, trying not to shudder. The last time I'd gotten involved with Richard I'd almost landed in jail.

"Is he any good?"

"There's no other like him."

"You think he'll help us?"

Us? I cringed. "I'm going to use Richard only as a last resort." I raised an eyebrow at Lilly and sent her my seasoned reporter look. "Elaine's messed with the wrong woman."

"Women," Lilly corrected.

"If there's one thing I've learned in my career it's to investigate all the facts before making my move. I won't point the finger of blame until I'm one hundred percent certain Elaine is guilty."

"How are you going to prove that?"

A brilliant plan wedged itself into my mind. "Simple. I'm going to do some fingerprinting of my own."

Aunt Lilly grabbed hold of my elbow. "Whatever you have in mind, count me in."

When Jake arrived after his shift, I'd already packed my bag and was ready to spend the night at his apartment.

"If you'd prefer, we can stay here," Jake said, capturing my mouth in a bone-melting kiss.

"But the window's broken, and it's rather chilly."

"I can tape on another couple layers of cardboard and seal it off with plastic. It'll keep out the cold."

That might be true but I wanted to search his place for traces of a certain female varmint.

"Besides, I'll keep you warm."

"Hmmm," I said against his neck, flicking my tongue over his earlobe.

Jake mistook my actions and started to pull me into the bedroom.

I needed to think of something—fast! I dug my feet into the living room rug and pulled away. I unsuccessfully summoned a tear. "I can't sleep in there. Just thinking about a stranger inside my duplex will give me nightmares." I clawed at the air. "I'd see his hulking form tearing at my books. Who knows what else he's done. For all I know he was in my bedroom. The very thought makes me feel sick to my stomach."

"I'm sorry, I guess I wasn't thinking. Let's go to my apartment."

On the ride to Jake's place, I stretched my arms and

yawned, did my best to sound matter-of-fact. "Is anything new with you?"

Surely he'd tell me he saw his ex.

"No, why do you ask?"

I wanted to smack him. But then I'd have to explain. "No reason, just trying to make conversation."

He nodded and smiled at me. He pulled into his parking space and, grabbing hold of my bag, escorted me to the second floor.

"How'd your day go?"

"Fine."

I wanted to ring his neck. "Nothing different?" *Did you arrange to meet Elaine for your break?*

He unlocked the door to his apartment and flicked on the light switch. "Why the third degree?"

"No reason. Blame it on the reporter in me." The fact he hadn't told me about seeing Elaine wasn't good. An innocent man would have confessed. Another possibility existed. An innocent man might have nothing to confess.

Had Elaine lied to me about meeting Jake? I'd seen the victorious look in her eyes. I believed her. However, she might have shown up and to be polite he'd invited her to join him for a cup of coffee. Either way, if he had nothing to hide, why hadn't he mentioned her?

While my mind ran amok, I studied every shadowed nook and cranny of Jake's living room, which wasn't easy in the dim light, looking for traces of incriminating evidence.

My reporter brain logged every small detail from the empty beer bottle—one bottle, phew, not two—to the balled-up Burger King bag on the couch cushion. I wanted to check under every cushion, every chair, every piece of furniture, but I couldn't do that without raising questions. So I'd bide my time and wait until Jake had fallen asleep. Meanwhile, I'd investigate the room most likely to produce clues.

"Be back in a sec," I said, taking several steps and shutting the bathroom door. I dug a small flashlight from my pocket and examined the hairbrush for signs of long blonde hair. Finding none, I turned on the water spigot to drown out the sound of my opening the medicine cabinet. Had I found a tampon or a bottle of Midol, I'd have gone into cardiac arrest. I checked Jake's razor for signs of foreign female leg hairs and finding none, felt light-headed with relief, proving to me Elaine hadn't spent much time in Jake's apartment.

A thought stuck me, wedged in my prolific mind like a splinter deep under one's flesh. The devious witch might do some checking of her own. So before leaving the bathroom, I ran my fingers through my hair, shedding loose follicles all over the room. I brushed and combed my hair, and for good measure, I dropped my jeans and shaved a swath down my leg with Jake's shaver. Convinced I'd done all I could do, I joined Jake on the couch.

"Are you all right?" he asked, taking my hand and rubbing circles with his thumb over my palm.

Tiny electrical jabs nipped my flesh. "Yes, I am now."

"I poured you a glass of wine to help soothe your nerves."

"Thanks." I took a sip and leaned back against the safety of his arm. "Did the fingerprints from my duplex yield any suspects?"

"So far we haven't found any matches."

As he spoke, I slipped my hand under the cushion and came up with a gum wrapper, a coin, what felt like either a Cheerio or a Froot Loop. No panties or bras—phew! My voice trembled with relief. "From your experience, what's our criminal's psychological profile?"

Jake tightened his hold around me. "I'll know more tomorrow. We're either dealing with a prankster or a mentally unstable person. His destroying the books doesn't concern me as much as the note he left behind."

"I have my own theory about that note. I think a woman wrote it."

"Do you have someone in mind?"

"Yes, but I need to do a little research before I say any more. You know me, cautious to a fault."

He groaned. "You better tell me what you know, or I'll take you into the station for withholding evidence."

I pulled an imaginary zipper across my lips.

"You're toying with danger. I don't know who broke into your duplex, but whoever it was may not be in his right mind. I want you to have an alarm system installed in your duplex and your mother's side, too."

"I can't afford that."

"Then I'll pay to have it done."

"If my reporter's instincts are correct, an alarm won't be necessary. I'll have a name for you very soon. Anyway, this could be just an isolated incident."

"Maybe, but I won't gamble with your safety."

His concern for me fueled my confidence and made me feel protected and loved.

"I know what I'm doing."

He pulled me onto his lap and kissed a path from my lips down to my neck. "The individual you're dealing with could be dangerous," he whispered, his voice already deepening with desire.

As I leaned into him, I thought of Elaine's delicate face, small breasts, thin hips, thinner waist, and perfect legs.

Dangerous was an understatement.

Chapter Eight

Fearing I'd later regret it, I met Richard at the mall during his lunch break. "Did you bring the stuff?"

He handed me a box wrapped in plain paper bound together by two elastics. "If you get yourself in trouble, forget you know me."

"Sheesh, what is it they say about a friend in need?"

"We aren't friends. I'm helping you out because I feel bad about that last time."

"And you should. For crying out loud, I was handcuffed and thrown into the back of a squad car like a thief."

"The charges were dropped, so stop bitching." Richard, a Howdy Doody look-alike, adjusted his Radio Shack nametag. "Instead of griping, you should thank me for allowing you to join forces with an experienced P.I. You gleaned valuable knowledge from that case and had access to the latest night vision technology."

"We're lucky we aren't serving time behind bars for armed robbery."

Richard set down his Moxie. "Everyone makes mistakes."

"How long do fingerprints last?"

"That depends on the temperature, the humidity, and the type of surface."

While Jake and Officer Williams dusted for prints, I'd slipped on my mittens and, when no one was looking, retrieved some of the shredded paper from the trash bag, hoping to find Elaine's prints. I'd stashed the possible evidence in the back of my closet. "That kind of generalized information doesn't help me one bit. Do you care to elaborate?"

He glanced at his watch. "In cold weather, prints on hard surfaces might vanish instantly, but in hot, humid weather those same prints might last for weeks."

Damn, damn, triple damn. "There's a twenty below zero wind chill factor outside. My toes are still frozen together from my short jaunt into the mall."

Richard offered me a fry.

I took three and frowned. "I certainly can't wait around for summer to arrive."

"What kind of surface are you dusting?"

"Paper and cardboard, and maybe ceramics and stainless steel."

A smile tugged at his mouth. "The good news is that unglazed paper can hold a print indefinitely, the bad news is you need to spray the paper with ninhydrin."

"Where do I find that?"

"I just happen to have a can in my van. Be sure you spray it in a well-ventilated area, preferably outdoors."

"Aye, aye, Captain," I said with a salute.

"The P.I. business is no laughing matter," Richard said as he headed out the door with me behind him. "You should settle down and take this seriously."

Since I needed his advice and equipment, I schooled my features into a sober expression and fought the urge to salute again.

Now that I had what I needed to incriminate Elaine, it was time to set my plan into action. I went home and called her.

She answered on the third ring. I heard the catch in her voice when I introduced myself.

My throat felt thick, my tongue dry. "I was hoping we could meet for lunch."

I heard a snicker. "You must be kidding."

BITCH! I shouted to myself. It took every shred of my self-control not to blurt out that word along with several others. "No, we need to talk."

"I've already told you everything I have to say. I've come back to claim what's mine."

Slut! "That's no reason for us to be enemies."

"Well . . ."

If she didn't agree to meet me, she'd ruin everything. When all else fails, lie. "Jake told me something, and I need to know whether it's true."

"Why don't you ask him?"

Good question. "If I were you, I'd be dying of curiosity." Short pause to allow my words to sink in.

A disgruntled sigh. "All right, what did he say?"

"I'll tell you when you meet me today at the Olive Garden."

"What time?"

"One o'clock." I glanced at the wrapped package Richard had given me. I needed time to practice. "On second thought, make that three o'clock."

Aunt Lilly shook her head and fluttered gloved hands in front of her face. "I can't drive."

"You have your permit, and you'll be with a licensed driver. Chances are you won't even need to turn the key. This is plan B, in case plan A fails. It won't fail."

"What if it does?"

"Then I'll jump into the backseat and you'll take off

84

around the corner and stop. I'll leap into the driver's seat and get us home safely."

"Gee, I don't know."

"All you need to do is watch us inside the restaurant. Order yourself something to eat, but don't let on that you know me. If all goes the way it's supposed to, Elaine will leave, and I'll slip her place setting into my purse, take it into the bathroom, and dust for prints."

"Stealing is a sin," Aunt Lilly said, sounding like Sister Mary Agnes, my parochial school teacher.

"I'm not stealing anything. I'm going to borrow it for a few minutes, then give it back."

"So why do I have to drive?"

"If something goes wrong, I may need to leave in a hurry. You'll drive the getaway car."

Lilly worried her lip.

"It'll be exciting, and later I'll have you help me compare the prints I collect in the restaurant to the ones on the shredded paper in my closet."

Lilly braced herself with a deep breath.

Ten minutes later I sat inside the Olive Garden wondering whether Elaine would show and watching Lilly, who looked ready to throw up, at a table across the room.

I'd almost given up when the wicked witch strolled to the table, dressed in clingy slacks, showing not even the tiniest roll of fat. "I can't believe we're here together."

I wanted to slap her silly, claw out her eyes, pull out every hair on her perfect head—one by one. I smiled. "There's no reason we can't be civil to each other."

"That's mighty big of you."

Did her words have a double meaning? Was she implying I needed to lose a few pounds? Was I again being paranoid?

The waiter arrived. Elaine ordered a small salad with dressing on the side, a glass of water and a wedge of lemon. Although I wanted chicken Parmesan, extra cheese, with a side of fries and a large chocolate milk, I told the waiter to bring me half a salad, no dressing, and a small glass of plain water. Certain I'd won this round, I sent her a smug smile.

"So . . ." Now that I had her here, I couldn't think of one thing to say.

She lifted one perfect hand and traced the edge of her linen napkin. "What do you want from me?"

My parochial schooling came to my rescue. "Though we may never be friends, there's no reason for us to be enemies . . . love your neighbor and all that good stuff," I finished with a wave of my hand, fighting the urge to knock over her water glass. "As I see it, the decision is not ours to make. Jake's the one who'll decide who he wants to spend the rest of his life with."

"Yes, and since you threw his ring back in his face, I see him as fair game."

The hairs at the base of my skull stirred. Jake had confided in her. He'd told her I'd refused his engagement ring. My heart clenched. I inhaled a deep breath for control and counted slowly to ten. *Twice!* "The phrase 'throw in his face' is a bit harsh." My voice shook with rage. I sucked in another breath for good measure.

Elaine picked up her butter knife and spread fat-free margarine over a bun, depositing loads of fingerprints. I decided I'd gather everything she touched and later return it, instantly wishing I'd brought along a larger handbag. Could I fit her glass, her utensils, and her small bread dish into my purse?

Our meals arrived. When I glanced down at my pathetic little salad, my stomach growled in protest. On the way home Aunt Lilly and I would stop for a burger and fries.

I smiled coyly. "I merely postponed becoming engaged."

Elaine drizzled vinaigrette over her salad. A little landed along the side of the bowl. "Which means he's free." She ran her finger on the edge of the bowl and licked off the dressing. I wanted to wrench her tongue from her throat.

I smiled, my lips aching from the effort.

She returned the gesture, but I knew by the glint in her eyes she disliked me as much as I disliked her.

More accurately—*we hated each other.*

"But," I said, pleased I'd found a suitable reply, "you ditched Jake for another man. You tossed him away like an old sock with a frayed cuff."

Elaine daintily nibbled her salad, slicing the larger vegetables into tiny bites. I suspected she was deliberately trying to prove a point. She was petite, and she knew it. I wasn't, and she knew that, too. I bet she pigged out in private but had been blessed with great genes and a speedy metabolism.

She pushed aside the last cucumber. "That's it for me."

We haven't even had the main course. "Aren't you going to eat dessert?"

"I couldn't eat another bite."

Give me a break! "My sentiments exactly."

She tapped her napkin to the corner of her mouth; her lips twitched.

I braced myself.

Her eyes widened with satisfaction. "When I broke off our engagement, he had tears in his eyes. I bet you've never made Jake cry."

"I wouldn't be so sure of that if I were you." The image of Jake, his eyes misty, ripped me apart. I didn't know the man could cry. He was my rock, my strength. I wanted to call Elaine a liar, but I couldn't do it without making a scene. My fingers itched to slap the victorious grin from her face.

I cracked, lost it, and became totally unglued.

87

Reaching for a bun, my elbow slammed into her water glass, which struck her chest at high velocity and landed on her slim thighs. The lemon wedge contrasted nicely with her forest-green pants.

She jumped to her feet. "I've had enough of your little game. I'm leaving. You'll get the tab for my cleaning bill." She turned and, with her head held high, sashayed from the room.

Several nearby people stole glances at me. When they turned away, I slipped on my mittens and slid Elaine's place setting into my purse, which bulged open so I threw my jacket over it. The waiter rushed over with a sponge to mop up the water. Shaking all over, I rose on wobbly legs. "Leave the bill on the table. I'll be right back." I ran to the bathroom.

I'd no sooner shut the door to the stall than Elaine's salad dish clattered onto the tile floor, shattering, some of the pieces landing beside a woman who stood by the sink.

Feeling like a fool, I dropped to my knees and, reaching beyond the partition, scooped up the ceramic shards and deposited them into my purse. I was a wreck. No way could I dust for prints in this atmosphere. I breathed in shallowly until, from lack of oxygen, spots flittered before my eyes. I waited until the bathroom door closed and the other woman had left before leaving the stall.

I removed a twenty-dollar bill from my pocket, figuring I'd drop it on the table as I ran by. More shallow gulps of air. Lightheaded and on rubbery legs, I wended my way between tables, left my money by my salad, and ran past the hostess who shouted for me to stop.

My heart slammed into my ribs as I hotfooted it outside and spotted Lilly behind the wheel of my Explorer. I opened the back door and threw myself facedown on the seat.

"Gun it," I shouted.

Nothing happened.

Sweat drenched my underarms. I sat up and rested a reassuring hand over my aunt's shoulder. "I'm counting on you. Push the pedal to the metal. NOW!"

The engine roared, tires screeched as the Explorer jumped the curb, took out a mailbox before careening back onto the street. People ran for cover. We missed a delivery truck by a hair, another by a lot less. My vehicle rounded the corner on two wheels. A cement mixer came right at us.

Aunt Lilly threw up her hands, closed her eyes, and screamed.

"Hell's bells," Aunt Lilly said while I inspected the damage to the right fender. "I never knew I could drive that fast."

I ran my hand along the broken headlight and wondered whether the hostess at the Olive Garden had gotten my license number. I heard sirens in the distance and prepared myself for the worst. The cruiser rushed past my duplex. *Phew.*

"I hear a strange hissing." Aunt Lilly cocked her head to one side.

I saw steam coming from under the hood. "I bet the radiator's shot to hell. Don't worry about it. I have insurance." *With a five-hundred-dollar deductible.* I groaned.

"Do you think you can still drive it?" Aunt Lilly asked, looking concerned.

"I'll drop it off at the garage on my way to work tomorrow and see what the mechanic has to say. But I expect to be without a vehicle for a few days."

"Get a loaner."

"My insurance doesn't cover that."

"Let me pay for it," she said, digging in her purse.

"I couldn't let you do that."

"It was my fault."

"It was my idea."

Lilly nodded. "True, but no one held a pistol to my head. And I did have one . . ." She yanked her spiral pad from her pocket and flipped through the pages, her lips curving happily. ". . . helluva good adventure. Worry not, we single women on the prowl need transportation. I'll find a suitable mode of transit." She hesitated a moment, then her eyes lit with excitement. "It's about time this single gal had a car of her own, a sturdy vehicle with a backseat large enough for my Cobbler."

"If you're serious, tomorrow evening I'll go with you and help you choose a sensible late-model used car."

"With your help teaching me to drive, I'm sure I'll have my license in no time."

God, no! Anything but that. "Sure," I said, surprised at how calm I sounded.

"Cobbler and I may just jog on down to the dealership tomorrow morning and have ourselves a look around."

"Be careful, these used-car salesmen are slicker than hair gel."

She nodded in agreement.

"Promise you won't make any decisions until you've had a chance to speak with me."

"It does my heart good to know you're looking out for my safety."

Feeling a deep sense of kinship, I hugged her and was surprised to discover I enjoyed Aunt Lilly's company. In fact, I was glad she lived next door.

A brisk wind whipped Aunt Lilly's coat around her legs. I pulled my collar against my neck and dug my keys from my purse. "Let's get inside before the cold air erases Elaine's fingerprints."

Chapter Nine

With Lilly looking over my shoulder, I picked up the stiff brush, dipped it into the black powder, and swept over the broken shards of Elaine's salad dish.

"Is that one?" Lilly asked.

I looked at the black smudge. "I think my mittens damaged the evidence. It's also possible the vinaigrette is causing the magnetic powder to clump, or Elaine doesn't have normal fingerprints, which would explain a lot. The woman is too perfect to be real."

Lilly inclined her head. "I sure hope something else yields a good fingerprint because I couldn't go through that ordeal again."

"Elaine would never agree to meet with me again so you have nothing to worry about. Anyway, I haven't given up. I still have to check her glass and her utensils."

I dusted the knife and salad fork with equally poor results.

Lilly sighed. "That's too bad."

"It's not over until you hear the elephants trumpet."

"I've never heard that expression before."

I cast a quick glance at my aunt. "Clichés are the mortal sins of journalism. Anyone who's been to a circus knows the elephants arrive last."

"Gee, I didn't know that."

"Now you do."

Aunt Lilly jotted in her spiral pad.

I eyed Elaine's glass, sitting on my bookcase shelf, my last chance for success. Since I'd worn mittens when I'd handled it, I didn't hold much hope. Plus I'd shoved it in my purse without thought of damaging the prints.

I dusted the powder over the smooth surface. My dark mood lifted. "Hot damn! If this isn't a print, then I'm not Monique St. Cyr, investigative reporter on the rise."

"I envy you. You have such an exciting life."

Feeling sure of myself, I rested blackened fingers over Lilly's hand. "You're on your way to becoming a vital woman, too."

"Hot damn!" Lilly said, sounding a lot like me. "By the time your mother returns from Europe, she won't recognize her little sister."

"That's what I'm afraid of."

"Tee hee hee."

It was no laughing matter, but since I wouldn't see my mother for months, I concentrated on a more pertinent problem—proving Elaine had broken into my duplex. After rereading the directions that came with Richard's kit, I unwound the tape and pressed it down, careful not to leave air pockets. I pushed my thumb hard over the print and with one swift motion yanked the tape off the glass, adhering my evidence to a special card. I placed the edge of the card under the glass to hold it in place.

Lilly leaned in closer. "That looks like a good one."

"Can't you do better than that? Great, marvelous, and at the very least, awesome."

"How about extraordinarily, brilliantly spectacular?"

"You catch on fast."

"I have a lot of making up to do." She paused a moment. "I bet Cobbler is lonely. I'm going to take him outside to do his business, then bring him in here to visit."

"Sure, and while you're doing that, I'll get the cover of my mother's book and the shredded paper out of my closet. Make sure you have on plenty of warm clothes because we'll be using a strong chemical on my back porch."

"Be right back."

I watched her leave. More than her hair color had changed. Lilly walked with a more confident stride. Until my mother arrived, I'd proudly take responsibility for her transformation.

Lilly returned with the dog a moment later. Cobbler sniffed every inch of the living room rug before stretching out on the couch next to my leather handbag. He put his head down on his paws and with one eye closed, peeked at me.

I recognized his don't-you-worry-I'm-a-good-boy look. *I knew better.* I grabbed my purse and set it on the top shelf of my bookcase before joining my aunt in the kitchen.

Lilly pressed the nozzle on the spray can. "Ick, this smells putrid."

"Don't inhale that. Richard made a point of warning me to use ninhydrin only in a well-ventilated area, which is why we're heading to the porch."

"Maybe it's too cold outside."

"I hadn't considered that, but since Richard didn't mention it, I'm assuming we're all set."

Lilly's brow creased with doubt. "After all we've been through, it would be a shame if you made a mistake."

"You're right. Normally I wouldn't bother Richard, but what are friends for."

"I'd like to meet Richard sometime. I've never rubbed elbows with a real honest-to-goodness private investigator."

The less I saw of Richard, the better. "He's a busy man so I don't know whether that'll be possible."

"Just keep it in mind."

93

"Sure." I picked up the phone, dialed Richard's number, and listened to it ring for several seconds. "No one's home." I slid my hands into plastic Baggies and picked up the spray can.

"Why are you doing that?"

"Because I don't want to smudge Elaine's prints with my mittens."

"You're the most clever woman I know."

"An investigative reporter's mind never rests."

"I can see that."

My chest expanding with pride, I was about to go outside when I heard glass breaking, not the loud explosion of a book hurling through a window, but a soft tinkling sound.

Lilly and I exchanged startled looks and dashed into the living room. Cobbler stood with his front paws on my bookshelf, the shattered remains of Elaine's water glass by his hind feet, the corner of the fingerprint card sticking out from the corner of his mouth.

While Aunt Lilly mumbled, "Goodness gracious, goodness gracious," I wrenched open the dog's mouth and dug out a slimy wad of partially digested paper.

"You better take your hero home before I'm tempted to skin him alive and bury his remains in the backyard."

Spreading her arms wide, Aunt Lilly jumped between us.

Yet, even as I threatened the despicable creature, I glanced at his lolling tongue, his expectant expression, and felt something inside me melt. The big lout knew I was a softy. As much as I tried to hate the beast, I knew the fault was mine. I should have been more careful.

Against my better judgment I reached around my aunt and patted his head.

"He didn't mean to do it," Lilly said, her eyes tearing.

"I know that."

"I'm so sorry."

I gestured matter-of-factly. "It's not your fault. Don't worry about it. I'm sure I'll think of something."

Jake showed up at seven. "If I didn't know better, I'd swear I smelled ninhydrin, a chemical used in finger-printing."

I sniffed the air and looked at him with what I hoped was wide-eyed innocence. "What use would I have for that?" This was a trick I'd learned back in parochial school. To avoid telling lies, answer with a question.

"True." He handed me one perfect red rose. "For my favorite girl."

Since he wasn't in the habit of giving me flowers, I concluded he was feeling guilty for not telling me about you know who. "Are you saying you have more than one girl?" This was the perfect opportunity for him to come clean and tell me he'd seen Elaine.

"You know better," he replied, sweeping me into his arms for a mind-numbing kiss.

My thoughts wandered off track for a moment as his hands connected with vital body parts. "Mmmmm, I've missed you."

"Same here."

"Really?" I asked. "Am I the only one you miss?"

He chuckled. "That depends on the day of the week," he replied in a teasing tone before flicking his tongue over my earlobe, then down along the tender flesh of my neck. "All day I've been thinking about you. I can't wait to make you mine."

Before he could again broach the subject of marriage, I ran

my hand over the bulge of his jeans and, nodding toward the bedroom, gave him a come-hither smile. "Copper, for the right price, I might be able to take your mind off your troubles."

His grin widened. "I should pick you up for solicitation of an officer."

I yanked off my sweatshirt and stood in my lacy bra.

I heard his rapid intake of air.

Pleased with myself, I leaned in close so he'd get a good view of my cleavage. "I don't usually do flatfoots, but in this case, I'm willing to give you a deal. Two for the price of one."

He lifted an eyebrow and seemed to ponder the offer. "Do you take Visa?"

I was prepared to give him a flip answer but his irises turned a smoky brown, rendering me speechless. He swung me into his arms, entered my bedroom, and set me down on the bed, stretching out alongside me. "I love you," he murmured. "Marry me and be my wife."

"I love you, too. Just give me a little more time." I threaded my fingers through his hair and pushed my tongue against his. Desire hummed through my body.

He looked down at me, his eyes filled with need. I saw love and a whole lot more. I was the woman he wanted forever. And I wanted him, too.

Jake already owned my heart, and when a moment later he claimed my body, I felt myself transported into another world, a place where men and women trusted and never hurt each other.

Afterward as we clung together, our hearts beating as one, being married to Jake seemed like the smart thing to do. Even having his baby and postponing my career seemed wise.

Jake was my whole life. Were he to run off with Elaine, to the casual observer I'd look the same, but deep inside I'd be a hollow shell. With effort I'd survive and go on as though nothing were wrong, but those close to me would know better.

I was tempted to tell Jake I'd made a mistake, but I needed to be certain, to allow my emotions to ebb, and to seek counsel from my best friend, Jeannine.

So I kept my thoughts to myself and slipped out of bed. "I bought a couple steaks, and there's beer in the fridge."

"Good, I'm starving," Jake said, jumping out of bed. The sight of his naked body stole my breath.

I padded toward the bathroom. Glancing over my shoulder, I sent him a saucy smile. "If you've nothing better to do, I need some help washing my back."

"You're an insatiable wench."

"Are you complaining?"

"I'm thinking I'm one hell of a fortunate man." He caught up with me and playfully slapped my fanny, his fingers tracing the contours of my behind.

When we stepped into the shower, I took the pleasure of running a soapy washcloth over Jake's chest and legs, paying special attention to that part of him that sprang from a nest of dark curly hair. Jake cupped my breasts with both hands, pebbling my nipples on contact. He lifted me above him, anchored my back against the tub wall and entered me. I arched back and moaned. He licked the droplets of water from my neck, once more taking me to heights I didn't think possible.

Sometime later I watched Jake wipe the water from his back with a thick towel. "Hey, before I forget, I have to work late on Friday, and I want to take you someplace special for your birthday."

I was pleased he remembered.

"You're reaching a milestone," he teased, combing his hair. "I've never made love to an old lady before."

Pretending to be angry, I scrunched up my mouth. "You really know how to stroke a woman's ego."

Laughing, he glanced at me in the bathroom mirror. "I aim to please."

I winked. "You sure succeeded earlier."

"You did a pretty good job of that yourself." His smile warmed my heart. "To save time, would you mind driving to my apartment Friday evening?"

"No problem."

"Wear something special."

"How special?"

"Wear something hot."

I saluted. "Aye, aye, sir. Where are we going?"

"You'll see."

"You know I can't stand surprises."

"Yup, which makes this all the more fun. No jeans and sweatshirts. I want you to wear something that'll turn a man's head."

"I'll do my best."

An idea quickly mushroomed.

Jake was right. This was a milestone, hence a day I wanted to remember. Always. If all went as planned, my birthday would be etched into both our minds until the day we died.

If, in his final years, Jake ended up in a nursing home in the advanced stages of senility, I suspected he'd glance at the nurses with a slightly perverted look on his face, a look brought on by a distant memory.

When I was through with Jake, he wouldn't speak of Elaine because he wouldn't remember who she was.

Great joy bubbled in my heart.

Some of my ideas were good, but this idea surpassed all others. I knew just the place to shop for the perfect getup. I'd pick out an outfit guaranteed to melt the socks from Jake's feet, guaranteed to widen his eyes and flair his nostrils, guaranteed to speed his pulse and race his heart. I doubted we'd ever leave his apartment in time for our reservation at the restaurant. For that matter, food would be the furthest thing from our minds.

Pleased with myself and anxious to put my plan into gear, I grinned. *I'd show Jake Dube what an old lady of thirty years could do.*

Sometime later Jake was outside grilling our steaks. Wrapped in a thick blue chenille robe, I threw together a salad, all the while wondering whether I'd made a mistake when I'd refused Jake's ring.

What harm was there in simply getting engaged? He knew how much my career meant to me. He wouldn't stand in the way of my dreams. Would he? Of course not, I told myself, the slightest shiver of apprehension sluicing through me.

Jeannine was ready to settle down and have Ted's baby. If she could focus on the present, why couldn't I?

Once I figured out what I wanted and set my priorities in order, I'd have a serious talk with Jake. If I accepted his engagement ring, Elaine could crawl back under her rock and leave us alone.

The thought took me aback.

Was I bending my principles because of her? Surely I wasn't so afraid of losing Jake that I'd resort to getting married before I was ready. Would I?

The truth hit me full force.

I was scared of Elaine, a gut-wrenching fear that started deep in my chest and consumed me, threatening my very being.

She was petite, successful, and in pursuit of the man I

loved. Damn right I was frightened, and rightfully so.

I might be a vibrant, intelligent woman, but in Elaine's presence, my self-esteem wavered. And Jake not mentioning he'd seen his ex-fiancée only made matters worse.

Chapter Ten

When the taxi dropped me off the next day after work, I was surprised to see a vehicle parked next to my mother's red Mustang. Wide, and low to the ground, the bright yellow monstrosity took up half the yard and then some. Instead of bumpers, thick metal pipes curved over the front and rear fenders.

I concluded Gramps had male company because no woman would give such a vehicle a second glance. I peered inside the windows at the two bench seats, wide enough for four grown men sitting side by side. Ample room for scratching, telling raunchy jokes, slapping each other good-naturedly, and stretching tired limbs after a hard day of beer-drinking and moose-hunting.

I dug out my key and unlocked the door to my duplex. From the corner of my eye I spotted Aunt Lilly jogging toward me with Cobbler trailing several yards behind. Barely winded, she came up beside me.

"What do you think?" she asked, reaching down to pat her dog.

"He looks exhausted."

"That's because he's done nothing but lie around. I'm whipping him into shape. Anyway, I didn't mean Cobbler, what do you think of my Hummer?"

I had no idea what she meant until she aimed a small device at the ugly vehicle in the yard. I heard the click of locks.

"It comes with automatic locks, power windows, and MT mudflats."

"What are MT mudflats?"

"I haven't a clue, but it sounds grand." She ran a gloved hand lovingly over the pipes that, in my opinion, enhanced the vehicle's hideous appearance.

"The last owner upgraded the brush guard to two-inch steel. There are roll bars, a roof rack, and backup radar to detect the distance to the nearest object. According to my salesman, even the most inexperienced driver could back up this beauty with one eye closed and one hand tied behind her back."

"That'll come in handy if you ever have to wear an eye patch and a cast on one hand."

"Tee hee hee." She opened the door and Cobbler hopped inside. "When I first saw it, I was flabbergasted. It has an appearance all its own."

"That's a fact." Nodding, I wondered whether it was too late for her to renege on the deal. A crafty used-car salesman had taken advantage of my aunt's naïve nature.

"It wasn't the best-looking car on the lot, but it's the safest. Because of its width, it's almost impossible to roll over." She glanced at me and shook her head. "I looked at a vehicle similar to yours. Did you know your Explorer is an accident waiting to happen? The salesman explained that popular SUVs have such a narrow wheelbase they tip over easily. When we rounded the corner at the Olive Garden yesterday, it was a miracle we weren't killed. I thought for sure we were going to roll over, which will never happen with my fly-yellow Hummer," she said with certainty.

"But it's so wide."

"Precisely, that's why I picked it. Plus think of all the

damage your vehicle sustained because of a minor collision with a mailbox. I bet I could flatten every mailbox in Portland and never even nick the finish."

"Why yellow?" I asked because it seemed a bit bright for a middle-aged woman.

"That's simple." She ran her fingers over a stiff red curl. "The red Hummer clashed with the color of my hair."

Her answer made me proud. Aunt Lilly had begun to think like a modern woman. "That makes sense."

"And the list of options goes on and on. In front there's a winch capable of pulling us out of any ditch. For that matter, the next time your Explorer flips over into a gully, give me a call, and I'll come rescue you."

"In all the time I've owned the Explorer, not once have I come close to rolling it over, except for the one instance you were behind the wheel."

"My point exactly. You have a dangerous vehicle." She speared me with a warning look. "I've always come unglued whenever I slide behind the wheel of other vehicles, but I sat in the driver's seat of my humdinger of a Hummer and hardly felt dizzy at all. Every day after my run with Cobbler, he and I will sit in the vehicle for no less than fifteen minutes. Once I've achieved success with that small feat, I'll venture forth and try turning the key and listening to the purr of the engine. For good luck, I've hung my favorite rabbit's foot from the rear-view mirror and adhered a small St. Christopher's statue to my dashboard with Super Glue. Within a week, I should be ready to drive this beauty on the road . . . with your help, of course."

NO!!! Gooseflesh peppered my arms. "Did you put down a deposit?"

"No."

Phew, it wasn't too late.

I tempered my comment because I saw Aunt Lilly was

happy with her selection. "Then maybe we should go back to the dealership and have ourselves another look." I'd point out other cars and try to change her mind.

"While there, you can test-drive the red Hummer. She's magnificent, and I'm sure my salesman will give you a good deal, too."

"Let's make sure I have all the facts straight. Did you sign any documents? Did money exchange hands?" I glanced at Cobbler who'd settled in for the duration.

"She's all mine." Aunt Lilly flashed bright eyes at me and rested her fingers on the hood. "I paid cash."

Common sense dictated I abandon my plot to acquire Elaine's fingerprints. Cobbler eating the first set of prints was an omen. However, if I were to believe that theory, the same would apply to the backseat of Jeannine's Camaro, Jake's shoes, several belts, a purse, and what remained of a one-sleeved leather jacket.

Unfortunately, the urge to know whether Elaine had done the deed festered inside and drove me wild. I had no choice but to forge ahead.

The next day I called Richard. "How good are your lock picking skills?"

He exhaled an impatient sigh. "We P.I.s don't divulge some details of our profession. Why?"

"If you don't know crap about breaking into someone's apartment, then I'll let you go."

"I know plenty," he said, his voice pulsating with pride.

Yippee! I'd found my man, the answer to my dilemma. If I stroked his ego, he'd be putty in my hands.

"I really need help, but if you're too busy . . ."

"Good, see ya around sometime."

"I'll hire a more experienced private investigator."

Someone who'd gotten his knowledge in the real world, not from a computer program.

"That's fine with me."

"Hey, not so fast. You needn't act so uppity." Sheesh, I was losing my grip. If I didn't calm down, Richard would hang up and refuse to talk to me. Granted, he was the worst private investigator in the whole state of Maine, probably in the entire country, but he was also the only one I knew. I couldn't allow him to slip through my fingers.

"I didn't want to embarrass you, but you have a fan who's desperate to meet you."

"You better not be coming on to me again."

"I wouldn't . . . I never . . ." On a previous phone conversation, my parrot, Long John, had blurted out, "I'm horny, let's screw." From that moment on, convinced I'd made advances toward him, gum-snapping, freckle-faced Richard, who looked all of twelve years old, kept a wary eye on me whenever we were together.

"Look," he said, in a condescending tone. "A lot of women go ape over me so I'm not blaming you."

If I were stranded on an island with Richard as my sole companion, I would swear off sex and have no regrets. My libido would shrivel up and waste away. If Richard were the last male specimen on Earth, I'd join the nunnery without a backward glance.

Never, no way, nohow!

I heard another sigh over the line. "I'm not trying to be cruel, but by now, you must realize I'm not interested in you."

I rolled my eyes and proclaimed the matter a lost cause. I was in a bind, and he was my only hope. "If I promise to behave, will you come over?"

"I'll think about it."

"My Aunt Lilly is here from Texas, and she'd be thrilled to

meet an honest-to-goodness private eye."

"I can understand why she would."

I decided to seal the deal! "She thinks all you guys are hunks."

"Gee," he said, sounding like a kid. "I'll see what I can do."

Later that evening, Aunt Lilly and I were standing around my kitchen table paying close attention to Richard.

"You'll never know how exciting this is for me to be standing next to an honest-to-goodness private eye. If I live to be one hundred, I'll never forget this day."

Right before my eyes Richard's head swelled a hat size. "Thanks," he said.

"Taking time out of your busy day is nothing to sneeze at," Aunt Lilly replied with an admiring glance.

"There are some who don't appreciate my efforts."

"It's not every day I get to see a professional working his trade. Have you busted many crooks?"

Richard puffed out his chest. "Some."

"Killers?"

Richard gave a strange half-nod, which I took to mean *absolutely not.*

Lilly didn't see it that way. "I bet you carry a real gun." Standing still, she seemed to be holding her breath.

"Yes, I carry a piece."

Aunt Lilly's eyes blazed with excitement. "Have you killed anyone?"

"There are some things I'd rather not discuss," Richard said, his brow furrowing convincingly.

I doubted Richard had ever fired his weapon. If he wasn't careful with his gun, he'd shoot off his own foot. But I kept my mouth shut and my opinions to myself. "Did you bring along your lock-picking gear?"

Lilly turned to me. "Are we going to break into someone's house?"

"No, we're not." *I'm going solo.*

Richard leered at me, his attempt at looking tough failed. "Wherever my gear goes, I go."

Two evenings later, dressed in black sweatpants, a black hooded sweatshirt, and with my face covered with soot, I pulled my Explorer into the back of a parking lot across the street from Elaine's apartment.

"I'm so excited I could wet myself," came Aunt Lilly's voice from the backseat. "How long do you think this operation will take?"

I recognized Richard's phrase and frowned. "With a bit of luck, I'll be back in a few minutes."

I heard the crinkle of plastic and turned to see my aunt with a black plastic bag over her hair, secured to her forehead with silver duct tape. We'd found no hat large enough to hide the glowing spectacle.

"My life sure took a turn for the better when I decided to stay in Anne Marie's apartment. I can't wait to tell her about all my adventures."

My mother would tan my hide. "Maybe you should wait until she returns. Just think how surprised she'll be to see the new you instead of hearing about your transformation in bits and pieces."

"I suppose so. Do you think it's safe parking here?"

"Sure."

"That sign says this is parking for the tenants of this apartment building, and all other vehicles will be towed."

"I'll be back before anyone notices. Don't worry about a thing. Meanwhile, stay down so no one sees you."

"Sure thing."

I watched Richard's white van roll into a parking space in front of Elaine's apartment complex. He couldn't have picked a more conspicuous location.

"Don't make a sound," I said, locking the door and sending my aunt a reassuring smile.

She cranked down the back window an inch. "Don't worry about me. If need be, I'm prepared to drive the getaway car."

"I'm hoping that won't be necessary." Our last escapade had cost me a five-hundred-dollar deductible. Plus my insurance premiums would skyrocket.

I crossed the street and looked for signs of Elaine's silver Porsche. Seeing none, I walked behind Richard's van, heard the door open, and felt a hand encircle my arm.

"Quick, get in."

I hopped into the back of the van, caught my foot under the edge of a torn rug, lost my balance, and flattened Richard beneath me.

Sounding terrified, he pushed insistent hands against my shoulders. "Get up! Your feeble attempt to seduce me has failed. For crying out loud, can't you control yourself for even a few minutes?"

"It was an accident," I said, getting to my knees and freeing him.

"That's what you say. Accept the facts. I'm not interested. Period."

To think that someone like pipsqueak Richard, who stood all of five feet in heels, wasn't interested in me rankled. My self-esteem shriveled. Anyone else would have taken their shredded pride and beat feet.

Insulted, I was tempted to ask him what was wrong with me. Fearing he might construe my question as another come-on, I let the subject drop. "Sorry."

"Once we get inside, you're to do exactly as I say."

"Don't I always?"

"If we hear sirens, it's every man for himself."

Sirens! My heart beat like a jungle drum. "Surely you don't expect trouble."

"Over the years I've learned to be prepared for the unexpected. It's part of being a professional."

I decided to take him down a notch. "Why would someone with your experience park a white van on a moonlit night right outside the person's house?"

"That's simple," he said while pulling a black hat over his red curly hair. "No one would ever suspect an undercover operation going on right under their noses. Which is why I'm the expert. You remember that."

I saluted. "Aye, aye, sir."

"Wipe that foolish grin from your face. This is no laughing matter. And wash that goop off your face. If anyone takes one look at you, they'll call the cops."

I dabbed the soot from my cheeks and glanced at my image in a small mirror he handed me. Frightened eyes looked back at me. Did I want to go through with this? I only had to conjure Elaine's image, and I was ready to go.

I followed Richard into Elaine's apartment complex. We took the stairs two at a time to the sixth floor, or rather I watched Richard scamper up the stairwell. My legs felt like mush and my heart threatened to explode by the time we reached the landing.

I gasped for breath and grabbed hold of the door molding. Looking no worse for wear, Richard unzipped a small leather case and made his selection.

"In the event someone shows up, be prepared to bolt."

"I need to recoup my strength," I said, inhaling another raspy breath.

"Did I mention I've expanded my business? I do repo work on the side."

"What exactly is repo work?"

"I repossess vehicles for banks and lending institutions after people default on their loans."

"Hmmm. Very interesting." My reporter's mind clicked into gear. *Potential story!*

"The last gig I did, the owner showed up just as I was pulling out of his driveway with his truck. The gunshot missed me by an inch, shattering the front and rear windshields."

Lately, Mr. Winters hadn't given me any good assignments so I was on the lookout for some of my own. I wiggled my nose. "I smell a story."

"Play your cards right, and I might let you tag along some night." He glanced down at his paraphernalia. "This is a sixty-two-piece lock pick set, the best on the market. I got a good deal on it at professionalburglar.com. I ordered other tools for breaking into cars and trucks."

I watched him unsuccessfully jiggle the pick. He chose another tool and, while turning the doorknob back and forth, he jabbed at the lock.

"Do you think it's going to work?"

"Of course. But I need absolute quiet," he said, in that same tone Sister Mary Agnes used with me back in grade school. He kneeled on one knee, leveled his right eye with the doorknob, and frantically wiggled the small metal object into the lock.

He made such a racket I assumed he hadn't heard the elevator doors open. A couple stepped out. I had my flaws, but over the years I'd honed my quick thinking to an art form.

Kicking aside the small leather case, I grabbed the back of Richard's collar, yanked him up against me, and planted a convincing kiss on his mouth. His kicking feet dangled in the air. Trying to escape, he pressed his palms against my shoulders, but I clamped insistent arms around him and tried to give him a signal. Either my actions scared him into submission or he'd gotten the gist of our predicament because he quieted.

The couple smiled at each other as they strolled past. Before they disappeared inside their apartment, in a low tone the woman murmured, "You think they'd take it inside."

I set Richard down and avoided his scowl. "Next time just tell me, and I'll scoot down the stairwell."

"There wasn't time."

"I bet."

A female can take only so much. "I'm out of here . . ."

The door clicked open, and my sentence trailed off as I reached in my pocket for my flashlight and dashed inside Elaine's living room.

"That's her," I said to Richard, directing the light beam at a photo of Elaine on the mantel over a fake fireplace.

He puckered his mouth and whistled. "Good-looking dame."

"She's not so hot. I bet the photographer did a lot of touch-up work."

"What's she done? Are you working on a story about espionage, drug lords, or child pornography?"

I turned an imaginary key over my mouth. "It's top secret."

"I have connections. If I wanted to know the scoop, I'd find out, but . . ." He threw me a frightened glance. "After that display in my van and in the hallway, I'm keeping a safe distance."

"The first was a mistake and the last a necessity."

"Right. Anyway, don't call me."

"Aren't I going with you on your next repo job?"

"No way. You blew it big time."

"Sheesh." I wanted to wring his skinny chicken neck.

"Do your thing, but I'm outta here."

"How will I lock up?"

"I'll leave you my pick, but you better not lose it."

"I don't know how to use it."

"Just do what I did," he said, opening the door, and cramming a small metal file with a hook on one end into my hand. "Don't worry about it. People forget to lock their doors all the time. Be sure you don't leave prints behind."

I pulled on wool gloves. "Got it covered."

He shook his head. "Anyway, if you get caught, you don't know me."

I heard a ring and the elevator door shuffled open. I was prepared to run for the stairwell, but Richard pushed me inside and softly shut the door. I lost my balance and tumbled onto the carpet. My flashlight rolled across the room.

"Damn that blasted Richard," I mumbled as I crawled toward the only source of light, circling my fingers over the cool metal of my flashlight.

My breath caught in my throat as I waited for the sound of footsteps in the hallway to pass by the door.

I heard Elaine's voice. "Jake, it was so sweet of you to come to my rescue and give me a ride home."

"It's nothing."

Nothing! I just bet. Like vehicles at a demolition derby, my thoughts collided, making it easy to jump to conclusions. Elaine would coerce Jake into her apartment. Once inside he wouldn't stand a chance. The seductress would overpower him with her feminine wiles.

I heard a key in the lock, then Elaine's voice. "That's strange . . ."

"What's wrong?" Jake asked.

112

What's wrong! You have no business being with Elaine! I considered showing myself and demanding an explanation. Fortunately my reasoning returned.

"I was sure I'd locked the door," Elaine said, turning the doorknob.

Looking for an escape, I chose the doorway to my left, plunged into the dark, and found myself at the foot of her bed. I tried to crawl underneath, but the space was too small. As Elaine flicked on the living room light, I dove into her closet and flattened my body beside her extensive shoe collection. As I waited, I discovered Elaine had one flaw.

Her feet stunk.

As I stood nose to sole with a pair of high-heeled shoes, I tried not to breathe in deeply and prayed I wouldn't pass out from the stench.

Chapter Eleven

Holding my breath and praying I wasn't discovered, I pressed my ear against the closet door and tried to listen to the conversation in the other room.

"I just happen to have a cold one in the fridge," Elaine said, her voice a purr.

"Thanks, but I should be going."

I cheered him on. *Jake Dube, he's my man, if he can't do it, no one can!*

"What's the hurry? Anyway, there's something I want to discuss with you. Certainly, you can stay for a few minutes . . . for old times' sake."

"Well . . ."

He was weakening. That worried me. I crossed my fingers and sent Jake telepathic messages. *Tell her you're sorry but you need to go home and wash the sink, cut your toenails, or take the dog for a walk.*

Since Jake didn't have a dog, I hoped Elaine would get the message and leave him alone.

"I baked a cake, your favorite," she said, in an overly sweet voice.

"Chocolate?" Jake asked.

According to my mother, the way to a man's heart was through his stomach. I'd never put any credence in that ridiculous adage.

I pictured Elaine eyeing Jake the way a female black widow did her mate—before snacking on him. "Chocolate cake with chocolate frosting and mint filling."

"Hmmmm, you drive a hard bargain."

Damn you, Jake Dube! I could almost hear him salivating. He'd abandon ship for a measly piece of cake. He'd switch teams for a few cake crumbs and mint filling.

Disappointment slammed into me. I wanted to dash into the living room and hit him over the head with one of Elaine's stinky shoes.

I didn't even know Jake's favorite dessert was chocolate cake with chocolate frosting and mint filling. I felt as though I'd lost this match. Big time. Elaine knew something about Jake that I didn't.

I'd thought I knew everything about Jake. Wrong again. Familiarity bred closeness, and at the moment I felt a world apart from the man I loved.

I heard footsteps going into the kitchen, the ping of ceramic dishes, and the clink of silverware. My fertile imagination filled in what I couldn't see. I saw Elaine with her skirt hiked up her thigh, a come-hither look on her face. I pictured her spooning cake into Jake's mouth, running her index finger along his lips to catch a small dab of frosting.

"What did you want to tell me?" Jake asked.

"Enjoy your cake. We can talk later."

Reasoning returned in the nick of time. Elaine was crafty, but still not a worthy opponent. I might not bake worth a damn, but I knew how to cook in the bedroom. Regardless of what my mother and Elaine might think, the way to a man's heart could not be found in the kitchen, unless I factored in that one time Jake had anchored my bare bottom against the kitchen counter and had his way with me.

Given the choice, I'd wager Jake would choose me with a

can of pressurized whipped cream in my hands over Elaine's crappy cake. Feeling better, I realized I hadn't lost this match because I hadn't yet had my turn. As Jake and Elaine made small talk, I planned my birthday outfit right down to my makeup and hairdo. When I was through with Jake, chocolate cake would be the furthest thing from his mind.

"That's the best cake I've had in a while," traitorous Jake said with an appreciative moan.

"Monique's not much of a cook, huh?"

I craned my head and waited for his reply.

"I don't have any complaints."

"It's too bad she turned down your engagement ring."

It hurt me to think he'd discussed our relationship with her.

"She needs a little more time."

"She's where I was a few years ago," came the syrupy voice, allowing some time for her comment to sink in so Jake could draw a comparison.

I was treading water, weighted down with cement booties.

"Only I've changed my outlook about settling down. I wasn't ready for marriage back then, but I am now," Elaine added.

"What are you getting at?"

"I'm here for you if you ever need to talk to someone. I know you care for Monique, and I can accept that, but if your relationship happens to hit a snag . . ."

Bitch!

My lungs constricted and burned from lack of oxygen.

"Elaine . . ."

"Don't say anything. I know I've come to my senses too late. At the very least, I want us to be friends."

I heard the sound of chairs scraping against the kitchen floor.

"Let me box up the cake so you can take it home with you."

"That's not necessary."

A very feminine laugh ensued. "I made the dessert especially for you so I want you to have it."

And a whole lot more, I figured, barely containing my rage.

"You'd be doing me a favor. I don't want all the extra calories going straight to my hips."

"If you insist."

I groaned. He hadn't put up much of a fight.

A moment later I heard footsteps, then a door opening. "If you'd like, come back after your shift tomorrow, I'll bake a lemon meringue pie."

Silence.

What was going on? I warded off visions of groping hands and clinging lips. I trusted Jake, but that didn't stop me from imagining the unthinkable.

Jake cleared his throat. "Elaine . . ."

A short pause.

I clenched my fingers and held my breath.

"There won't be a next time. I doubt Monique would approve of our getting together for old times' sake, and I don't intend to do anything that might jeopardize our relationship. You should know I'm going to marry Monique just as soon as she'll have me."

Phew!

Tears flooded my eyes. I wanted to wrap my arms around the big lug's neck and kiss him senseless. Unfortunately, that wasn't possible.

First I needed to escape from the closet and Elaine's smelly shoes.

After several hours I finally dared to push the closet door

open and, while staring at Elaine's sleeping form, tiptoed across the bedroom. A floorboard under the carpet creaked, its sound echoing across the room like a sonic boom. My heart slammed against my ribs. I froze for a moment, expecting to hear Elaine scream or reach for the bedside phone to call the police. I heard a soft sigh and watched the small mound under the covers stir.

I gulped a deep breath and forced one foot in the front of the other until I'd inched my way across the bedroom and the living room. Holding my breath, I wrapped trembling fingers around the doorknob, stepped out and closed the door. I ran into the hallway and down the stairs until I stood, hands on knees, inhaling ragged breaths. Looking up at the starlit sky, I was thankful for my freedom and glad to have escaped undetected.

Holding tight to a pair of Elaine's shoes that I'd borrowed in hopes of gathering fingerprints, I dashed across the street and into the parking lot. I looked all around and saw nothing in my parking space. Thinking I was mistaken, I checked the parking lot of the adjacent building. Same results. My Explorer was gone and so was Aunt Lilly.

I was well beyond panic mode when I heard what sounded like bagpipes. I looked up to see a yellow Hummer with my aunt behind the wheel, taking the corner on two tires. Brakes screeched.

"Hop in," she shouted in a crazed voice.

In the moonlight, her red hair glowed like flames. I ran into the street and hopped onto the front seat next to Cobbler, who'd already feasted on half of my leather purse. I threw Elaine's shoes on the backseat.

The tires squealed as a wild-eyed Aunt Lilly pushed her foot to the floor mat and punched the air with one hand while holding onto the steering wheel with the other. "Isn't this bitchy!"

"Where's my Explorer?"

"It got towed."

"I could have sworn I heard bagpipes."

"It's my horn," Aunt Lilly said, pressing the device for good measure. A bagpipe rendition of the "Beer Barrel Polka" reverberated in the frosty night air.

We missed a lamppost by an inch. Certain I was about to meet my demise, I squeezed my eyes shut and peeked out through the narrow slit of my eyelids.

Seemingly calm, Aunt Lilly reached down and patted Cobbler's head. "While the mechanic was hooking your Explorer to the wrecker, I grabbed your pocketbook, crept out of the car, and jogged on home. It took me a while to get up the courage to drive, but I couldn't abandon you."

She swerved around a parked car. I ground my teeth to a pulp.

"The first mile was the worst," she said, waving her hand and letting go of the steering wheel for a second. "After that it got easier. Then a feeling of power took hold. I'd never felt anything like it in my entire boring existence. I was in control."

For the moment she made eye contact, I saw pride and self-confidence.

And my life passing before my eyes!

The tires on the passenger side jumped the curb and back down again; one of the heavy pipes around the front fender struck a trash can that exploded on impact. Garbage flew everywhere; a banana peel and a partially chewed hamburger struck the windshield.

Cobbler lifted his head and sniffed. He planted his front feet on the dashboard, pressed his nose against the window, and barked at the tasty morsel on the other side of the glass.

Aunt Lilly snapped her fingers. "Cobbler, lie down."

Much to my surprise, the dog hopped onto the backseat and lowered his bulky frame.

"Isn't this just bitchy?" Aunt Lilly threw back her head and uttered a maniacal laugh. "I'm in control!"

"Watch that . . ." I screamed seconds before impact and a loud clunk. The mailbox flew twenty feet into the air before landing upside down in the crook of an oak tree.

Minutes later the Hummer came to a screeching halt inches from my front door. Fearing Aunt Lilly might take off again, I jumped out and tried to stand on trembling limbs.

My aunt climbed out of the vehicle and, with a small flashlight she took from her pocket, closely examined the fenders and doors. "Just as I thought, not one nick, not even one tiny scratch."

As hard as it was to believe, she was right. I couldn't see any damage.

"It's a good thing I had the forethought to buy this Hummer. It's practically indestructible."

"I wish I could say the same for the mailbox you hit."

"I sure hope no one saw us and took down your mother's license plate number."

"What's this about the license plate number?"

"Well, since I wasn't planning to drive my Hummer for some time, I saw no point in paying for the registration. But then tonight you were in trouble so I borrowed your mother's plates. I didn't think she'd mind. Besides, since she's in Europe, she doesn't need them."

I groaned. "If the police had stopped you, you'd have gotten a hefty fine." My right eye blinked uncontrollably.

She blinked back and shrugged.

"What happened to the temporary plates the dealer gave you?"

"Cobbler ate them." She shrugged. "Oh, well, nothing ventured, nothing gained."

"That's the second mailbox you've hit. You could go to jail for destroying government property." I didn't know this for a fact but figured I somehow needed to get through to Lilly. She had no business driving.

"Tomorrow I'll call the local post office and ask what the going price is for a mailbox. I'll explain I'm putting some cash in an envelope to pay for the damage."

Aunt Lilly opened the back door and out hopped Cobbler with one of Elaine's high heels in his mouth.

"Not again!" I screamed, wrapping my bare hands around his muzzle and trying to wrestle the shoe free.

"Don't speak too loudly, or you'll traumatize the poor dear. Anyway, I can tell he's sorry." Aunt Lilly tried unsuccessfully to wedge the shoe free, which disappeared by degrees into the slobbery mouth.

Hoping to find Elaine's other shoe, I climbed into the backseat. But after checking every square inch, I had to accept facts. Cobbler had swallowed it.

Aunt Lilly shoved the dog into her duplex and came up beside me, resting a consoling hand on my elbow. "I'm sure you'll think of some other way to get Elaine's prints. And if there's anything I can do to help, just give a holler."

All the hours I'd spent holed up in that closet—for nothing!

Over the years my mother had drummed into my head that if I couldn't say anything good, then I should keep my mouth shut.

So I said nothing. At this rate, I'd never obtain Elaine's fingerprints.

"Well, what do you think of my driving?" Lilly asked, a sparkle in her eyes and a lilt to her voice.

"Doesn't my fear-struck expression give away my reaction?"

"Tee hee hee, you're a hoot."

Clearly, she hadn't taken me seriously. I held what remained of my favorite leather purse with shaky fingers and tried to figure out a diplomatic answer. According to my mother, Lilly was very sensitive. I didn't want to hurt her feelings. But I had to get through to her.

She must never drive again.

"You scared me out of my wits," I said, losing my cool for a moment. "From now on, only sit behind the steering wheel of the kiddie cars at carnivals." On the trip, my eye had developed a nervous twitch. My lid batted open and shut several times.

Aunt Lilly winked back and sent me a sly smile. "I just love your sense of humor. We had ourselves a rootin' tootin', humdinger of a good time."

I decided to postpone our serious talk until later because I needed some rest. I unlocked the door to my duplex and was about to say good night when I spotted a brightly wrapped package in the middle of my living room floor.

"Holy shit!" I couldn't wait to see what was inside.

Aunt Lilly nudged past me. "What do you think it is?"

"I bet it's a peace offering from Jake." I figured Elaine's chocolate cake had formed a hard ball in his stomach. Consumed with guilt for spending time with his ex, he'd dropped over, bearing gifts.

"Maybe he brought you an early birthday present," Lilly said, lifting the box an inch. "It's too heavy to be clothes."

I tried to slide my fingernails under the paper, but all the seams were taped shut. Running into the kitchen, I grabbed a steak knife and, after dashing back into the living room, I slit the paper along the top and side. Aunt Lilly and I tore the wrapping off in a microsecond.

I removed the lid and stared down at crumpled news-paper. Reaching into the bottom of the box, I pulled out part of a book cover. Upon closer inspection, I realized I wasn't looking at crumpled newspaper but ripped pages from my mother's erotic fiction.

Lilly gasped. "Should I call the police?"

"That's not necessary."

"Are you sure?"

"Elaine did this," I said with certainty.

"How can she be responsible? You were with her half the night."

"There was a window of opportunity between the time I left to meet Richard and the time she arrived at her apartment with Jake."

"I don't see why she'd go to this extreme to harass you." Looking frightened, Aunt Lilly chewed her lower lip.

"A woman scorned is capable of anything. These are hardcovers; at $26.95 a pop, she's spending big bucks to take out her vengeance on me. If she keeps this up, my mother will make the *New York Times* Bestseller List."

"What are we going to do?"

We? No way!

"I'm going to set a trap."

Chapter Twelve

I called Jeannine the next day and asked her to come right over. I needed to bounce some thoughts off a levelheaded female, and she was it. When it came to common sense, she had more than most and had helped me out of jams several times. I needed to hear her say I was finally on the right track.

I poured myself a glass of Merlot and filled another glass with ginger ale. I sliced cheese and grabbed a box of crackers. Taking everything into the living room, I sat on the couch and sipped some wine.

A warm feeling started in the pit of my stomach and rushed to my arms and legs, due either to the alcohol entering my bloodstream or my excitement—I'd decided to accept Jake's engagement ring.

Last night's fiasco in the closet had proven to me how much I could trust him. He'd answered all the questions correctly. He'd even defended my cooking, which under the best of circumstances would qualify as poor.

Now that I'd made up my mind, I couldn't wait to tell Jake the news. As soon as possible I wanted to take another trip to the mall and pick up my ring. A beautiful marquise solitaire. My heart pumped erratically. I couldn't wait to show off my diamond ring to family, friends, and co-workers.

When Jeannine arrived a few minutes later, I knew by her red-rimmed eyes something was seriously wrong.

My heart clenched. "Is everything all right with the baby?"

"My baby's fine." She unbuttoned her long woolen coat and dropped it over my computer chair.

That left only one other possibility—man trouble. "Do you want to talk about it?"

With a sigh, she sat on the couch and grabbed a slice of sharp cheese and a cracker. "My life's a mess."

"You heard from Ted?"

Blinking back tears, she nodded and bit down on a cracker. "He's not coming back. He's asked for a transfer. His father was never ill. He used that as an excuse to make his getaway."

"That louse."

"He offered to pay for an abortion." Jeannine stared across the living room and heaved a long, weary sigh. "I told him to go screw himself."

"Good for you."

She dropped the cracker on the table, turned, and grabbed hold of my forearm. "I'm frightened. I'm going to be a single mother."

A gamut of emotions streaked across her face: fear, love, and bewilderment.

"I'll help you," I said, wrapping an arm around her shoulder.

Jeannine collapsed against me; her body shook as she cried.

I patted her back with my hand, trying to think of things to say that might make her feel better. "Maybe he'll change his mind."

"Ted said he was sorry, like that would make a difference. Sorry for what, I asked him, for making a baby or for lying when he said he loved me? He didn't even bother to answer."

"He can't walk away without a backward glance. We'll see

a lawyer and make sure he pays child support."

Jeannine straightened and wiped the tears from her face. "I led him to believe I was going to have an abortion. As far as Ted's concerned, there'll be no baby. I want nothing from him. I'm going to raise my child by myself. And I'll never again depend on another man."

"All men aren't alike," I said, a tremor racking my body.

"I thought you were stupid not to take Jake's engagement ring, but you're the smartest woman I know. You're goal-oriented. I admire you."

"I'm not that smart," I said, my heart clenching.

"I honestly don't know how I'll provide for myself and a newborn. How will I manage to work and pay for day care?"

"I'll help you," I said, hugging her, realizing I could barely pay my own bills, much less anyone else's.

"You'll never find yourself in my predicament because you'll have a career to fall back on."

I shrugged and bit the inside of my cheek. "I'm thinking of accepting Jake's proposal."

The muscles of her back stiffened beneath my fingertips. She lifted her head and faced me, her features twisting harshly. "Don't do it. You need to stay on course, or you could end up just like me."

"That's not what I thought you'd say."

"You need to be able to stand on your own two feet before you can rely on anyone else. I like Jake, but . . . be true to yourself before you commit to him or any man. If not, you could regret it for the rest of your life."

She sighed and cupped her hands over her abdomen. "My baby is growing inside, and I don't know how I'll provide for him. College costs so much, and I want the very best for my child. You shouldn't ask me for advice right now. But you've always known what you wanted. Go for it, stick to your guns and reach for the stars. In time, you'll become a well-known investigative reporter."

Well-known investigative reporter had a nice ring.

So did Mrs. Jake Dube.

What had started out as a simple discussion with a good friend had become complicated. Instead of hearing words of encouragement, I'd been warned to proceed with caution.

I arrived at work the next morning ten minutes late. I threw my purse in the desk drawer and leafed through the day's assignments. Four obituaries, a recipe for fried haddock for my weekly cooking column, and information on a church bazaar. My career as an investigative reporter teetered between *downright boring* and *going nowhere*. Neither held much hope.

I looked up and saw Jeannine, her nimble fingers typing away. To a stranger she looked the same, but beneath the smile she aimed at me, I saw the sadness in her eyes, the slight puffiness of her face that meant she'd spent the night crying.

"How are you doing?"

"Better."

She didn't elaborate, and I didn't pry.

"Look busy, Doris Cote is heading this way full bore."

Glancing up, my heart skipped a beat when I stared into Doris's feral eyes. My copy editor, a harbinger of bad news, thrived on finding other people's mistakes. By her mile-wide smile, I knew I was in deep trouble.

I inhaled a calming breath and forced a casual pose, which wasn't easy with my wobbly limbs threatening to give way.

She slapped an obituary on my desk. "Walter Freedman's widow just called, and she was hysterical."

"That's to be expected. Her eighty-nine-year-old husband passed away three days ago."

"The obituary you wrote had a small boo-boo."

Doris never used words like boo-boo, which meant only one thing. She was in a jovial mood.

I was going to be fired.

My stomach twisted. "What have I done?"

She aimed one manicured nail at the third paragraph and read, her voice ringing with joy, " 'Walter Freedman was a man with a big heart. He'd give the shirt off his back to a stranger. Everyone was proud to call him a fiend.' "

Friend, it was supposed to say friend. "My fingers must have missed a key."

"Apparently. Give the distraught widow a call. Offer to take her to lunch and make it up to her. It's your mess. Clean it up." Doris's sharp gaze pierced through me. "If I hadn't been home yesterday battling the flu with a temperature of one hundred and three, I'd have caught the error. Unfortunately, even I get sick once in a while."

I took the yellow Post-it note with a phone number and a name she jammed into my hand and wondered what I was supposed to do. Nothing I'd say to Mr. Freedman's widow could change the printed word.

"Oh . . . I almost forgot," Doris said, glancing over her shoulder as she marched away from my desk, her mouth curving into a rare smile. "Mr. Winters wants to speak with you."

As I marched toward Mr. Winters's office, I tabulated the facts: Doris's high spirits—not good, my obituary mistake—even worse, add to the scenario the gray ominous clouds outside and the raindrops pelting the windowpanes. A bolt of lightning sliced across the sky. From my years at parochial school, I recognized the signs. The Man upstairs was sending me a coded message.

Life looked bleak.

Either my boss would hand me my walking papers, or he'd shoot me and hide my remains inside his cavernous metal cabinet, which he kept locked at all times. Many in the newsroom had speculated on its contents, but no one knew for sure what he kept hidden inside.

Lightning sluiced across the sky. Another message, which if decoded probably meant "run like hell." Through the glass panel in his office door, I admired the colorful crocheted granny afghan tossed over a chair, adding a touch of warmth to his otherwise gloomy office. When I scanned the top of my boss's desk for weapons and watched his fingers wrap around the plastic letter opener, a shiver raced down my back. I eyed the storage unit and deduced it was large enough for one if not two bodies.

Rationally, I knew Mr. Winters wouldn't hurt me, but the obsessive, jump-to-conclusions side of my brain wasn't so sure.

Since on occasion I'd been accused of overreacting, I double-checked my facts: Doris's smiling face, the missing "r" in the obituary, and another ear-shattering clap of thunder. Lights flicked off and on again. My arms pebbled with gooseflesh. Clearly doomed, I lifted my hand and, hoping not to make a sound, I lightly brushed my knuckles against the glass panel.

Mr. Winters raised his head. His glum expression fueled my apprehension.

Sweat beaded my forehead, my throat thickened with dread, and my size-nine shoes were rooted to the floor.

"Come in, come in," he said impatiently, waving his hand. I pictured that same hand raised in a final farewell in a few minutes as I drove away with the contents of my desk in a cardboard box.

I managed to force one foot in front of the other until my

thighs were pressed against his desk. I looked down into his cold gray eyes.

"Doris Cote had a talk with me this morning."

Gulp! My fears mushroomed.

"She showed me Walter Freedman's obituary. No doubt the old man is rolling over in his grave. I can't say I blame him. He was a generous philanthropist, and he deserved better than to leave this world portrayed as a fiend, a maniac, a beast."

The lines around Mr. Winters's mouth deepened.

"Everything happens for a reason," I said, paraphrasing my parochial school teacher, Sister Mary Agnes.

"Consider this a warning. I'm not pleased with your work."

His announcement drowned out the next jolt of thunder.

"Depending on how it's used, 'fiend' isn't all that bad."

Mr. Winters's pupils narrowed to pinpricks.

I clenched my fingers and proceeded. " 'Fiend' also means enthusiast, devotee, obsessed."

My boss's eyebrows winged sharply.

I took a moment to regroup. "When we're through with our discussion, I'll call his widow, apologize, and offer to take her out to lunch. My treat, of course." I looked for understanding on Mr. Winters's face and saw none. "I'll explain the mistake and throw myself at her mercy. I'm sure she'll understand."

"I hope so. Meanwhile, I have an assignment for you."

No doubt he'd hand me a recipe for chicken soup, or expect me to cover the opening of the new Jewish deli around the corner.

"Mailboxes have been vandalized, and I want you to get to the root of the problem."

"How many mailboxes?" I asked, crossing my fingers and praying to hear any number but *two*.

He dropped the letter opener, and I released a breath.

"Two so far. The one outside the Olive Garden was knocked off its base, the other ended up upside down in a tree."

For lack of a better word, I muttered, "Oh." I pictured Aunt Lilly wearing stripes because of my exposé, which had won me fame and critical acclaim . . . What was I thinking! I couldn't turn in my own aunt.

"I can't write this story."

Mr. Winters scowled. "Why not?"

Conflict of interest. Unable to come up with a suitable reply, I clamped my lips together.

"I'm not taking no for an answer."

Maybe Lilly would consider jail time another adventure. I quickly dismissed the thought.

"Talk to the postmaster, then write a great article. Your job depends on its outcome."

I nodded. My gaze again strayed toward his cabinet. Not one but two locks. Hmmmm. My newswoman curiosity was piqued. No one went to such trouble unless he had something to hide.

A deep, dark secret.

A hideous past.

As I left Mr. Winters's office, I wondered what skeletons lay hidden in his cabinet.

As I drove to the post office, I pondered my stagnant career. Unless I dredged up a news story guaranteed to knock the socks off Mr. Winters's feet, I'd be writing my name on the back of my unemployment checks.

I shuddered when I thought of my obit blunder and

131

blamed my shoddy work on boredom and my wandering mind. It was becoming increasingly difficult to focus on dead-end assignments.

Were the circumstances different, I might be eager to solve the mystery of the vandalized mailboxes. Since I personally knew the vandal and had witnessed the destruction firsthand, I dreaded this assignment.

How could I properly cover the story without incriminating my aunt? *Or me!* I exhaled slowly and saw the white puff of my breath. Trying to warm up, I slid my gloved hands along the steering wheel and tapped my left foot. Two days ago the heater in my Explorer had quit working. The driver's side window didn't shut tight, and it was twenty degrees below zero. I wondered whether Aunt Lilly ramming my vehicle into the first mailbox had caused more damage than we'd originally thought.

When I pulled into the parking lot, my feet felt like blocks of ice. I hopped out of my vehicle, slammed the door shut, and admired the candy-red Corvette parked a few feet away. Corvettes were my favorite sports car, low, sleek, and they shouted success. As I rounded the front of my Explorer, I spotted flecks of *mailbox-blue paint* on my bumper. My heart ricocheted from my throat to my knees and back again.

I bent down, removed my gloves, and rubbed at the spots with my thumbnail and watched the evidence flake off. A howling, icy gust of wind peppered my face with loose gravel. Hoping I'd destroyed all the evidence, I dashed inside the post office.

As I waited for Bill, the postmaster, to finish with the customers, I obsessed about my vehicle. What if I'd missed some of the blue paint? Could I be jailed as an accessory to the crime?

I was ready to go outside and take another look at my bumper when Bill motioned for his assistant, Ed, who arrived with two large boxes. "These packages are addressed to you, but they're for your mother."

I saw they were from her publisher. "I bet these are her author copies. She told me to expect them."

"She's getting to be quite the celebrity. Her post office box is always crammed with fan mail. Would you like me to take them out for you?" Ed asked.

"Sure, the car's unlocked. Just put them on the backseat of the green Explorer."

The next customer was a man with a Mohawk, a nose ring, half a dozen eyebrow piercings, and star tattoos on his earlobes. On the back of his leather jacket were the words, "Up yours!"

Same to you!

Bill weighed his package. "Do you want to track that?"

"No." The punk collected his receipt and turned to leave.

I felt a moment's guilt for judging the young man so harshly, a by-product of my years of parochial schooling. I tried not to shiver when he cast black, demonic eyes toward me. His smile was sinister, mean, and stole my breath.

As a reporter I had an innate ability to tell a person's character at a glance.

Punk—too mild a word.

I settled on *serial killer* and was relieved when he left the post office without drawing a gun.

Leaning on a thick cane, engraved with a serpent's head, an elderly woman handed Bill a large envelope. "I'd like this to go Priority."

As she hobbled out the door a moment later, I dug my notepad and pencil from my purse. "I'm here to get the

133

scoop about the mailbox capers," I said, turning to the post-master.

Frowning, he pushed his wire-rimmed glasses up his nose. "When they find the culprit responsible for the vandalism, I'm pressing charges."

Tapping my pencil on my notebook, I pictured Aunt Lilly behind bars. "Maybe it was just an accident."

"Not a chance."

Phil replaced Bill at the counter.

"How can you be so sure?" I asked, my heart drowning out my words as I followed Bill into his office.

"According to the police, there are at least two people responsible for the crime."

"Two?"

"Yup, and the officers found a bit of green paint on the first mailbox."

Yikes! Not one minute earlier, I'd blurted to everyone within hearing range that I owned a green Explorer. Had Phil seen blue paint on my vehicle?

"When they finally got the second mailbox out of the tree, the police concluded a second vehicle was involved, something large with pipes for fenders."

I gripped my pencil so hard it snapped in two. I steadied my voice. "Do you know how the second mailbox ended up in a tree?"

"They think it was struck hard by a heavy-duty truck. Would you like a glass of water? You don't look so good."

I sucked in a calming breath and waved away his concerns. "It's probably nothing more than a bunch of teenagers playing a prank. I can picture them hauling the mailbox up the tree with ropes."

"Because of its weight, it would take considerable strength to lift it that high. But the police dismissed the idea because we'd had snow flurries earlier that evening. There were no footprints around and the tire tracks led right up to the mailbox."

"Oh," I said, with a nervous chuckle.

Bill's eyes hardened. "It's a federal offense to tamper with government property. When they find the people responsible for the damage, I hope they throw them in jail and lose the key."

What would happen to me when my mother discovered I was responsible for her sister's incarceration!

"Maybe those responsible are nice people who made a mistake."

Bill's eyes bulged with disbelief. "Their mistake was tampering with federal property. Uncle Sam doesn't look kindly upon thugs like these."

Thugs—too strong a word. "Don't you think you're being a bit harsh? Maybe some nice gray-haired lady who didn't know how to drive struck the mailboxes."

Aunt Lilly's hair was now fire-engine red, but gray sounded better.

He pointed at my nose. "Not a chance. The police calculated the vehicle's speed at the time of impact at being between forty and fifty miles per hour. There were no skid marks, which proves the driver never touched the brakes. It was a deliberate, direct hit. I hope the bastards rot away in jail."

I was overcome with an immediate sense of urgency to go double-check my bumper for traces of blue paint. I raised my finger to signal I'd be right back when Bill looked out his office window.

His head jerked back a fraction. "Did you say your vehicle was green?"

Cornered, unable to deny the truth, I nodded. Assuming

he'd spotted blue paint from this distance, cold sweat drenched my underarms. I pictured myself spending jail time with a muscled babe named Bubbarette as my cellmate.

"Yes, why?"

My wobbly tone shouted *guilty!*

"Because it's on fire."

Chapter Thirteen

Rushing outside, I heard crackling and popping as the flames devoured my only vehicle. My reporter's fine-tuned mind was numb, as were my fingers and toes from the brutal cold. I was vaguely aware of sirens, a fire truck pulling into the parking lot, and firemen hosing down the blaze.

The acrid smell of smoke filled my nostrils. Water hissed against the hot metal.

As I stood in a trance, wondering how I'd dredge up the money for another car payment, I thought I saw a trace of paint on the lower front bumper.

Could it be?

Was I hallucinating?

I squinted hard, crossed my fingers, prayed I was mistaken, but sure enough, there was a speck of blue paint about the size of a quarter.

Mailbox-blue paint!

The incriminating evidence taunted me. I no longer focused on the fire, but instead on the bumper.

Paranoia set in.

Expecting the postmaster to make a citizen's arrest, I watched his every move. Bill seemed fixated with my green Explorer. Was he staring at the flames or my bumper? Were his eyes zeroing in on the blue paint?

My much-cherished freedom passed before my eyes.

Prison garb would magnify the extra ten pounds I'd been meaning to shed; stripes or neon-orange would emphasize every flaw.

Maybe if I bribed the guards, I'd be allowed to wear my favorite black jeans with the industrial-strength zipper that held back the floodgates. I was debating whether to flee to Mexico or Canada when the firemen dropped their hoses and ran.

"Move back, she's going to blow!"

Several small pops preceded a large boom. The Explorer shattered. Flames leaped into the sky. Metal flew; people ran for cover.

A while later a myriad of emotions bombarded me as I stood staring at the charred remains and bits of singed paper drifting into the sky:

Confusion—what had caused the blaze?

Anxiety—where would I scrape up enough money for another set of wheels?

Relief—my Explorer was destroyed, but so was the last tiny speck of mailbox-blue paint.

"Arson!" My heart rumbled like a runaway train later that evening.

"Yes." Jake pulled me against him. I drew comfort from his strong arms.

"Are you sure it wasn't an accident?"

"Positive. Someone used an accelerant to torch your Explorer."

I shivered. "If I'd put the boxes in the backseat and driven off, I'd be toast." *Burnt toast.* "Why would someone torch my vehicle?"

An idea struck and gelled. Because it was difficult to think of anything but sex that close to Jake, I pulled away and inhaled a deep breath to clear my mind. "That's it! I'm sure of it. The arsonist wasn't trying to harm me. I bet this is the same person who's been sending me shredded copies of my mother's books. You find that person, and you've found your culprit."

"Had you been driving around with your mother's books for a while?"

"Well, no. Ed carried the boxes out to the Explorer about twenty minutes earlier."

"That's a very small window of opportunity."

"Meaning?"

"If I'm to believe your theory, either Ed is the arsonist or the person hell-bent on destroying your mother's books saw him putting the boxes into your vehicle. How would the arsonist know the contents of the boxes?"

"You can wipe that smart-aleck look off your face. When Ed showed me the boxes, I explained to him they were author copies. Everyone in the post office knew the boxes contained books."

"How many people were in the post office when you arrived?"

"Maybe half a dozen."

"Can you remember anyone who looked suspicious?"

"As a matter of fact, there was one guy who gave me the creeps. My reporter's instincts pegged him as a troublemaker the instant I saw him."

"Can you describe him?"

"Of course. I'm a trained professional. He had a Mohawk, a nose ring, half a dozen eyebrow piercings, and star tattoos on his earlobes. He had demonic eyes. I bet he's the one. He left right after Ed took out my boxes."

Jake's cocky smile irritated me. "He's not your man."

I grumbled under my breath. "Just because you're a cop,

you think you know everything."

Jake's grin widened.

"What?"

"If I tell you why, you have to promise not to repeat what I say."

Curiosity flourished. "Yes, yes, get on with it."

"Babe, this time your reporter's instinct let you down. The guy you described sounds like Larry, who works under-cover for our vice squad."

I pounded my fist against his chest. "You think you're so smart."

Another maddening grin.

He moved closer, tucked my head against his chest. I knew he was trying to throw me off track. He succeeded a moment later when he slipped his hand under my chin and pressed his lips to mine.

His mouth was soft and insistent.

I'd had a close call. A few minutes more and I'd have been behind the wheel.

Boom!

A woman doesn't almost meet her Maker without reper-cussions. I grabbed hold of Jake as though there were no to-morrow and tugged at his shirt. His devilish smile encouraged my efforts. Buttons flew. We never made it into the bedroom or managed to shed all our clothes. I had my way with him right there on the living room rug.

Not that he complained.

Then he picked me up, carried me into the next room, dropped me on the bed, and gave me an encore perfor-mance.

No complaints there, either.

Much, much later, we lay in each other's arms, naked and content, my mind floating blissfully.

"When are we getting married?" he asked, bringing me back to earth in a hurry.

My stomach clenched. "I've been thinking seriously about it."

He ran a finger along the side of my face. "And?"

"I was almost ready to take the plunge, but . . ." Should I betray a confidence and tell him about Jeaninne? I decided to wait and at least discuss it with her first.

"You make marriage sound like jumping off a cliff."

I kissed him, but his lips weren't pliant. "I don't mean to. Let's not argue."

"Time's running out," he said, causing a shiver to race down my spine. "I want an answer."

"Give me another week."

He playfully jabbed my chin with his knuckles. "You've got yourself a deal. I'm holding you to it."

"I promise," I whispered, somewhat apprehensive but pleased with my reply.

Jake uncapped a bottle of beer and poured me a glass of Merlot. "Remember to wear something nice tomorrow night for your birthday."

"I like the Olive Garden, but make the reservation for late because I might want to do a little pre-meal celebrating if you get my drift," I said with a look that left no doubt what I meant.

"We aren't going to the Olive Garden. I've planned a little surprise for you."

I had a little surprise for him, too. "On my way home today, I bought something special to wear."

"Good."

Little did he know! When I was through with Jake, Elaine would be permanently erased from his mind. With a little extra effort, he would no longer remember her name.

Once more I wondered why he hadn't mentioned seeing her. Did he have something to hide? I trusted him, but I didn't trust her, and that was reason enough to worry.

"Is anything new?" I asked, giving him another chance to confess.

"No, why do you ask?"

I wanted to slam my fists into his chest. I wanted to grill him with questions until he confessed. I forced a smile. "No reason."

He leaned into me and kissed my cheek. "What story are you working on now? Have you irritated the hell out of anyone and given them a reason to come after you?"

"To hear you talk, you'd think I was a pain in the butt."

"I plead the Fifth," he said, raising his hands in surrender.

I made a rude gesture.

His smile intensified.

Turning my back to him, I sat down, sliced cheese and pepperoni, arranged crackers on a plate, and set them on the kitchen table. "I'm doing a piece on mailbox vandalism. That's hardly exposé journalism."

Jake pulled out a chair and sat next to me. "Have you stepped on anyone's toes or caused a stir lately?"

"Sheesh," I said, rolling my eyes. "Ninety-year-old Virginia Helms is bent because I featured her sister's vegetable soup instead of hers in my cooking column. Then there's the missing 'r' in the obituary, but that's hardly reason to try to charbroil someone."

I stacked cheese and pepperoni on a cracker. Not exactly a healthy snack, but I'd start my diet after my birthday.

"Can you think of someone who'd want to harm you?"

"You're starting to frighten me."

"You should be frightened. I want you to be careful. Keep an eye out for suspicious people, and don't go out alone, especially at night, until we've solved this crime."

"I'm a reporter. I can't do my job if I'm hiding indoors."

"I want to keep you safe. Meanwhile, make a list of the names of anyone who'd benefit from having you out of the picture."

I gave it some thought.

Only one name surfaced.

ELAINE!

She didn't strike me as the sort who'd stoop to murder to win her man. But a woman scorned . . .

Not believing Elaine capable of such an act, I toyed with the possibility. Had desperation sent her over the edge? Had she come to her senses and realized she didn't stand a chance with Jake?

Not wanting to give Jake the opportunity to defend his ex, I said nothing.

For one perverse moment I pictured Elaine decked out in stripes and neon-orange. She looked perfect, and the guards stood wide-eyed, admiring her petite butt. Just wait until she took off her shoes. Those same guards would run for their lives, and the prison wing would have to be fumigated.

I chuckled.

"What's so funny?" Jake asked, breaking into my reverie.

Aunt Lilly lifted a disposable camera up to her face and snapped a picture of the Explorer's remains. One door was cocked at a strange angle; the other door was missing.

"Goodness gracious, it reminds me of that turkey you tried to cook for Thanksgiving when you were twenty."

"How can you remember something that happened so long ago?"

"Until moving in next door to you, it was the most memorable moment of my life. Not anymore," she said, waving her manicured nails decorated with tiny dog decals. She knelt and snapped several more pictures. "I hope these suffice for the insurance company."

"I only had liability." I heaved a discouraged sigh and leaned against my rental vehicle—an older model truck with oversized tires, no tailgate, and sporting so much rust, it was hard to guess its original color.

"Still, I don't understand why you insisted on renting this rattletrap. I could have driven you wherever you needed to go."

Precisely! After riding with Aunt Lilly that last time, I planned never to repeat the experience.

I almost blurted out that I didn't want to impose, but since my near-death experience, I didn't want to press my luck and later find out that white lies did count.

Instead I said nothing and patted Cobbler, who rubbed against my sleeve and left behind a thick thread of slime. I reached into my coat pocket, rubbed at the mess with several tissues, and frowned.

Aunt Lilly fluttered lashes thick with mascara. "Don't look so down in the dumps. Sometimes these things happen for the best."

Was she referring to my Explorer going up in smoke or the dog spittle on my sleeve? *Had Aunt Lilly lost her mind?*

"Look at me," she said, tapping her spiked red hair. "I dreaded the thought of the long drive from Texas. I even considered not coming, but here I am, and I'm glad."

"So?"

"If I hadn't made the effort, look at all the fun and excitement I'd have missed. Your mother's wedding was the turning point in my life. I've had more adventure in the last week than I've had in my entire life."

"What does that have to do with my Explorer?"

144

"Maybe fate intervened, that's what. Maybe this accident is the start of a new adventure. Now you can buy a safe vehicle, and I won't have to worry myself sick whenever you're out. And next time, I suggest you dangle a rabbit foot from the rearview mirror."

Aunt Lilly craned her neck and looked at several charred book covers. "Are those Anne Marie's books?"

"Yes, what's left of them."

"I'd heard her books were hot . . ."

I interrupted. "What do you mean, you've heard? Haven't you read your sister's books?"

Her face turned crimson. "I started one once, but . . . well . . . I stopped because I felt rather dismayed that I would never experience any of it."

"You're still young and vibrant," I said, having some doubts.

"Since moving in next door to you, I feel much younger. I haven't reached vibrant yet, but there's still plenty of time before Anne Marie returns."

I smiled approvingly.

Lilly lifted a gloved hand to her mouth. "Tee hee hee. If we can spread the rumor that Anne Marie's prose set the car afire, she might get her some good press."

"I bet you're right."

"Anyway, to get back to fate and your Explorer. The fire destroyed a potentially dangerous mode of transportation. I'll go shopping with you for a better model. We'll have a grand old time."

"Easier said than done," I said, looking over my shoulder. "I'm really worried."

"If it's the money, I can help."

"I keep expecting this truck to blow up, too."

"Try not to fret. Accidents happen."

145

I looked into her face and realized she didn't understand the situation. "This was no accident. The arson squad did an investigation. Someone doused the backseat with a flammable liquid."

Her face paled. "You mean someone deliberately tried to harm you?"

"Or the books."

She ran a shaky hand over her forehead. Her eyes rolled up into their sockets. She batted her eyes closed and braced her hand against my Explorer.

I grabbed her arm. "Are you going to faint?"

She blinked her eyes open, her cheeks turning a delicate pink. "Good gracious, no. Old habits die hard. I've never . . . well . . ."

"You've never what?"

Guilt clouded her eyes. "Fainted."

"But . . . ?"

"Long ago I learned that fainting not only gained me attention but helped me to escape unpleasant situations. It was my way of fleeing reality."

"I can't believe it. All these years you've fooled my mother," I said, with a measure of pride.

Chapter Fourteen

I arrived at the Saltwater Grill at noon and, because it was bad for my image, I hid the rusty rental truck in the back of the parking lot next to the Dumpster. No successful investigative reporter worth a damn drove a vehicle ready to fall apart.

Granted, it wasn't my truck, but the initial reaction was still the same. That truck said—LOSER. When Joyce, Walter Freedman's widow, arrived, I wanted her to see an intelligent career woman.

As I sauntered toward the entrance, a cold wind whooshed off the Atlantic and sent a shiver down my spine. I lifted the collar of my long woolen coat against my neck and collected my thoughts. I'd buy a round of drinks and hope Mrs. Freedman understood I'd made an honest mistake. I'd appeal to her generous nature and explain my job was at stake.

Maybe she'd even call Mr. Winters or Doris Cote and smooth their ruffled feathers. *Ruffled feathers,* I decided, was a cliché that fit perfectly. If Doris were a bird, she'd be a vulture. I chuckled at the image of my copy editor picking a carcass clean.

A few minutes later a white stretch limo pulled in front of the building. The chauffeur, a ten on the male Richter scale, scooted to the back and opened the door. He offered Mrs. Freedman his hand, which she took and held a bit too long.

147

My reporter's nose smelled trouble.

Joyce Freedman was a looker, probably mid-thirties, sleek black hair, pale complexion, and not an ounce of fat on her slim figure clad in navy blue.

I instantly hated her.

During my years at parochial school, Sister Mary Agnes had drummed into my head not to judge a person on appearances alone. I'd done my best to follow those teachings, but I'd been blessed with an inner sense, which at the moment contradicted the good nun's advice.

This time my reporter's nose was right. Joyce was trouble.

After introductions, she peered from behind a thick veil and tapped a lace handkerchief to the corner of her eyes. She sniffed and wrapped firm fingers around mine. "Shall we go inside?"

Since my goose bumps had sprouted goose bumps, I nodded and stilled my rattling teeth. I followed her into the restaurant and to a table overlooking the ocean.

A waiter arrived a moment later, his admiring gaze locked on Joyce. "Can I get you ladies something to drink?"

"A glass of water with lemon," she said, her voice wavering.

Although I didn't like her, I felt empathy for her loss, and worse knowing my mistake had compounded her worries.

"I'm having a glass of wine, would you like one?" I asked.

She hesitated. "Since you're having a drink, I will, too. Make mine a double martini."

The waiter left and I chose my words carefully. "I must apologize for the error in the obituary. I don't know how to make it up to you."

Her lower lip disappeared beneath her top lip. "Your mistake has caused undue embarrassment to my husband's memory. He was a good man, kind and generous, willing to help the homeless and those less fortunate." She lifted her hankie to her nose and patted gently.

"Yes, I know all that. Walter Freedman was a generous philanthropist to our community, and he'll be missed."

She sniffed and swiped at her eyes with the back of her hand.

I rested my fingers over hers. "I feel really bad about the pain I've caused you. Did you know that according to *Webster's Unabridged Dictionary*, fiend can mean obsessed, a zealot, or addicted?"

"My husband never did drugs," she said, sounding a bit miffed.

"No, no, I wasn't insinuating that. I was thinking more along the lines of—Walter Freedman was obsessed with helping people and a good-hearted zealot. He was addicted to assisting those less fortunate than he."

"I thought a fiend was a diabolical demon."

"It can be, but when used in reference to your husband, it's the highest compliment a person can receive."

"I never thought of it that way."

Neither had I.

"Unfortunately, most people think a fiend is a monster."

"It's a shame the public doesn't have a better command of the English language. I could write an article about your husband and how his donations over the years have aided our community."

She toyed with the veil over her face.

I forged ahead. "I doubt many people saw the obituary, but if I can persuade Mr. Winters to put my article on the front page . . . Wouldn't that undo the insignificant damage of my missing 'r'?"

"You'd put an article about my husband on the front page?"

"You bet I would!" Now all I had to do was convince Mr. Winters.

Joyce's double martini and my glass of Merlot arrived. I took a sip and congratulated myself on my diplomacy.

"How long were you and Mr. Freedman married?"

"One year, three days, and four hours," she said without a pause. "He meant the world to me. I don't know how I'll manage without him."

"Are you saying he didn't provide for you in his will?"

A silly laugh bubbled from her throat. "No, no, not at all. I meant I don't know how I'll survive emotionally. We were so close. I'll miss him. The money means nothing to me. I'd give it all away if I could spend one more evening with my precious Hug-a-Bug."

A corny endearment for an eighty-nine-year-old, but hey, I'd been to parochial school. I didn't judge such things.

Joyce ordered another double martini with extra olives. I passed because I had to drive. I removed a small tape player from my purse. "Would you mind if I record our conversation? I want to be sure I keep the facts straight about your husband."

She chugged half her drink and waved her hand. "Whatever floats your boat."

I clicked on the machine. "Tell me about your husband, his hobbies, his friends, what he did for fun."

She finished her drink and set her glass down with a clunk. "Walt was the salt of the earth, he was the breath in my lungs, the reason for my existence. I loved him with all my heart." She dabbed at her dry cheeks, and I nodded sympathetically.

"He loved sailing." She laughed. "Sometimes I wondered whether he loved that sailboat, the *Miz Tilly*, more than me."

"Men with their toys, they're all the same," I said, encouraging her to continue.

"Damn straight. He'd run his fingers against her gunnels and get an orgasmic look on his face. That old fart was crazy about that boat." She giggled and raised a hand to her lips. "Of course, I mean old fart in the most complimentary way."

Our meals arrived, and I dove into my plate of fried clams. Joyce nibbled on her Caesar salad.

"Would you like another drink?" I asked.

"I shouldn't."

"I'd have one if I had a chauffeur."

"You make a good point. In that case . . ."

I waved our waiter over. She ordered another double and I figured I'd have to take out a loan to pay for our meal.

Joyce removed her hat. I'd expected to see red, puffy eyes.

I was wrong.

We finished the main course and ordered dessert, cheese-cake with strawberries.

I'd done my research and knew Joyce was Mr. Freedman's third wife. He had four sons. "Were you close to Walter's children?"

She broke off a tiny wedge of her cheesecake and chewed. "They hated my guts, but I showed them."

"How'd you do that?"

"They didn't expect our marriage to last."

"Imagine that." A little over a year was hardly a world rec-ord, but since I was here to pacify her, I kept my big mouth shut.

"They insisted Walt's lawyer add a clause in his will. In the event of his death I would get nothing unless we were married at least one year."

Was that a greedy glint in her eyes?

"The bastards wanted the lawyer to make that five years, but I persuaded the old fool to cut the time down to twelve months."

151

Her voice was cold, calculating. I assumed the liquor had loosened her tongue.

She winked. "Between me and you, I made out good on this deal."

"How much of a windfall?" I asked, not expecting an answer.

She leaned in close, brought her mouth near my ear. "The old coot left me over fifty million dollars."

"Holy shit," I said, before I could stop myself.

She threw back her head and laughed. "Stick with me, friend, and I'll help you find another old geezer."

Because I wanted to see her reaction, I said, "With my luck I'd marry an old man who lived to be one hundred and twenty, and needed me to change his Depends."

Her calculating smile sent a chill up my back. "With a little help, 'till death do us part' doesn't have to last a long time."

The clams I'd eaten settled like rocks in my gut.

My reporter's instinct, which had made mistakes in the past, zeroed in on the facts.

Joyce Freedman, seemingly grieving widow, had killed her husband for his fortune.

Unless I uncovered the truth, *she'd get away with murder.*

I arrived home and set my tape player on the kitchen table. I could hardly wait to present my evidence to Mr. Winters. Joyce hadn't come right out and said she'd murdered Walter, but I had enough of her conversation to raise doubts.

I brewed a cup of tea and pressed the play button. Every word was clear, and I congratulated myself for having the foresight to use a recording device.

Unfortunately, I soon discovered I didn't have the entire conversation. When it had mattered most, the machine had run out of tape.

Damn, damn, double damn.

I'd blown my shot at a great story. I wanted to beat my hands against the wall, but there wasn't time. I needed to get ready for my birthday.

A short while later I heard Aunt Lilly's Hummer rumble into the driveway. I needed to have a serious talk with her about driving without a license, without a registration, and using my mother's plates.

I heard Cobbler's deep bark as she shut the door to her duplex. A moment later the phone rang, and I knew by my caller ID it was Aunt Lilly. Thinking she might want to come over for another woman-to-woman chat, I ignored the phone.

I had lots to do before meeting Jake this evening for my birthday celebration.

And what a surprise it would be.

The door burst open and slammed against the wall. My aunt stood with a dust mop raised over her head. "Are you alone?"

"Yes."

She winked. Then took off at a gallop, dust mop thrust before her like a sword, dashing from room to room.

She came to rest a few feet from me. Looking disappointed, she said, "You are alone."

"I told you I was."

"In the movies on television there's always a maniac lurking behind a door with a weapon trained on the victim. I thought . . ."

"You've been watching too much television."

She put the mop down and raised her hand to her chest. "Goodness gracious, you gave me a good case of heart palpitations when you didn't answer the phone. So I grabbed the

153

only weapon I could find, mustered my courage, and ran over here."

"I'm touched that you'd enter a potentially dangerous situation for me."

"I never gave it a second thought, except for now." Looking distraught, she lowered herself onto the couch. "What was I thinking?"

I remembered her determined expression. "You looked ready to do battle. God pity the person who encountered your wrath."

"You think so?" she asked.

I nodded. "Definitely."

"I've been thinking about your situation, and there's only one answer to our dilemma. Each of us should carry a piece and learn something about self-defense."

"Who have you been talking to?"

"I called Richard," she confessed after a pause. "I'm worried sick about you so I sought a professional's opinion. Richard says you need to cover your back at all times. That man doesn't look like much, but did you know he needs to register his hands as lethal weapons?"

"I doubt that very much." I rolled my eyes.

"Don't let Richard's size deceive you. There's a lot of force per inch in his well-tuned body."

No doubt, those were Richard's exact words.

"Lucky for us, he's given me a deal on his complete self-defense course. It's one of my birthday presents to you."

The last thing I wanted was pipsqueak Richard showing me maneuvers he'd learned from a book or off his computer. But Aunt Lilly looked so pleased.

My mother hadn't raised a rude daughter.

"That's great," I said, silently cussing.

"Anyway, tomorrow first thing, you and I are going shopping for pistols."

"I hate guns. They're dangerous. We could kill someone! Besides, have you ever fired a gun?"

Her face blanched. "I've never even seen a real gun up close." She sucked in a deep breath. "But I've worked up the gumption, and before the sun sets tomorrow, we're going to be carrying concealed."

"Shit."

"It'll be another adventure," she said, rising from the couch and leaning in close. "Do you notice anything different about me?" She shook her head. Large metal rings hanging from her ears, clinked together.

"Did you have your ears pierced?"

"Sure did, three times, both sides." Looking pleased, she pulled back her red hair and showed off her earlobes. "They add a certain amount of pizzazz, don't you think?"

They were a bit large for my taste. "They're really nice."

"I can't wait to show Anne Marie the new me."

Would my mother blame me for Lilly's transition from dull middle-aged woman to middle-aged punk rocker? "I'm sure she'll be astounded by the change."

Lilly nodded. "I have a whole list of things on my agenda I plan to do. By the time your mother returns from her honeymoon, she won't recognize her little sister."

"You're fine the way you are. I hope you aren't changing anything else about yourself."

"I've already thrown caution aside, purchased some jewelry, and had one other itty-bitty thing done."

I examined my aunt from head to toe and saw nothing different.

She raised her hand and showed off a ring with small diamonds surrounding a deep blue stone. "I've indulged myself with this sapphire. I figure it's about time I spent some money on frivolity."

"Good idea."

Her face brightened. "Yellow carnations are my favorite flower so I got one of them, too."

"You should surround yourself with flowers," I said, glad my aunt was finally enjoying life.

"Tee hee hee, for now, one yellow carnation is enough. But I'm sure if I ask, the tattoo artist would gladly do more."

Sleet pelted the windshield as I carefully maneuvered the rental truck over the icy road. I hoped to make it to Jake's apartment without being involved in an accident. The thought panicked me. How would I explain my outfit to the paramedics, the police, or the accident room staff? Who'd believe me? For months I'd be the topic of conversation at both the police precinct and the hospital.

Which explained why I was crawling along at a conservative twenty miles an hour. When I turned the next corner, the rear tires skidded. After a near-miss with a fire hydrant, I regained control and released my breath.

The windshield wipers left behind an icy coating, impairing my vision. Even with the heater blowing a blast of hot air, I was chilled to the bone. My long woolen coat couldn't combat the cold. I wished I'd worn slacks over my fishnet stockings and boots instead of spiked heels. But in my excitement to make my grand entrance, I'd thrown an approving glance at myself in the full-length mirror in my bedroom and scurried out the door.

Turning thirty was a milestone in a woman's life. Before tomorrow dawned, I'd prove without a doubt, Monique St. Cyr wasn't just getting older, she was also getting a hell of a lot better.

I rolled into the parking lot adjacent to Jake's apartment and killed the engine. I wrenched open the door and hopped out. The shiny soles of my new heels kicked up in separate directions. My overnight bag cushioned my fall.

I stood, inched across the ice, and reached the stairs. Grabbing hold of the railing, I made it up the three stairs that led to the door. In the hallway I checked my fishnet stockings for holes and was relieved to find them intact.

I walked on wobbly heels to the second floor. Standing outside Jake's door, I pulled my compact from my purse, examined my makeup and glittered hair swept up in outrageous curls and highlighted with blonde streaks. I caught a glimpse of my large hoop earrings from which hung small male and female body parts that occasionally joined depending on how I moved my head.

Tacky?

I preferred the word *inventive*.

Earlier this week, disguised in black apparel and large dark glasses, I'd sneaked into Condom Mania and had chosen my garment, battery-operated tassels that swung in opposite directions, complete with tiny flashing lights, a large jewel for my navel, and a pair of leopard-spotted, glow-in-the-dark thong underwear. I'd complemented my outfit with fishnet stockings and five-inch heels that made walking almost impossible.

Since I wouldn't be standing long, that wasn't a problem.

I looked around to make sure no one was in the hall. Certain I was alone, I dropped my coat onto my bag which contained a change of clothes in case we later went out to eat, and turned on the tassels, which looked great, if I did say so myself.

I shoved open the door, staggered inside, was surprised to

157

see flickering candles on a birthday cake, was even more surprised to hear voices.

Not just Jake's voice!

My heart did a double take when the lights came on.

"Surprise . . ." petered out as the guests took a gander at the birthday girl.

I gasped and lifted my hands to cover my breasts. One tassel wound itself around my finger, trapping it like a bug in a spider's web.

In slow motion, I saw Jake flying toward me, Aunt Lilly fainting into Mr. Winters's arms, and Jeannine's lower jaw hitting her chest. Doris Cote cracked a smile. Gramps missed my entrance because he had his back toward me.

Jake threw an afghan around me and, to the sound of disbelieving murmurs, escorted me into his bedroom.

Chapter Fifteen

Once the bedroom door closed behind us, Jake helped to free my fingers from my tassel.

Pulling me against him, he kissed my forehead. "Change into something more appropriate and go mingle with your guests."

"Are you crazy? I can't go into the living room. Tomorrow, I'll pack my belongings and move across the country. I'll never again be able to show my face in this community."

He glanced down appreciatively. "Your outfit doesn't show off much more flesh than a bathing suit."

I stole a glance in the mirror and shuddered to see the amount of cheek exposed by my thong. Fortunately, I'd had my back to the wall. "Do you think everyone is shocked?"

He grinned. "Probably, but you still need to go out there. I'd better join our guests before they have something else to gossip about," he said with a wink, cupping my behind with warm hands and pulling me against him for a kiss that threw me off balance.

He rested his hands on my shoulders, his lust-filled eyes locking on mine. "Your outfit is sexy as hell, and I definitely plan on a private showing later this evening."

"I wanted to knock your socks off," I said, tracing the angle of his jaw.

"You knocked everyone's socks off," Jake said, as he stepped out.

I shed my tassels and pulled the jewel with the double-sided tape from my navel. I saw no reason to remove the fishnet stockings or the glow-in-the-dark thong. I put on slacks and a nylon blouse over a lacy bra, slipped my feet into sensible shoes and, after taking several fortifying deep breaths, went to face my friends and relatives.

"There she is," Aunt Lilly announced, sounding a bit flustered.

Avoiding eye contract, Mr. Winters looked anywhere but at me.

Doris Cote's mile-wide smile said it all; I'd made her day, her week, probably her entire year.

Jeannine hurried to my side. "Loved your entrance."

"It's not funny."

"No kidding," she said, barely stifling a laugh. "I've felt sick and depressed all day. You really know how to lift a pregnant lady's mood."

"I'm glad I could be of help." I pulled her close. "Do you mind if I tell Jake about your condition?"

"Sure, go ahead. I won't be able to keep my pregnancy a secret much longer."

"Have you heard from Ted?"

She pulled her shoulders back and raised her chin. "Ted who?"

"Hatred is good for the soul."

"That's not what Sister Mary Agnes taught us."

"Sister Agnes didn't know any better because she never went out with Ted."

"Thanks," Jeannine said.

"For what?"

"For being my friend." Before she turned away, I saw tears in her eyes.

Blushing, Aunt Lilly sidled up next to me. "I would have never dared to do what you did. You have gumption. You have spirit. You're my inspiration in life."

"Thanks, I think."

"Oh, before I forget, I spoke to Anne Marie, and for your birthday, we're going in on something big."

I blew out a breath. "I've had enough surprises for one night."

Aunt Lilly jerked her head. "Tee hee hee, goodness gracious. I didn't know your earrings did that!"

I'd forgotten about my coupling jewelry. I slipped them off and slid them into my pocket.

"Maybe later this weekend when we're alone, you'll give me a few dating pointers," Aunt Lilly said, staring at my bare earlobes. "And I hope I have an occasion to borrow those earrings."

Jake's phone rang. He handed my aunt the handset. "Your sister wants a word with you before talking to our birthday girl."

My mother!

"Yes, it's all taken care of," Aunt Lilly said, aiming a scheming smile my way. "It's due to be delivered first thing tomorrow morning."

"What's being delivered?" I asked, leaning in close and trying to catch the other side of the conversation.

"I won't keep you," Aunt Lilly said, "but before I go, I must mention I now have red hair and pierced ears."

I groaned. Cold fingers wrapped themselves around my heart and squeezed hard. When my mother stepped off the plane and didn't recognize her own sister, she'd direct her wrath at me.

Lilly handed me the phone.

"Hi, Mom, how's the honeymoon going?" I asked,

heading into Jake's bedroom for some privacy.

"Your new stepfather has a stick of dynamite you wouldn't believe!"

"Mother!"

She laughed. "Calm down, I was only trying to get a rise out of you."

"There are some things a mother shouldn't say to her daughter."

"Why not?"

"Because . . . that's why," I said, using the same reply my mother had used on me when I was growing up.

She laughed again. "In erotic fiction there are just so many words to call the male anatomy, so I've been racking my brain for something more original. What's your opinion about 'stick of dynamite'?"

"It sounds explosive."

"Perfect," she said with a low chuckle. "I've missed our conversations. Is everything all right with you?"

"Yes, I'm fine."

"Lilly mentioned you'd had a mishap with your Explorer."

"It's gone to the junkyard in the sky."

"So I heard. The main thing is that you're all right. So Lilly's put a red rinse in her hair."

Fire-engine-red hair dye was not a rinse. "The color covers her gray."

"I would think that would be an improvement."

"It definitely changes her appearance."

"Lilly tells me the two of you are getting along famously."

"She's enjoying her stay in your duplex."

"And she can't say enough about Cobbler. It was very kind of you to give her your dog."

"Thanks." I never thought I'd get rid of that slobbering, leather-chewing mutt. I cheered silently.

"Lilly tells me she had her ears pierced. I'll keep my eyes open for a small pair of Eiffel Towers or Arc de Triomphe earrings."

"She'd probably prefer a pair of Michelangelo's Davids with a jeweled stick of dynamite."

My mother laughed again. "It's good to know you haven't lost your sense of humor."

I woke up late the next morning in Jake's arms, feeling tired, sore, but definitely content.

After the guests left, I'd donned my tassels and . . . the rest was history.

Mission accomplished!

Jake stirred, opened his eyes, and smiled at me. "I'll never forget last night."

"That was my intention."

"Let's run off and get married."

My heart clenched; old habits died hard.

I knew Jake would be pleased with my reply. "As soon as we're dressed, I want us to go to the mall and pick up my engagement ring."

"Are we setting a date?"

"Not so fast. I figured we take it one step at a time. First we get engaged. In a while when we've had more time, we'll pick out the perfect date for our wedding."

Jake sat up and anchored his elbow on the pillow. "There's no point in you wearing my ring if you aren't ready to set a date."

"You said nothing about that the first time when you offered it to me."

A vein in his temple pulsed. "Things have changed since then."

"What's changed?"

He glanced across the room.

My stomach clenched. "What aren't you telling me?"

"I've seen Elaine."

Although I already knew that, the impact of hearing him say the words lodged in my stomach like a sharp rock. "Why didn't you tell me before this?"

"Because I didn't want you to overreact."

"You're seeing your ex-lover, and I'm not supposed to overreact!"

He brought his fingers down over mine. Knowing I was being childish and unable to stop myself, I yanked my hand away. "Do you still love her?"

"No, of course not."

I gave him credit for his speedy reply. "Then what does Elaine have to do with us?"

He kicked the blankets off, stood, walked across the room, and glanced out the window.

Though my nerves were frazzled, I wasn't too upset to admire his wide shoulders, narrow hips, and tight butt.

When he turned, I saw fear in his eyes. "Seeing her again made me realize I'm repeating my mistakes. I wasted a lot of time waiting for Elaine to make up her mind, and now I'm doing the same with you. I'm beginning to think you'll never be ready for marriage. There'll always be another story or another reason to postpone our wedding."

I climbed out of bed and went to him. "I'm not like her," I said, realizing physically I came up short.

I read so much on his face. Without a doubt he loved me, and I was responsible for the pain I saw etched in the creases around his eyes and mouth. I felt cherished, confused, and terrified I'd make another mistake.

"You're different in a lot of ways," he said, the timbre of his voice rough.

I kissed his chin, ran my hand along the back of his neck, felt his taut muscles beneath my fingertips. "I'd never leave you for another man. You're the only man I want."

"But your career comes first."

"I wouldn't put it that way."

"The wording is a technicality, but the results are the same."

"I love you, but I need to prove myself. What's wrong with that?"

"I'm not asking you to give up your career. Why can't you be both a reporter and my wife?"

He'd left out "mother of his children," but I knew it was part of the package. If I married Jake, would I, in time, give up my dreams to take care of our family?

Many women managed to do it all: work full-time, be a super mom attending all the school functions and baking cookies in her spare time while catering to her husband's needs. What spare time! Eventually, exhausted, I'd have to either give up or postpone my dreams of fame and fortune or simply writing a great story.

I thought of Jeannine's predicament. A sinking feeling settled in the pit of my stomach.

"Jeannine's pregnant," I blurted out, "and slimeball Ted has run off, leaving her to raise the baby alone."

Jake's expression softened. "Surely you know I'd never abandon you."

I bit my lower lip and nodded.

He pulled me tight against him. I absorbed his warmth, his strength.

As I rested my head under his chin, I prayed I'd find the right words to help him understand. "Jeannine is worried about being able to provide for her baby. If she'd focused on a career, she'd be earning more money and . . ."

"I understand your need to get ahead, but I have needs, too. Why can't we grow together as a married couple?"

I slid a hand down his abdomen. "I thought I'd satisfied your needs last night."

His smile never reached his eyes. "Monique, I love you, but I'm through waiting. I want an honest answer to my question."

He paused, looked at me for a moment.

My heart stilled. I didn't want to lose him. I tightened my grip on his shoulders.

"When will you marry me?"

I didn't like being put on the spot. My fingers clenched with frustration. A small voice inside warned me to calm down and choose my words carefully. "I understand where you're coming from, but this is a big decision."

If it hadn't been for *bitchy* Elaine, I wouldn't be standing here naked, the day after my birthday, trying to make the biggest decision of my life, fearing I'd make a mistake I'd later regret.

"Look," he said in a gentler tone, "you don't need to answer today. But I want an answer soon."

"How soon?"

For a moment my tongue wouldn't budge. I looked into his chocolate brown eyes and saw love and concern. If I were more athletic, I'd have kicked myself in the butt. What was wrong with me?

"If it were up to me, I'd choose today, tomorrow, at the very latest this summer."

I threw him a saucy grin and rubbed my bare breasts against his chest. "I'm not exactly dressed for a church wedding."

"No, but you're perfect for the honeymoon." The laugh that rumbled from his chest sliced through the tension.

Jake was everything I wanted in a man. At age eighteen, at age twenty-two, or even at age twenty-five I'd have taken a flying leap into his arms, declared my goals frivolous, and ridden off into the sunset with my knight in shining armor.

Past disappointments had changed my outlook on life. I'd matured the hard way. I was no longer satisfied being a man's significant other. I needed to be me, to find myself, and to be proud of my accomplishments.

As he brushed his fingers along the side of my face, I knew without a doubt I also needed Jake in my life. I couldn't afford to lose him. He complemented me in ways I hadn't thought possible.

Not sure if I'd later regret my answer, I pressed my mouth against his, tasted him, and felt his heartbeat beneath my palm. I moved away a little and knew in my soul that being with Jake was no mistake.

"In two weeks we'll set the date for our wedding."

Chapter Sixteen

Overnight the highway department had sanded the Portland streets, and the temperature had skyrocketed to a whopping zero degrees, making driving less treacherous. I was warm in my long winter coat, woolen slacks, thick socks, and fur-lined boots. As I drove home I thought of my promise to Jake. In two weeks, I'd set our wedding date. Before leaving his apartment, I'd vowed not to change my mind.

As the loose gravel on the roadway pelted the rental truck's undercarriage, I realized I was happy. Instead of panic, I felt confident I'd made the right decision.

I decided to stop by the *Portland Enquirer* and talk to Mr. Winters regarding Walter Freedman. I pulled into the parking space next to my boss's silver Volvo, hurried across the snow-packed pavement, and dashed into the building.

A moment later I stepped out of the elevator and made my way toward Mr. Winters's office. I spotted Doris Cote sashaying toward me with a puzzling smile.

I expected a wise comment about last night's outfit, but instead she said, "Thanks for inviting me to your party. I had a really good time."

Me invite her! Was she out of her mind!

And why was she being nice?

"I'm glad to hear that."

Raising her index finger, she motioned me to wait a moment. I watched her open her desk drawer and remove an envelope.

Thinking she was giving me a belated birthday card or possibly a poison pen letter, I was surprised to see the name, Abe, on the envelope she handed me.

"It's for Abraham, your grandfather. I was hoping you'd give him this," she said, her cheeks pink, her eyes bright.

My curiosity went into overdrive. Why would the *Wicked Witch of the West* send Gramps a card? What was she up to?

A bizarre thought slithered through my mind; maybe Gramps and Doris had hit it off last night. I dismissed the idea as preposterous.

My grandfather was too smart to allow Doris to sink her talons into him.

"Sure, I'll give it to him." I took the envelope. My fingers tingled on contact.

What I'd give to know its contents. Unfortunately, opening someone else's mail was a federal offense. Even if it weren't, I would never stoop so low.

I smiled back at Doris, changed my direction, and headed toward the staff photographer's office.

What a shame he wasn't there, but then he rarely came in on Saturdays. How had I forgotten that important fact? I checked behind me to be sure I wasn't being watched. Certain that no one had seen me enter his office I shut the door and turned on the light box. One more glance over my shoulder and I slipped my grandfather's envelope over the light box.

Since the note was folded, I couldn't make out much. I squinted and focused. Words came into view: "thanks," "good time." Much to my chagrin, I noticed Doris referred to herself as his little *filly*.

Worse still, my grandfather as her *stud-muffin*.

The envelope slipped from my fingers and landed at my feet. My stomach churned. I stood in shock, my breath lodged in my throat, my fingers shaking.

No granddaughter wanted to think of her grandfather as a stud-muffin. Grandfathers were on the same plateau as saints, Santa Claus, and the Tooth Fairy. Grandfathers lived their lives doing good deeds and reading bedtime stories to their grandchildren.

I wasn't exactly sure what stud-muffin meant, but stud conjured visions of wild sex and orgies.

I cleansed the blasphemous thought from my mind.

Plain and simple, the note was a mistake.

Maybe because I was reading through two layers of paper, I'd misinterpreted the words.

Still feeling somewhat uneasy, I picked up the envelope, tucked it into my purse, and went to speak to Mr. Winters, while trying to ignore the words pulsing through my brain.

Stud-muffin, stud-muffin, stud-muffin.

Mr. Winters waved me into his office. "Just the person I wanted to see," he said, refusing to glance my way.

I blamed my grand entrance last night for his inability to face me. Which added to my discomfort. It would be easier to stand here if he pretended I hadn't made a jackass of myself. So I blushed crimson and gulped a breath.

Maybe he was going to fire me for ruining the paper's reputation. I saw the headline: "Star reporter fired for tassel violation."

"Star reporter" was a stretch, but this was my daydream, and I'd do it up right.

Since Mr. Winters seemed preoccupied with his thoughts, for a moment my mind wandered. The large metal cabinet in the corner with the locks caught my attention. Why two locks? Either something valuable was hidden inside or it was something my boss wanted no one to see. The same questions had bothered me before but more so now.

Mr. Winters cleared his throat. "I don't want you to write the story about the mailbox vandalism."

I should have thought *phew*, instead I asked, "Why?"

"The why isn't important, just forget about it. I've already called the postmaster and told him unless he has more specific details, there really isn't a story."

His request struck me as strange, especially since my boss never gave up on a story. But who was I to turn down a gift, especially since I didn't want to implicate my aunt or me.

"Sure. Do you have another assignment for me?"

"All I have right now is a blueberry cobbler recipe for your column."

Damn, damn, triple damn.

Since he wasn't looking at me, I rolled my eyes. "I apologized to Mrs. Freedman and all seems fine."

"Good. I'm not surprised you managed to get your neck out of the noose."

Cringing, I decided to tell him the rest. "I told Mrs. Freedman I'd make up for the embarrassing obituary by writing an article about her husband being a generous philanthropist that would appear on the front page."

"You had no right to tell her that." Mr. Winters never met my gaze, but instead focused on the knit coaster beneath his coffee mug.

"But I promised . . ."

Uttering an exasperated sigh, he said, "Then you'll just have to break that promise because it's not going to happen. The front page is reserved for news-breaking stories: a drug bust, rape, or murder."

"What if I have a lead to a murderer running amok?"

"If you can prove there's a killer on the loose, write the story, and I'll print it on the front page."

"I'm certain Joyce Freedman killed her husband," I blurted out.

Mr. Winters's eyes finally locked with mine. "Before you make a statement like that, you'd better have proof."

"I do, kind of, or I did, but then the tape ran out." I removed my tape player from my purse, pressed the play button, and watched my boss's reaction as he listened to my conversation with Joyce.

"You can tell by the sound of her voice, she hated him."

"That's not a crime, Miss St. Cyr."

"But after the tape shut off, she implied she killed him."

"All you have is hearsay, nothing that'll hold up in a court of law."

"But the tape . . ."

Mr. Winters's stony expression stopped me mid-sentence.

"All your tape proves is that Walt Freedman loved *Miz Tilly*, Joyce is a millionaire, and you'll never change an old man's Depends."

I pulled into the yard. Wearing a wool cap beneath his white Stetson, Gramps dug into the bucket of gravel with a plastic cup and sent a spray of dirt over the icy driveway.

"How's it going?" he asked in a voice heard for miles when he spotted me getting out of my rental.

"Fine." I was grateful he'd missed last night's excitement. There were advantages to being nearly deaf.

"Lilly's gone on an errand, but she says the two of you will go shopping for guns and ammo when she returns."

A tremor started in my big toe and worked its way up my spine. In theory guns didn't kill people, people killed people. I understood all that and had heard it repeatedly from several people, including Jake. That didn't ease my mind.

The mere mention of a firearm sent my pulse racing and my heart tangoing with my ribs. Some people were not meant to carry a real gun. My name belonged on the top of that list.

"Tell Lilly I'm going to take a nap and that we can go shopping later this afternoon." My night of fun and games with Jake had taken its toll, and I could barely keep my eyes open.

Unaware I'd spoken, Gramps continued toward his duplex.

"Oh, you have a note," I said as he shut the door.

Damn. As I dashed after him, I considered keeping the envelope and steaming it open. Since Gramps was my responsibility, it was my duty to make sure Doris wasn't terrorizing him.

The words "stud-muffin" and the graphic visual it conjured could send an elderly man into cardiac arrest.

I'd reached my door when I realized I couldn't go through with it. In the event the post office ever discovered my Explorer had rammed into a mailbox—destruction of federal property—I didn't want to push my luck by tampering with someone else's mail.

So I knocked on the door and handed Gramps his mail, and without success tried to gauge his reaction. "Thanks, darlin'," he said, barely sparing the envelope a glance.

If he'd acted excited, I'd have worried, but his complacent response set my mind at ease. Doris had a crush on my grandfather. Fortunately he didn't reciprocate the feeling.

I'd fallen asleep when I heard knocking on my door.

"Monique, get up quick," came my aunt's voice, followed by pounding footsteps in my living room.

I hopped out of bed and tripped over the jeans I'd thrown there earlier.

Lilly ran into my bedroom. "Hurry, I can't wait another minute."

Certain Doris Cote's note had wreaked havoc with my grandfather's heart, I asked, "Have you called 911?"

My aunt looked puzzled. "No, whatever for?"

"I thought Gramps had a heart attack."

"There's nothing wrong with your grandfather." She raised her hands over her mouth. "Tee hee hee, your present has arrived. And I'm so excited, I could pee my pants."

I sat on the bed and shoved my legs into my jeans.

"I just know you're going to love it. When your Explorer caught fire and blew up, I knew it was a sign. As I said, everything happens for the best. Fate," she said, stressing the word. "I called Anne Marie and told her you'd need another vehicle."

I got the message. Loud and clear.

A new car! Well, if not brand-new, a good used car—something that shouted success.

Tears of joy sprang to my eyes. I couldn't wait to see it, to slip my behind onto the thickly padded seat, and to cruise around Portland, enjoying the envious glances aimed my direction.

"What color?" I asked, slipping my feet into running shoes and not bothering to lace them.

"Red."

Be still, my heart. My imagination filled in the few facts I didn't know. True, the only thing I knew for certain was the color. Mention *red vehicle* to anyone and they'd jump to the only possible conclusion.

A red sports car with tinted windows, leather bucket seats, and a surround-sound stereo system.

I jumped to my feet and zoomed past Aunt Lilly, in my excitement almost knocking her over. Even before opening the door, I glanced at her over my shoulder. "You shouldn't have. You and mom are the greatest."

With Lilly at my heels, I ran out on the stoop. I searched the driveway, stretched on tiptoe so I could see the curb over the Hummer.

Confused, I turned to my aunt.

Her eyes glinted like hubcaps struck by sunlight. "Isn't she a beauty?"

Figuring I'd missed my sports car the first time, I gave the driveway a slow perusal. I noticed a strange vehicle parked next to Aunt Lilly's. It had the same ugly pipes instead of fenders, and it was very wide, extremely wide, dreadfully wide.

It couldn't be.

This ridiculous-looking Hummer wasn't mine.

My heart thudded. My eyes misted.

Though my mind refused to accept the possibility, I could not ignore one teeny, tiny, insignificant fact.

It was *RED!*

Aunt Lilly hugged her black purse to her chest. "How's it handle?" she asked from the passenger seat.

"Swell."

"I knew you'd love it. The vanity plates were your mother's idea. CUTIEPIE sounds cool, don't you agree?"

I ground my back teeth together. "Yup."

"Finally, when you're out at night, I can sleep peacefully, knowing you're safe."

"Yup."

"With the heavy-duty winch you can pull yourself out of any ditch. The oversize tires are brand new. The last owner put the roll bars on so you can flip over three hundred and sixty degrees or go end over end, and your

Hummer won't sustain even a scratch."

"I'd rather not test out that feature."

"Tee hee hee. Your Hummer is loaded with safety features. You can drive anywhere, through mud, on ice, even over a shallow riverbed. You can't get lost. It comes complete with a computerized Global Positioning System. The first time I sat behind the wheel of my Hummer, I was struck with a sense of power. Can you feel it?"

The only thing I felt was *ridiculous,* but I couldn't hurt my aunt's feelings. Until I figured out a way of getting rid of the monstrosity, I'd pretend I loved it.

"I know what you mean," I said, my jaw straining from my fake smile. "I keep thinking everyone is watching me."

"I knew you'd understand."

Cringing, I wished it weren't red. I would have preferred a dull gray or drab olive green, any color but *r-e-d.*

Red shouted, *Everybody look at me!*

I preferred to remain incognito.

I pulled in front of Rob's Guns & Artillery Shop. I hopped out, almost sprained my ankle jumping from that height.

"Aren't these oversize tires something?" Aunt Lilly said, looking proud.

Nodding, I noticed the Hummer took up the entire width of the parking space and half the street. I left it right where it was, hoping fate would again intervene and this time send a sixteen-wheeler to flatten my bright red birthday surprise.

Aunt Lilly sprinted into Rob's Guns & Artillery Shop. Since I dreaded the thought of even looking at guns, I dragged my feet but eventually joined her at the counter. Dressed in army fatigues, ammo belts crisscrossing his chest, Rob joined us a moment later. Two large, menacing-looking guns hung in holsters at his hips, next to a couple of long knives and what I assumed was a hand grenade.

"What can I do for you two young ladies?" he said, his hands braced on the glass countertop.

Aunt Lilly turned to me and whispered, "Isn't he a polite man?"

I tried to roll my eyes, but paralyzed with fear, I managed to jerk my head to indicate I wasn't deaf, just terrified.

Lilly turned to Rob. "We want guns."

"What kind of gun did you have in mind?"

"What are my choices?"

"We have big guns, little guns, guns you strap to your ankle, guns you carry in a purse or pocket. Then we have the bad-ass guns, capable of taking out a man just like that!" He pointed his finger, cocked his thumb, and fired an imaginary bullet. "Pow!"

Aunt Lilly hopped back, then bent and studied the weapon selection in the display case. "I never realized there were so many different types."

Meanwhile I stared straight ahead, doing my best not to consider the possibility we'd be leaving with real guns that shot real bullets.

"Are you feeling all right?" Rob asked, directing his question to me.

I tried to say, "Sure," but it came out garbled. I saw concern in his eyes.

"Before either of you can buy a handgun, you'll need to fill out some paperwork. I'll need to know whether you have a prison record or have escaped from an insane asylum."

Thanks a lot.

Lilly covered her mouth and tee hee heed. "Isn't he a riot?"

I uttered a pathetic-sounding laugh.

Rob threw me another look before concentrating on *the*

smart one. He didn't say it out loud, but I knew what he was thinking.

I blew out a breath and gathered my wits. "Let's get out of here before we kill someone."

Lilly didn't budge. "I'm not moving one iota until we have a means of protecting ourselves."

"If you're looking for firepower, I'd recommend a .45 caliber." He indicated several guns to his left.

I bit the inside of my cheek and looked down at the ugliest guns I'd ever seen. Plain black, clearly designed by a man for men.

"Then there's the Beretta 9mm." Rob's eyes glowed like neon lights as he stroked the weapon with his index finger as one might a lover. "This little beauty has an effective range of one hundred and thirty-one feet, two hundred and sixteen millimeter barrel length. A lot of the cops in Portland carry Berettas. The detectives seem to prefer Glocks. I make the most of both worlds by having one of each. And these little babies are with me even when I sleep," he said, nodding to the guns hanging from his belt. "You can bet your ass this is one store in the Old Port that has never been robbed."

"What kind of weapon is that?" Lilly asked, tapping the glass and pointing toward a gun with a round canister on top. The design reminded me of a plastic water bottle, which would come in handy in hot weather.

Rob's voice rose with excitement. "That, my friends, is the Calico Model M-950. It holds a fifty- or one-hundred-round magazine and has an effective range of one hundred and ninety-seven feet. But you can't buy this baby without a dealer's license."

"How about that cute little one?" Lilly directed her gaze toward a small but still lethal weapon.

"That's the Glock 36, slim-line model, and the first choice

for many who carry concealed."

"We'll take two of those," Lilly said, opening her purse.

"Don't," I said, unable to mutter another word. My throat closed in on itself. I forced air into my lungs.

"You're sure edgy," Rob said, reaching for his belt and tossing the hand grenade at me.

Shit! Even in my state of mind, I leaped to my left, whipped out my hand, and grabbed it with the tips of my fingers. I'd watched enough war movies to know I needed to hold the pin in. Knuckles white, my fingers cramped from the force.

"Are you crazy!" I shouted, a statement of fact.

He walked around the counter, took the grenade from my trembling hand, and flicked it open.

Flames leaped from . . . the grenade-shaped cigarette lighter.

Lilly waved her hands and tee hee heed.

A deep moronic laugh burst from Rob's throat.

I threw up at his feet.

Chapter Seventeen

Aunt Lilly wrapped one arm over Rob's shoulder and the other around me, and we escorted her to my vehicle.

"Goodness gracious, I never imagined holding a gun could make me so dizzy."

"I know where you're coming from," I said, relieved Aunt Lilly hadn't purchased the cannons in the display case.

"It's mighty chivalrous of you to escort me from your shop," she said, looking at Rob as though he'd saved her life.

His chest expanded several shirt sizes. "It's nothing."

I agreed. If it weren't for his frightening guns, none of this would have happened.

Since I made a point of not picking fights with men wearing an arsenal, I gritted my back teeth and helped my aunt climb onto the seat. Once she'd snapped the seat belt shut, color started returning to her cheeks.

"Nice wheels." Rob cast an appreciative gaze over my red monstrosity.

"Thanks."

"How's she handle on the road?"

"Like a tank."

"Maybe you'll let me drive her sometime."

Not on your life! "We'll see."

I tried not to judge Rob strictly on appearance, but I could easily imagine him driving a getaway car with bullets whizzing overhead. I could also picture him mounting a missile launcher on top of my Hummer.

"I have one just like this," Aunt Lilly said proudly, "only mine is fly-yellow."

"If either of you gals ever need a chauffeur, you know where to reach me."

I threw him a no-nonsense look. "Yeah, right, when pigs sing 'The Star-Spangled Banner.' "

Aunt Lilly tee hee heed.

Rob chuckled. "I like women with a good sense of humor and a nice set of wheels."

I turned the key and put my Hummer into drive. Since my vehicle took up half the street, a line formed behind me because the cars couldn't pass until the other lane cleared.

Horns honked.

A man in a green pickup stuck his head out his window. "Cutiepie, get the lead out!"

Rob frowned. "Want me to kill him for you?"

Lilly turned to me. "Isn't he a hoot?"

My aunt thought Rob was kidding.

I wasn't so sure.

As I pulled from the parking space, Rob saluted. "Ladies, enjoy your weapons, and give a holler if I can be of any assistance."

Aunt Lilly shoveled a narrow path through the snow and set up empty bottles on my ice-encrusted picnic table in our backyard. "I don't think I've ever been this nervous or excited."

"Piece of cake," I said, adjusting my shoulder holster over my L.L.Bean jacket.

"I like the handle of your gun better than mine," Lilly said, admiring my weapon's carved ivory butt and the barrel's engraved floral pattern.

"Thanks, but yours is nice, too."

"I chose this one because Rob said it was more accurate and more powerful."

"Instead of precision, I went with style. My gun will look terrific with a black turtleneck and a string of pearls."

"Good thinking," Lilly said, loading her gun's chamber.

She took aim and fired. Looking disappointed, she peered in the distance. "It didn't hit a bottle. Where did the bullet go?"

"Beats me. Let me show you how it's done."

I'd had some experience at this. First Jeannine's father had instructed me, then Jake. Neither occasion conjured good memories.

Trying to look like a marksman, I widened my stance, brought my weapon to my face, and sighted down the barrel. "The trick is to pull the trigger back slowly and to remain steady."

Lilly's head almost touched mine when I fired.

Glass shattered.

"Bull's-eye," I shouted, then noticed the broken kitchen window.

Lilly and I went inside. I cut up a cardboard box as a temporary patch to keep out the cold until I picked up a piece of glass.

Meanwhile, after Lilly swept the floor, she scrubbed the blue paint off my counter and sink. "This stuff makes a mess."

"Personally, I prefer to load my weapon with soapy water and blind the culprit before he can escape."

"That makes sense to me," Lilly said.

"It doesn't work worth a damn if the assailant is wearing

glasses. Whereas a paintball leaves the barrel of a gun at such a velocity, it will not only cover the lens with paint, blinding the perpetrator, it'll slam into his face, leaving a welt and knocking his eyeglasses to the floor. I've come a long way since my high-powered water pistol days. My weapon of choice is now a paintball gun."

"I like my gun, too, but I still prefer my yellow paintballs to your blue ones. And I can't figure out why you didn't get the red ones that matched your Hummer."

I shrugged. "Now that I have a piece, I'm ready to do some serious damage."

"What do you mean?"

"There's a killer on the loose," I said and watched Lilly shudder. "Joyce, an innocent-looking widow, murdered her husband."

"Goodness gracious, why would she do that?"

"For his money."

"How did she kill him?"

"That's what I'm going to find out."

"It sounds dangerous."

"It could be." A shiver wiggled up my spine. Fear wedged itself into my heart and stole my breath.

"What are you planning to do?"

"I don't know," I said, speculating how dangerous this really was, and for all my efforts, would I get what I needed to write a front-page story?

"You should wear a wire. It's what everyone does in the movies I watch on television."

That had never entered my mind. "That's not a bad idea. Unfortunately, I don't have any of that equipment."

"I bet Richard does, and he's such a nice young man. I don't see why he wouldn't lend you everything you need."

I looked off into space and wondered whether it would be

worth degrading myself again by calling Richard and pleading for his help.

"I'll think about it."

"After you've thought about it and get the device from Richard, plan on me driving the getaway Hummer."

The thought frightened me more than facing a potential murderer.

The next evening while waiting for Richard to arrive, I stretched my feet on the coffee table and noticed Lilly's pensive expression. "What are you thinking of?"

"Well, I wasn't going to tell a soul, because it's kind of embarrassing . . . or it could be embarrassing if . . . but I could sure use some advice, and . . . ."

"You can tell me anything."

"Well . . . I have a date."

Rob was the first person who popped into my mind. "Who's the lucky man?"

"I had a long talk with Anne Marie last night, and she warned me if I didn't tell you right away, you'd pester me until I did."

"So what's his name?"

"I can't tell you until I know for sure the gentleman is going through with the date."

"You need to have confidence in yourself. Of course, he'll go through with the date. Why wouldn't he?"

"In the past, I've been . . ." Uneasiness clouded her face. "Stood up. I'd told everyone, then felt like a fool. This time I'm not taking any chances. I'm not going to jinx this date by sharing the particulars with anyone."

Before I could badger her with my questions, there was a knock on the door and Richard walked in, wearing a white outfit with a black cloth belt around his waist. He looked nervous when he spotted me on the couch.

"You better remember what I said on the phone. One wrong move and I'm outta here with my gear."

Lilly looked confused.

I wasn't. Richard was convinced I lusted after him while I slept and during every minute I was awake. To look at the terror on his face, I knew he expected me to lunge off the couch and strip him naked.

Never in a zillion years!

He was safe, more than safe. He could be the last man alive and he'd still be safe. I was speaking for the entire female population.

Because I didn't want to frighten him off, I kept a safe distance and watched him unpack his gear.

He didn't seem to mind Lilly close to him.

He threw a cautious glance at me over his shoulder.

I gave him the peace sign and watched him frown. "Why are you wearing pajamas?"

"This is my martial arts uniform."

"Nice."

"This is serious business," he reminded me as he did each time we were together.

"I should say it is," Lilly said, saving the day by looking at him with adoration. "I don't know how you got so smart."

Richard basked in her compliment. "It's hard for me to believe you and Monique are related."

"We're a lot alike," Lilly said.

"Not that I can see," Richard replied, casting another worrisome glance at me.

Richard uttered a strange sound, leaped across the living room floor, and raised his hands at sharp angles. "You need to stay focused at all times, be ready to defend yourselves at a moment's notice. You never know when the viper will strike."

"My," Lilly said, eyes wide with adoration. "Isn't he something?"

"He sure is."

Richard pranced across the room and twisted his face into a snarl that looked comical. "I'm going to take it easy on you ladies, but rest assured when I'm though, you'll be a danger to mankind."

He kicked his right foot in the air, then his left, he shouted more nonsense, and waved his arms.

He insisted Lilly and I repeat each motion. I felt like a fool, but I needed Richard so I kept my comments to myself. With luck, when confronted by a robber or killer, they'd laugh and drop their weapon, giving me a chance to run away.

He grabbed hold of Lilly's arm and twisted it behind her back. "See how easy it is to immobilize your victim. If I wanted, I could snap your wrist in two. Fortunately, I know my strength, and I'm holding back."

"Right," I said, out of the corner of my mouth. "What I really need is some of your equipment. Maybe you could put off the fun and games for later."

His eyebrows meshed in the center of his forehead.

Lilly came to the rescue. "I feel safer already."

"Me, too," I said, biting back a smile.

Grunting under his breath, Richard turned and unzipped a small gym bag, all the while keeping a close eye on me. "What did you have in mind?"

"I want to record a killer's conversation without her knowledge. I figured I'd wear a wire . . ."

Lilly interrupted. "Of course, I'll be in the vehicle listening to every word so if something goes wrong, I can run in with my gun . . ."

"You have a gun?"

"Yes, Monique does, too. We're carrying concealed," Lilly added, looking pleased.

"Do you have a permit?"

"I don't sweat the small stuff."

No kidding. Lilly still didn't have a driver's license or a registration for her Hummer.

"Forget the wire."

"But I thought . . ." I said, somewhat disappointed.

"That's why I'm the professional. The problem with using a wire is that the range isn't always good and if you're behind cement walls, sometimes it doesn't even work. What I have in mind is a sure thing. Only I hate letting it out of my sight."

"You know you can trust me."

"You still haven't given me back the lock pick I lent you."

"I may need it to do another job. Does the lock pick do metal cabinets?" I asked, knowing I could never in good conscience break into Mr. Winters's cabinet—no matter how much I wanted to know what he'd hidden inside.

"Just don't lose it. It's part of an expensive set."

"Have no fear. I won't let it out of my sight. I'll even sleep with it under my pillow."

"This is no laughing matter."

"Aye, aye, sir."

Groaning, Richard dug in his bag and held up what looked like a regular cell phone.

"Big deal, I have one of those."

He lifted one eyebrow and looked at me as one would a dumb kid. "If it looks like a cell phone, feels like a cell phone, and rings like a cell phone, then it must be . . ." He turned to Lilly, who looked confused.

"A cell phone?"

"No and yes. That's the beauty of it. No one who sees it will ever suspect it's anything else. It's a fully operational mobile phone, the first choice of spies across America. It has two modes. One is normal. Two is spy mode. Monique, you can plant this baby anywhere you want. Lilly will dial the secret code to activate the phone. It doesn't ring so those around won't have a clue they're being taped."

"Are the display lights on when it's activated?" Lilly asked, her question so smart I wished I'd thought of it.

A sly grin pulled at the corners of Richard's mouth. "The phone appears to be turned off. No one but the two of you will know what's going on."

"Goodness gracious, I never knew such a phone existed. I wonder why they don't use these on television."

"It's top secret," he said, loading it on thick. "Only the FBI and a few top-notch private eyes use this equipment."

"Gee, you must have studied a long time to know so much."

"It's not so much the schooling as the experience," he said, flashing a Howdy Doody smile, his red, freckled face beaming.

"What else you got in there?" Lilly asked, craning her head toward the bag he'd set on the table.

He opened up a small metal case measuring roughly six-by-ten inches. "This is a voice-activated tape recorder. Once you turn on the spy phone, you can take a nap because there'll be nothing for you to do. This device will turn itself on if a fly buzzes past it."

"Gee, that's amazing," Lilly said, craning her head to look inside the gym bag. "What's that for?"

Richard pulled out a small calculator. "This is a bug. You leave it on someone's desk and hear everything going on in their office."

"What a good idea," Lilly said.

"It can be, providing the person leaves it where you put it.

The last time I used one of these, some kid borrowed it from his father and brought it to school. I listened to math equations for two days."

"What's this gadget?" Lilly asked, pointing inside the bag.

Richard took out a small square device. "This is really neat. It's a state-of-the art, wall-contact microphone capable of hearing through walls sixty centimeters thick." He set the gismo next to the tape player and the phone. "What I'd recommend, is plant a seed of doubt in the killer's head, then ask to use their bathroom. While in there, listen through the earphones of the wall microphone and you could be surprised what you hear."

"That's a great idea," I said, impressed with Richard's suggestion. "I'll definitely do that."

I made the mistake of touching his arm.

He stepped back, cast a you-better-watch-yourself warning look and peered across the room. "What happened to the window?"

"My weapon misfired," I said to save face.

"What's the blue haze on the counter and on the floor?"

I noticed the residual paint from my ammo. "It could be blueberry Kool-Aid."

My answer seemed to satisfy him.

I'd replied without actually lying; instead I'd stated a possibility, not a fact.

Even Sister Mary Agnes would have trouble finding fault with my logic.

"When is this operation going down?" Richard asked.

"I'm not sure. I'll need to call and set up a time."

"Why not call her now?" Lilly said.

"Good idea." I looked up Joyce's number and punched it

in. She answered on the third ring.

"Hi, Joyce, it's Monique. I have a few more questions about your husband. When would be a good time for me to come over?"

There was a pause and voices in the background. "How about tomorrow evening around eight?"

"It's a date," I said and hung up.

"It's going down tomorrow night," I said, waving my arm and feeling nervous.

"No can do," Richard said. "I have work on a case tomorrow night."

"Gee, isn't that a shame. It looks like Lilly and I will have to work solo." I silently sang the "Hallelujah Chorus."

"I never let my equipment out of my sight."

"You have to. This is my big break."

"What if it's lost or damaged?"

"I'll guard it with my life."

"Yeah, but what if you take a bullet right through my spy phone, blasting it into a million pieces?"

Gulp. "I don't want to think about that."

"Neither do I." He waved a frantic hand over his supplies. "That phone alone cost thirteen hundred bucks."

"That much?"

"You'll just have to reschedule."

"I can't do that. I need to strike now."

Front-page story. My byline. My hopes and dreams realized. Need be, I'd throw myself on my knees and beg.

"I need to protect my gear."

"I won't take my eyes off it. And, if by some freak coincidence it gets lost or damaged, I'll give you the money to replace it." Never mind that I didn't have that sum in my account, but since I didn't plan to lose it, it wasn't a concern.

"You better not renege on our agreement."

"Don't worry. Your equipment is safe with me."

Later that night I'd fallen asleep when I was awakened by the unmistakable sound of footsteps in the other room. I lay there tense, every muscle cramping from stress, my imagination going wild.

I pictured a thick-necked behemoth, jagged scar along one side of his bearded face, inside my duplex. Or maybe it was one of the cats jumping off the counter.

Only one other possibility existed, and this one struck a chord. Elaine was out there, slinking about, ready to cause havoc.

I pictured her prancing like a flower girl at a wedding, tossing shredded pages of my mother's books around my living room.

My fear evaporated, replaced with vengeance. This was perfect. Even better than perfect: wonderful, fantastic, and super-duper-terrific! If I yanked every hair from Elaine's head or scratched her flawless face, no one could blame me.

The lights were off.

I was protecting my home.

Heart drumming, I crept out of bed and reached for my weapon on the nightstand, every cell in my body energized. Ready to do some serious damage, I tiptoed across my bedroom floor. Springing into action, I leaped into the living room and shouted, "I've got you now!"

From the dim light coming through the window, I made out the shape of a silhouette. I widened my stance, tried to sight down the barrel, impossible in the dark, and fired off several rounds.

Paintballs splattered against walls and furniture. I heard glass break and Jake's agitated voice.

"What the hell is going on here?"

Chapter Eighteen

I switched on the lights and noticed the mess along with the disgruntled look on Jake's face. Not only had I broken another window, but I'd also struck Jake's forehead where a blue welt had started to form.

"Why didn't you say anything when I shouted?"

"I thought I was in for another treat. How was I to know 'I've got you now' meant my life was at stake?"

"I thought you were . . ." *Elaine,* which I couldn't say without taking the chance he'd defend her. ". . . a burglar, or a bomber."

"What are you doing with a paint gun?"

Good question.

I hesitated and tried to figure out a suitable response. I knew Jake wouldn't approve.

"Tell me you aren't planning to use this on a story."

"Not unless I need to."

"Didn't you learn your lesson last time?"

"Of course I did." I put my gun down next to my computer. "I'll use it only if I have to scare someone off."

"Do you realize how dangerous that can be? If you insist on carrying a weapon, it should be a real gun. Don't go pointing a toy because you can't defend yourself."

"You know how I feel about guns," I said, remembering the last time he'd brought me to the shooting range. They'd had to replace several ceiling tiles after I left.

"If you handled them more, it would become like second nature. I want you to promise you won't go running around with that thing," he said, frowning at my weapon with the carved ivory butt.

"My paintball gun is prettier than your Glock."

"That's true, but it's also more dangerous than a real gun."

"No way! My gun can't kill anyone."

"My gun isn't responsible for killing. I'm the one who makes the decision whether to fire," he said, taking a step toward me. "At least if I point my weapon, I know I can protect myself. If a robber mistook your gun for the real thing, he might shoot to defend himself. I want you to promise me you won't use this except for target practicing."

"Aunt Lilly and I did some target practicing this afternoon."

"Good, I'm glad that's settled."

"Me, too." Not that I'd promised anything, but Jake hadn't noticed, and that was fine with me.

He smiled; his face filled with tenderness. He came to me and wrapped his arms around my shoulders. "I'm sorry if I frightened you, but it won't happen again. Tomorrow, first thing, I'm calling to have an alarm system installed."

"That's not necessary."

"I've been worried about you. An alarm will give us both some peace of mind."

"But . . ."

He swiped paint from his cheek with the back of his hand. "I've put it off too long already. Consider it done. This way, when I decide to drop in after my shift, if you hear a noise, you'll know it's me. And I won't need to worry about losing an eye."

★ ★ ★ ★ ★

The next night Aunt Lilly killed the engine of her Hummer a block from Joyce's estate.

I adjusted my shoulder holster, its stiff, tooled leather digging into the side of my breast. I'd worn a loose-fitting cardigan under my winter coat, hoping to hide the bulge, and if necessary, I could quickly access my weapon.

"Where's our list?" Aunt Lilly asked, looking in her purse. "I was sure it was on the front seat." She turned and eyed Cobbler suspiciously. "You better not have eaten it."

The dog licked its chops.

"I don't understand why you had to bring him along."

Lilly reached behind her to pat the dog's thick head. "He gets lonely at home alone with Gramps and Long John."

"I remember what we wrote on the piece of paper, but to be sure we're all set, let's go over everything," I said, my stomach queasy. "My gun's right here. Richard's phone is in my purse. I have a small tablet and pen to pretend I'm jotting down notes so Joyce doesn't get suspicious."

"It sounds like you have it all covered."

"When I get inside, I'll pretend I'm waiting for a call so I'll put the phone on the table."

Lilly lifted her finger. "And I'll activate it by calling the special number, and I'll record every word of the conversation with the voice-activated recorder."

"Right."

"This is so exciting. I wish I was going in there instead of you."

I threw back my head and grinned, hoping to conjure the appearance of a self-assured investigative reporter. "Once I'm inside, pull your vehicle close to the gate, just in case I have to make a quick getaway."

"Will do." Lilly gripped my arm. "Maybe we should forget

about this. It's dangerous, and you could get hurt."

"There's nothing to worry about. Besides, Joyce and I bonded. I bet she's looking forward to our meeting as much as I am."

I walked past the gates, up the winding driveway, and pressed the doorbell.

Joyce opened the door and stepped aside to let me enter. "It's good to see you again."

"Thanks. I expected a servant to greet me," I said, admiring the granite floor in a foyer larger than my entire duplex.

"I gave the staff the night off."

That worried me. Did she suspect my real reason for coming? Did she have plans of her own?

If she'd killed once, she wouldn't hesitate to kill again.

I harnessed my wandering imagination and told myself I had nothing to worry about.

She hung my coat in a closet and escorted me to the spacious living room overlooking the lights of the city. "Nice."

She sat on a sofa near a stone fireplace and motioned for me to do the same. "So what do you want to know about Walter?"

How you killed your husband. "I want to give my article about your husband a more personal feel. I was hoping you could give me more details about his life."

"Did you have anything in particular in mind?"

I dug out Richard's phone from my purse and set it on the coffee table between us. "I'm expecting an important call," I said in a calm tone, my expression composed, my hands steady. I yanked out my tablet and jotted down Joyce's name, a smiley face and several wavy lines. "Could you elaborate a bit on your husband's love of boating?"

"I can't tell you much. I only went with him twice because all that rolling and swaying made me seasick. I ended up throwing up my guts. I prefer steady ground beneath my feet."

I nodded sympathetically.

"I could use a martini. Would you like one?"

Martinis weren't my style, but I was afraid if I refused, Joyce wouldn't drink. I needed to loosen her tongue.

"Sure."

She rose to her feet. "Great, I'll pour us each a double."

I decided to take tiny sips and leave most of the drink untouched.

She returned a moment later with an entire pitcher and two glasses. After filling our glasses, she took hers and stretched out on a chaise longue near the fireplace where a fire roared and cast a warm glow in the room.

I silently cheered her on when she gulped most of her drink. "Is there anything else you want to know?"

How you killed your husband? "Did he have any hobbies?"

She threw back the rest of her martini. "Off the record?"

"Sure."

"My husband collected women, the younger the better."

"You didn't mind?"

"I knew it when I married him. I got what I wanted, and he had me to parade around at functions. It was just a matter of time before his eyes wandered."

"Oh."

"Ours was an open marriage."

"I see."

"But you can't write about any of that in your article."

I shook my head, drank a couple more sips, and twisted my fingers over my mouth. "My lips are sealed."

She laughed. "I like you."

"Thanks." I noticed instantly that martinis were stronger than wine. My head was fuzzy already. I set down my glass and picked up my pencil. I drew a bunch of three-dimensional cubes and shaded them in. "Was he a golfer?"

"No."

"You mentioned his sons didn't like you. I was surprised to learn they never asked for an autopsy after their father's death."

"There was no reason for them to expect foul play. They were here when he died."

"Had your husband been sick for a long time?"

"He was healthy until the moment he dropped dead."

"Isn't that strange?"

"I guess his heart just gave out."

Because I was getting nowhere, I tossed back the rest of my drink.

"Let me refill your glass," Joyce said, standing and pouring the martini to the very top.

I felt light-headed and giddy, but with her looking on, I reached for my glass and took a tiny sip. "This drink is beginning to grow on me."

"They're my favorite," Joyce said, downing most of hers.

An hour later we were sitting side by side on the couch, arms slung around each other's shoulders, singing our childhood favorites. "Row, Row, Row Your Boat" tripped us up each time we started.

"You're a lot of fun," Joyce said. "How much do you earn in a week?"

The answer didn't immediately leap into my head.

"If it's less than ten thousand a month, you're wasting your time."

"Then I'm wasting my time," I said, still not remembering

the exact figure but certain it was way below what she'd mentioned.

"I should set you up with one of Walter's friends."

"Really, what's he like?"

"He's old and rich. The perfect combination."

"Sounds good to me," I said, waving my hand over my glass so she wouldn't refill it. Joyce wouldn't take no for an answer.

To be sure I didn't miss a word, I tapped my finger over the spy phone on the table, hoping Lilly would pay special attention from this point on.

"As I said, I'm not in the market for wiping drool from an old man's chin."

She threw back her head and laughed. "A woman can put up with a lot if the rewards are worth the struggle. I'd do just about anything for a few million bucks. Wouldn't you?"

I nodded, admired the large fish tank across the room, and found its continual gurgle soothing. "With my luck he'd outlive me."

"Not if you take the right precautions."

Because I didn't trust Richard or his equipment, I reached for my phone and tried to see whether it was working. I knew it wasn't supposed to be lit, but I still felt uneasy.

"What kind of precautions?"

"Let's just say there are ways."

"I wouldn't look good in prison attire," I said. "Unlike you, my hips are too wide."

She flapped her hand at me and laughed until tears ran down her face.

"Before I jump into a situation with an old man, I'll need to know some particulars. I don't want to take a chance of being on bedpan patrol for the rest of my life."

She stretched and pulled a book off a shelf. "I took up writing as a hobby. The Internet is filled with authors who are experts in just about everything. One of the mystery writers suggested I buy this book when I told her I was researching poisons."

A shiver raced up my spine. If it weren't for the martini-induced fog enshrouding my brain, I'd have been crafting the perfect first sentence for my article.

She handed me the book, titled *The Amateur's Guide to Murder*. I thumbed through the pages and saw it covered poisonous spiders, snakes, plants, and even prescription drugs.

I slid my phone closer to Joyce. "Are you saying you poisoned your husband?"

A wry smile curved her mouth. "What do you think?"

I wanted proof. I needed to hear the words. I couldn't stop now. "I think you killed him."

"That's such a harsh word. I prefer to think of it as freeing him from his earthly troubles and giving him a helpful shove toward his heavenly reward."

"Adulterers don't go to heaven," I said, thinking of their open marriage.

She laughed. "I know. The bastard got what he deserved."

I had what I needed so I rose to my feet. Steadying myself by gripping the back of the couch with both hands, I noticed the blonde chauffeur who'd brought Joyce to the Saltwater Grill standing in the corner of the room. I didn't like the way he was staring at me, but hey, after several martinis, frankly I didn't care. I reached for the spy phone and was shocked when he rushed across the room and grabbed the phone from my hand.

"Joyce, you're too trusting."

I bet her husband, Walter, would disagree with that statement.

"Monique's a friend."

"And a reporter."

"We're pals," I said, trying to pull the phone from his grasp.

"I bet she's wired."

"I'm a bit buzzed if that's what you mean," I said, silly grin on my face, noting for a moment there were two of him.

He started to pat me down, his hand brushing the side of one breast. I pressed my arm down over my gun, hoping he wouldn't continue his search. "Hey, no one touches these unless I say so."

"Lift up your blouse or I'll rip it off."

"Lilly, call the police," I shouted, before he clamped a hand over my mouth.

I bit down hard, and he slapped me across the face.

I thought he'd broken my jaw, and I expected Joyce to come to my defense. Instead she tucked her hands around her chest.

"Tony, I like her."

I turned to her. "Lover boy's making a big deal out of nothing. I want in on this old man deal. I won't blow the whistle. I could sure use the extra cash."

"I think she's legit," Joyce said, sending a pleading look at Tony.

Tony wrenched the phone from my fingers and hurled it into the fish tank. I watched the thirteen-hundred-dollar device settle at the bottom of the tank.

"Why'd you throw out my cell phone?"

"I've been watching you with it. I'd bet that's a listening device." He ripped my purse from my hand and emptied the contents on the table. "Just as I thought. She has a wall microphone. She's up to no good."

"I'm sorry," Joyce said, looking sincere. "I don't know what you had in mind, but I'm sure I wouldn't like it."

"Get her a bowl of salad greens, heavy on the onions," Tony said.

What were they up to? Why feed a guest a salad? I decided to tell the truth.

"Look, I can understand why you'd be upset. I came here hoping to write an exposé about this case. But along the way, I changed my mind. Joyce and I bonded." I waved two fingers twisted together. "Just like this. We're like sisters."

Joyce scurried from the room and returned with a dish of lettuce, tomatoes, and onions. On a tray she had assorted salad dressings.

"Would you like croutons?" she asked.

I glanced at the book, *The Amateur's Guide to Murder*, and I knew. "That's poison, isn't it?"

"Sorry," she said, glancing away.

Lover boy placed a hand on my shoulder and shoved me into the chair. "Eat."

"I'm on a diet."

"You have two choices. One, you eat and feel no pain. Or two, I force the onions down your throat. Personally I prefer two, but it's up to you."

By now Aunt Lilly had called the police. I knew help was on the way. I needed to stall. I turned to Joyce. "Was it salad that killed Walter?"

She poured me another martini. "This will help everything go down easily." After a pause, she thumbed through the book and pointed to an entry—scientific name, *Zygadenus venenosus*, also known as poison sego lily. The paragraph explained the bulb-shaped onion had killed cattle and many humans.

"Why didn't Walter's sons insist on an autopsy?"

"They'd consumed the same meal and were relaxing after dinner when their father felt sick. He went in to take a nap and never woke up."

"His sons didn't get sick?"

"I made their salad with regular onions. Walter's was special."

"I see." Hoping to waste some time, I carefully selected the bottle of ranch dressing. "Wow, two hundred and forty calories for a measly two tablespoons. Potent stuff."

I reached for the second bottle, but Tony beat me to it. "What difference does it make?"

"I don't want to put on any weight."

"It won't matter when you're swimming with the fishes."

Could I blast him with paintballs and make it across the room before he caught up to me?

"The hell with the dressing, eat an onion!"

I glanced over my shoulder at Joyce. "I don't know what you see in this man. He's a pig, and I don't care for his tone, either."

Tony grabbed a fistful of my hair and forced an onion into my mouth. Because I had no choice, I chewed and swallowed.

"Do you want me to force-feed the rest to you, or are you going to do it by yourself?"

I nodded. My pulse pounded in my ears, and I wondered whether it was because of fear or the poison in my system. "How many onions do I need to eat to finish me off?"

"You ask way too many questions," Tony said, his gaze raking over my body. "I bet it'll take more for you than it did the old man. You're a lot heavier."

A woman can only take so much. "You're an insulting swine."

I gasped, grabbed hold of my chest, and gritted my teeth. "I think I'm having a heart attack."

Joyce and Tony exchanged surprised glances.

I threw myself facedown on the couch and tried to pull my gun from my holster.

Behind me came Tony's rough voice. "Your ploy isn't working. Sit up and eat." His hand settled over my shoulder.

I spun around, aimed my gun, and fired. Windows broke. The fish tank shattered. Ammo hit the ceiling, the walls, and the floor, but not one paint pellet struck Joyce or Tony.

Tony yanked the gun from my hands and shoved another onion in my mouth. I tried to spit it out, but he clamped fingers over my mouth until I swallowed.

"Nearly everybody in Portland knew I was coming here. You won't get away with this. When they find my body, you'll be spending the rest of your lives in jail."

"There'll be no body," Joyce said, her voice sweet and friendly. "Tony will make you a pair of stylish cement shoes and throw you off the *Miz Tilly*."

"Eat up," Tony said with a laugh. "It won't be long now."

Hoping to calm down, I tossed back the rest of my double martini.

Feeling dizzy, sometime later I sat on the couch, my eyes at half-mast.

What had happened to Aunt Lilly?

Where was the SWAT team?

What had gone wrong with Richard's damn spy phone?

Chapter Nineteen

I was floating in a tunnel toward a bright light. I'd seen talk shows about near-death experiences so I knew what was happening. I braced myself for the thrill of a lifetime.

Lifetime?

Was that word still appropriate?

I heard the hum of voices, probably my ancestors coming to greet me, and the clang of metal, which didn't make sense. I heard the spinning of soft rubber wheels, also confusing.

Something was wrong!

I searched my mind for a similarity with what I was experiencing and what I'd read in books and seen on television. Except for the bright light, there were none.

My head hurt like the devil.

I gagged. It felt as though I had a hose down my throat.

Where was the peace and the calm?

Where were the multicolored lights and the feeling of being enveloped in love?

Through the fog, one hand reached out. Certain I'd arrived at my destination I grabbed hold of the fingers that felt cold to the touch.

The icy grip was familiar, but no matter how much I racked my brain, I couldn't put a face to the memory.

It wasn't my dad; his large hands had felt warm and safe.

My grandmother's hands were much too small and soft.

A form came into view, shrouded in black, a crooked wimple over her head, her mouth twisted into an I-told-you-so grin.

Sister Mary Agnes!

I instantly released my grip.

In a distance I saw the pearly gates.

Sister Mary Agnes turned and whispered something into a man's ear. He looked noble, wise, and extremely holy. I assumed he was Saint Peter. Instead of long, flowing robes, he was dressed in shorts and a striped tank top.

Strange.

Because this was the worst possible time to be judging people, I forced myself to think only good thoughts. Within seconds I loved his outfit. Even his hairy, bowed legs brought on a barrage of silent compliments.

Since he probably read minds, I expected him to skip the questions and hand me an engraved invitation. *Go directly to heaven.*

"Welcome, my child."

At this point, I decided He was God. In all my years of parochial school, He was the only Being Who referred to people as "my child."

From far away I heard Lilly crying. My work on earth wasn't done. My aunt needed me to guide her. What would happen to her now?

Sorry, Lilly, but I must go.

I recognized Jake's voice.

Sorry, my love, Heaven awaits me.

God pressed a button by his side, and the large gates creaked open. I saw shock on Sister Mary Agnes's face. Before I could stop myself, I stuck out my tongue. Instantly repentant, I cleansed my mind of bad thoughts and sent her an apologetic, angelic smile.

I took two steps toward an eternity of joy. Never again would I worry about money or life's other troubles.

As I gingerly stepped from cloud to cloud, nearing my destiny, my feet sinking up to my knees in the marshmallow consistency, a terrible thought struck.

What would happen to Jake?

Would he grieve for me until his death and become a wizened old man who spoke of his one true love to anyone willing to listen?

Or . . .

As if in a large-screen movie, a smiling face hovered before me.

Elaine!

I came to with a start.

I was on a gurney with a sheet up to my neck. A doctor wearing green scrubs pulled a tube from my throat.

I gagged uncontrollably. When the reflex stopped, thankful to be alive I sucked in a breath. I felt dizzy. Had the paramedics arrived in time? Was I going to die? Now that I knew what awaited me, I was in no hurry to depart this world.

Lilly stroked my left hand. "Goodness gracious, you frightened me something fierce."

Frightened—past tense.

Phew!

I glanced to my right and saw Jake looking down, his eyes filled with relief and love.

At that moment I knew I'd marry him soon.

Very soon.

My eyes misted.

"They're keeping you overnight for observation, but you'll be fine," he said.

"I can't stay. I have a story to write."

Something streaked across Jake's face, but before I could question him, the doctor spoke.

"You're one lucky woman." He pulled off his gloves. "We've pumped the poison from your stomach, but you'll have one hell of a headache for a while."

"Because of the poisonous onions."

"Because of the booze."

"Sip some ice, that'll help soothe your throat. Meanwhile, consider drinking less."

"I usually consume only one or two glasses of wine," I said in defense of my martini-drinking binge. "Besides, when I found out I was about to eat my last meal, I tossed back a few to dull my pain."

"When the high from the alcohol wears off, you'll regret having those last drinks. I've given you a shot to help you rest. I'll see you in the morning."

"I can't stay," I said to his retreating back.

Lilly squeezed my hand. "I don't know what would have happened if Richard hadn't arrived when he did. In a way the man saved your life."

"Richard?" I said in a raspy voice, praying it wasn't so.

I didn't want to be forever indebted to pipsqueak Richard.

"I was sitting in my Hummer, craning my neck, trying to pick up the faintest sound from the spy phone. I hadn't heard one word, not one syllable for some time. I lost the connection shortly after your rendition of 'Row, Row, Row Your Boat.' I was debating whether to knock on the door or call the police when Richard pulled up behind me in his white van. He'd tried calling, but you'd already left. He'd been scouring the streets of Portland hoping to find us. Thankfully, he found me in the nick of time."

"Let me guess, his phone was broken."

"There was nothing wrong with the phone, but he'd forgotten to charge the batteries."

"When I see him, I'll wring his chicken neck," I said, forcing the words over a raw throat.

"All's well that ends well. As I said before, everything happens for a reason."

I closed my eyes and relaxed as the attendant pushed the gurney through the hall and into the elevator. I heard the soft whoosh of the wheels and clanging of metal. I concluded I hadn't had a near-death experience, but instead a nightmare.

I allowed my mind to drift back to my conversation with Joyce.

A short while later the attendant helped me slide over onto the mattress and left.

Even with my eyes closed, I felt Jake beside me.

"I still don't have the confession on tape," I said, looking at him. "Is Joyce going to walk?"

"No, she and her boyfriend confessed."

I pushed myself up in bed. "I need to get out of here."

He shook his head. "You're staying if I have to handcuff you to the bed."

I sent him a saucy smile. "I have a story to write. Otherwise I'd take you up on your fun and games. Where are my clothes?"

"Accept the facts. You aren't going anywhere."

"Then borrow a laptop from work. Mr. Winters will want this story in tomorrow's paper."

"You need to rest," Jake said.

"I'll rest after I've written my story."

"You've been through a lot. Your health is what's important."

"We're talking front page. This kind of opportunity doesn't happen every day."

That same look I'd seen earlier scooted across his face.

"What's wrong? Did the doctor tell you something he didn't tell me?" In all the movies I'd ever watched, the sick person was always the last to know their condition.

"If I'm dying, I want to know." I braced myself for the worst.

"You aren't dying."

"Phew, then what is it?"

"I was hoping to tell you tomorrow after you'd gotten a good night's sleep."

He paused, the suspense wrapping around me like a wet blanket.

"If I'm not dying, then what is it?"

"Doris Cote is writing the story."

"What!"

"Mr. Winters didn't think you'd be up to it, and news like this can't wait. The doctor gave you a shot for the pain that should put you out."

"Of course, I'm up to it. Call and tell Mr. Winters I'm on my way. I don't feel the effects of the shot. I'm all right. I couldn't be stronger."

Planning to throw on my clothes and head to the *Enquirer*, I leaped off the mattress and fell into Jake's arms. The room spun, my head throbbed, my vision blurred, and my knees buckled.

Strong arms wrapped around me.

For a moment there were two Jakes.

I kissed the one on my right, then the one on my left. They smiled, lifted me in their arms, and set me down on the bed. As I lay my head back on the pillow, they pulled chairs beside the bed and held my hand.

"Jakes," I said in a slurred, sexy tone, surprised to see three of him. "You guys are the best."

Lilly arrived with a change of clothes the next morning. "How are you feeling today?"

"Like I have a pickaxe chipping away at my brain."

"Tee hee hee."

"That wasn't supposed to be funny."

"Just wait till you get home and see your surprise."

I gritted my back teeth. "I haven't gotten over my last surprise yet."

"It's nice to know you like your red Hummer as much as I like mine."

Aunt Lilly was immune to sarcasm.

"Anyway, this surprise isn't from me. It's from Jake."

My curiosity was piqued. Maybe he'd decided to give me the engagement ring without setting a date. Or maybe he'd purchased the wide-screen television he was always talking about. There was the king-size bed.

"Give me a hint."

"Every kick-ass investigative reporter should have one of these."

"You're still collecting terms?" I asked.

"You bet your sweet bippy I am."

Aunt Lilly wore a faux fur leopard coat with brown leather boots and a green knit cap with a white pompom on the top. Her spiked red hair poked helter-skelter through the cap's yarn, resembling barbs of wire.

"You shouldn't be driving by yourself," I said, not looking forward to the ride home.

"I know that. A friend gave me a ride."

I was in too much discomfort to question her. I figured I'd find out soon enough. I stood and pulled on panties and jeans. I slipped on a sweatshirt, threw my arms into my jacket, grabbed my purse, and called it good enough. If my aunt hadn't insisted on helping with my shoes, I'd have tucked them under my arm.

My head throbbed; the tiny hairs on my eyelids thudded. My brain pulsated against my skull. I minimized my motion.

As Lilly grabbed hold of my arm, I dragged my feet along the floor. "I will never again drink a martini. I've even sworn off olives."

Lilly nodded. "That's probably for the best."

We continued down the endless hall, past the nurses' station, toward the elevator. I doubted I'd ever walk at a normal pace or even blink again. I'd never raise my voice, or dare to lift my chin. The tiniest flick of a muscle sent a sharp jab to my brain, where bass drums boomed.

A nun leaped in front of us. "Young lady, where do you think you're going? You should be in a wheelchair."

"Great idea," Lilly said.

I squinted at the woman, her no-nonsense expression capable of making an armed man drop his weapon and run. She reminded me of Sister Mary Agnes. Determined to win this battle, my rebellious nature surfaced. "Thank you, but I can make it on my own. We investigative reporters are a strong lot," I said in a martyred tone and imagined the saints in heaven smiling down at me.

Her eyebrows winged sharply.

I turned and pressed the button for the elevator. Insistent hands wrapped around my waist. For a moment I held my ground. My feet lost contact with the floor, and I found myself airborne. Once my behind hit the cushioned sling of the wheelchair, she bent down and pinned me with a frosty gaze. She didn't say a word, but she didn't need to.

She'd won. I was her prisoner.

I slipped my feet onto the supports. "Ready when you are."

Very cautiously she wheeled me into the elevator. A man got on and stood beside to me. Under his arm was a folded newspaper.

I craned my head to get a closer look.

In bold print: "Black Widow Spins a Deadly Web of Deceit," by Doris Cote.

Front page, newsworthy article—it should have been my story with my byline.

I bit back a curse.

Doris was lower than pond scum.

As I grumbled under my breath, I spotted my photograph beneath the article. Looking like a drunken escapee from a mental institution, my gun with the carved ivory butt at my feet, I was sprawled on the couch, my mouth curved into a silly grin, martini glass in one hand and a fork piercing an onion in the other.

I groaned.

Unfortunately, for once my name was spelled correctly.

I climbed into the backseat of Aunt Lilly's Hummer and was greeted by Cobbler tugging at my leather purse.

"You riding shotgun?" came Rob's voice from the front seat. He wore a camouflage shirt. Ammo belts crisscrossed his chest.

I'd been too immersed in pity over my lost article to notice him behind the wheel.

I managed a feeble nod. A bolt of lightning pierced my skull, and I blinked in pain.

"Tied one on last night," he said, his loud voice rattling my brain. "I read the piece in this morning's paper."

Doris was lower than the mold that formed in the tiny crevices of a shower.

"I never would have guessed you had the balls to take on a killer by yourself."

"The article said that?" I asked, grabbing my head with both hands, relinquishing my handbag to Cobbler.

Lilly hooked her seat belt and turned around. "That and lots more. Doris gave you credit for doing the research. She made you sound like a brave, adventure-seeking heroine."

Suddenly my head didn't hurt quite as much. "She did?"

"You're freaking famous!"

Chapter Twenty

I slipped out of Lilly's Hummer, managed to drag myself to my door, and stabbed the key in the lock. I wanted nothing more than to drop onto my mattress and not open my eyes for days. I craved peace and quiet.

The torturous ride home with Rob at the wheel, blaring the horn at traffic, had drilled through my skull. I pushed the door open.

Relief.

Home at last!

Glorious silence greeted me.

For a microsecond I noticed the silly grin on Lilly's face and the expectant look in Rob's eyes.

Sirens blasted. Trying to figure out where the shrill sound originated, I covered my ears with my hands and looked around.

The deafening noise pulsated through my brain, surrounded me, and jabbed at every nerve from my head down to my large toe.

I watched Lilly turn and punch numbers into a keypad near the door. *Where had that come from?*

Long after the sound stilled, my ears rang. "What in the hell . . ." I said, each word softer than the previous, each syllable carving a crater into my skull.

"It's your surprise. Jake pulled a few favors and had your

security system installed overnight," Lilly said.

Cobbler barreled into the living room with the remains of my purse. With a sigh, he stretched out in front of the couch.

"Every door and window is wired," Rob added. "I volunteered to stand guard and blow away all intruders, but Jake turned me down. The offer still stands." Grinning, he ran his fingers over the ammo belts crisscrossing his chest.

I shook my head to decline and immediately regretted the action.

"If you change your mind, you know where to reach me," he said, cupping the palm of his right hand over the Glock pistol by his side.

"There are motion detectors everywhere. Check this out." Looking pleased, Lilly pressed numbers on the keypad and waved her hand in the air.

The ensuing sharp clamor sliced through my head. I escaped into my bedroom, threw myself face down on the bed, and covered my head with a pillow.

I'd had enough surprises to last a lifetime.

I awoke sometime later feeling much better. I stretched out in bed and ran my fingers through Taffy's fur. The cat craned its neck and purred. I was 100 percent safe. No one could sneak into my duplex and leave behind shredded remnants of my mother's books. Thanks to Jake, I could relax. My duplex was burglar-proof.

Or in my case, Elaine-proof.

I could understand why Elaine would want to cause me grief. I couldn't understand why she wanted to pulverize my mother's books. Had she torched my Explorer because she hated my guts or because the backseat was loaded with books?

Was she opposed to women's erotic fiction?

Had her jealousy toward me warped her mind, and she could no longer control her actions?

I needed to catch her in the act. If, by some slim chance, Elaine wasn't to blame, I had to find out who was.

I needed a plan, a surefire way of catching the devious witch.

I was deep in thought when the burglar alarm went off. I leaped from my bed, dashed into the living room and realized I didn't know the code.

Damn, damn, triple damn.

The racket became a living entity, browbeating me as I pressed every button on the control pad.

Lilly dashed into my duplex and silenced the alarm. "What happened?"

"I was lying in bed when the damn thing went off."

My aunt's gaze traveled over the inside of my duplex. "Either, one of your animals crossed a motion detector or . . ."

Her face paled. "Or someone is inside."

My knees shook, and I gulped a breath.

Hand in hand we rushed from room to room and found the kitchen window ajar. I opened the door and spotted an open box of destroyed books on my stoop.

I dug a hand into the box and pulled out a tattered cover, *Thrust or Bust*, by Busty Galore.

A shiver raced down my spine. Was I dealing with Elaine or a madman?

"This has got to stop," I said, infuriated and frightened.

Lilly turned and started toward the phone. "I'll call 911."

"Stop," I said, for the first time seeing this situation as an opportunity. I raised my hand to indicate the books. "I don't know why I didn't think of this before now. Maybe this is a potential front-page story?"

"You think so?"

"Damn straight." I spread my hands in front of me.

" 'Love Triangle Drives Woman Insane.' Catchy title, don't you think?"

"Damn straight," Lilly mimicked me.

"We need to bait a trap for the rat."

Lilly jumped back and stared at the floor. "Where's the rodent?"

"This is a figurative rat, but the trap will be real."

"When are we going to do whatever you have in mind?"

"You might want to reconsider. This could be dangerous," I said.

"Goodness gracious, that's precisely why I want to be included. Plus I'm not worried. If Elaine is the perpetrator, we can subdue her with one arm tied behind our backs."

"What if she isn't the person responsible?"

Lilly's eyes brightened. "Then I think we should ask Rob to come along."

I cringed. "No way."

"He's really a very nice man."

For all Lilly knew, he killed people for sport. "I'd rather we tackled this job alone, sort of a women's night out."

"Gee, I hadn't thought of it that way." She nodded. "A women's night out sounds like fun. So what are we going to do to catch this person?"

A great idea popped into my head. "I'll advertise a book sale this weekend at my duplex, offering autographed copies of my mother's latest works."

"Do you have autographed copies of Anne Marie's work?"

I inclined my head the way all well-known reporters did on television. "No, that's the beauty of my plan. When customers arrive, I'll say my mother's bookplates with her signature didn't arrive in time, but if they'll leave their names and phone numbers, I'll call them when the books are ready. I'll make sure I have empty cardboard boxes all around the room so those who show up will think they're filled with books."

"What makes you think Elaine is going to show up?"

"I plan to send her a brochure with the information."

"What if it isn't her?"

"Then I'm hoping the person responsible sees my advertisement in the newspaper. How's Saturday evening sound to you?"

Lilly's features clouded with worry. "I can't . . . Sunday would be much better."

"What's wrong with Saturday?" I asked, my curiosity already in overdrive.

She paused and bit the inside of her cheek. "I have a date—that's if the gentleman doesn't stand me up."

"You need to have confidence in yourself. Think positive."

"I'm trying."

"Good, then fill in the blank and repeat after me . . . 'Mr. *Blank* will definitely take me out this weekend.' "

Lilly covered her mouth. "Tee hee hee, Anne Marie warned me about your tricks."

"Spill the beans. I need to know who he is."

"I can't jinx what could be my very last chance to nab myself a man."

Nab a man. At first I thought she was joking, but I realized by her expression she was serious. "You're a vibrant, attractive woman. You'll have plenty of opportunities to find the right man."

"I've heard those same words since I was a teenager. I don't believe them anymore. I'm tired of being alone."

"You have Gramps."

"That's not the same."

"I know it isn't, but you have me, too."

"And I have Anne Marie's manuals to help me along."

At first I didn't understand, but when I realized she was referring to my mother's erotic novels, I cringed. "Yikes, those books could get you into a lot of trouble. The covers should come with a warning: *Beware, dangerous material inside.* Much too much information for a first date."

"I have lots of catching up to do," she said, seemingly deep in thought, glancing across the room. "Anyway, I haven't read Anne Marie's books yet."

"Phew."

"But I intend to study every word. I'm tired of being a spinster. I'm tired of missing out. I'm tired of being me."

My throat clogged with tears as I rested my hand over my aunt's arm. "You need to believe in yourself. Any man would be lucky to have a woman like you. When your date sees you, his eyes will pop out of their sockets. Once he's caught his breath and is able to speak, I guarantee he'll wink and say, 'Lilly, honey, you're babe-a-licious.' "

"What I need is a guarantee he'll show up."

After Lilly left, I sat on the couch and counted my blessings.

Jake came in number one.

Jake and I had grown so close, I felt as though he were an extension of me, as though I couldn't function without him in my life. I still wanted to become a top-notch reporter, only now I trusted Jake, believed I could be both his wife and a career woman. In time, I'd be the mother of his child, but not for a while.

I realized how much my aunt wanted to share her life with someone special. I'd already found my soul mate.

So what was I waiting for?

My close brush with death had opened my eyes and my heart.

It was time to take our relationship another notch.

The final notch.

The hairs on the back of my neck stirred slightly. Not an all-out cry of alarm but a minor tweak of apprehension. I brushed aside my last vestige of concern and made a decision.

When Jake arrived, we'd set the date for our wedding.

Jake arrived at six. I was ready. Candles bathed the room in a soft glow. A bottle of Merlot and a bottle of Budweiser chilled in an ice bucket on an end table.

I wrapped my arms around his neck and pressed my mouth against his. Too excited to put off my announcement I cut the kiss short.

"Not so fast," he said and tried unsuccessfully to pull me in for another foray.

"I need to tell you something, and it can't wait. Quick, sit down."

I giggled like a schoolgirl. Tugging at his hand, I sat close to him on the couch, my knee touching his, the fingers of one hand entwined with his. I handed him a bottle of beer, and lifted my glass of Merlot in the air.

"I want to make a toast to our upcoming . . ." The last word wedged in my throat for a moment. "Nuptials."

He looked down at me, his chocolate brown eyes filled with intensity, warmth, and love. "Are you sure?"

I leaned my head against his shoulder. "Yes, I'm one hundred percent sure." *Well, at least ninety-nine point ninety-nine percent sure.*

"I still want a career."

"I know that's important to you. I promise never to stand in the way of your career."

He pinged his bottle against my glass. "Here's to us."

I sipped my wine, he chugged his beer.

Tears of happiness rimmed my eyes. I dashed them away with the back of my hand. "You better not make me regret this decision, copper." I playfully jabbed his jaw.

"We haven't even tied the knot and you're already getting bossy. Did you have a month in mind?"

"I want my mother to help me plan my wedding. July would be a good month unless you'd rather wait for fall."

"Hot damn," he said, slapping his hands together. "There's no way in hell I'd postpone our wedding. Which weekend did you want to get married?"

I thought for a moment. I wanted our wedding date to stand on its own and not be part of another holiday. "Let's stay away from the Fourth of July."

"Fine by me."

"Then let's get married the second weekend of the month."

"It's a deal," he said.

We kissed and laughed and kissed some more.

His expression turned serious. "And you won't change your mind?"

I lifted two fingers in the air. "Girl Scout's honor."

"You were never a Girl Scout."

"What difference does that make?"

He grinned. "Then let's make this official." He grabbed my hand, threw an afghan around my shoulders, and pulled me out the door toward his truck.

"It's below zero. I should be wearing a thick coat and fur-lined boots, not a blanket and open-toed slippers. I'm freezing. Have you lost your mind?"

"Yes, the day I met you," he said, his eyes twinkling in the moonlight.

"Where are we going?"

"Nowhere, everywhere. I love you, Monique," he said,

opening the door to his pickup and reaching into the glove compartment. He withdrew a small dark blue velvet box, popped it open, and stood watching me.

The diamond ring I'd seen at the store, a lovely marquise solitaire, sparkled brighter than the stars overhead. "But . . . I thought . . ."

"Even after you turned me down, I bought it. I told the clerk to go ahead and size the ring. I wanted to be prepared, just in case."

He took the ring from the box and slipped it on my finger.

"It fits perfectly."

"That's because we're perfect together." He kissed me and, grinning, cupped my rear in his hand. "We better go inside before you freeze your cute ass . . . ets."

As a gust of wind pelted us with frozen snow, we rushed into my duplex.

I realized I could weather most storms with my foul-mouthed, hot-blooded cop at my side.

Chapter Twenty-one

That night I had difficulty sleeping. Every few minutes I turned on the bedside lamp to look at my ring. My heart beat double time.

Jake had fallen asleep instantly, but not me. Tears clouded my vision each time I peeked at my engagement ring. I'd never expected to feel this excited about getting married.

I'd vowed never again to trust a man, any man, but Jake wasn't any man. He was *"The One."* For a while I didn't believe in the magic of love, and I'd pitied the women who flashed their diamond rings around the office like trophies.

But no more.

I'd switched sides and belonged to the silly, blissful, this-doesn't-have-to-make-sense team. I was happy, content, and ecstatic. I'd won the megabucks of love, and I'd lived long enough to know there were few winners. But I'd aced it. I had both everlasting love and a career; I'd soon be Mrs. Monique Dube and a top-notch investigative reporter.

The next morning I was vaguely aware of Jake kissing me good-bye. "See you this evening."

I cracked an eyelid open. "What time is it?"

"Six. You look exhausted."

"I had trouble sleeping."

"No regrets?"

"None," I said, opening my eyes and seeing the concern in

his eyes. "I'm looking forward to being your wife."

"Continue thinking good thoughts."

I swung my legs out of bed.

"Don't forget to set the security alarm when you leave," he said, glancing over his shoulder as he went out the door.

I nodded and admired my ring.

I heard the knock on the door a moment later and assumed he'd forgotten something.

"Did you come back for a quickie?" I shouted, opening the door, surprised to see Richard hopping back in fright.

"You never catch on."

"I didn't mean . . . I thought . . . it was an innocent mistake."

"Yeah, right." Careful to keep his distance, he hurried into the living room.

I slammed the door shut. "What do you want?"

"I've come for my money."

"What money?"

"You're kidding, right?"

I shook my head and tired to figure out what he meant.

"The money for the spy phone you ruined the other night."

"I could have died, and you're here griping about your phone."

"Against my better judgment, I allowed you to take my equipment. I should have made you wait until I could go with you."

"That wasn't possible."

"That's what you said the other night. You also said you'd pay if my equipment got damaged. You ruined a thirteen-hundred-dollar phone, and I can't afford to replace it."

He stretched out his palm as if waiting for me to slap money into his hand.

"I can't afford to give you thirteen hundred bucks."

"If you'd told me that the other night, I wouldn't have let

you take it. A promise is a promise. You owe me, big time."

"I could have been killed . . . all because your phone stopped working."

"Yes, I feel bad about that, but I still need my equipment replaced. A private eye isn't worth jack without the tools of his trade. And if I hadn't arrived when I did, you wouldn't be standing here right now."

"I'll pay for it, but it'll take a while. I can give you twenty-five to fifty bucks a week."

"I run a business. I can't afford to wait months to replace my phone."

"Maybe I can work it off?" I said, cringing and praying he'd turn me down.

He mulled the matter over. "As a matter of fact, that might not be a bad idea. I've overbooked my schedule and there's a small job that would be perfect for you."

"How much does it pay?"

"Because I feel bad about you landing in the hospital, do this job for me, and I'll consider us squared away."

As I waited for nightfall, I sat in Lilly's Hummer and flicked on the overhead light so I could see my ring.

"It's a beauty," Lilly said in a wistful tone, taking my hand and looking again at my diamond. "Jake is a great catch."

"You make it sound as though I have him dangling at the end of a hook."

"Too bad that isn't so because I'd cast my line in next to yours."

"Have you heard from your mystery man?"

She nodded.

"And, how's it going?"

"I can't say."

"Why not?"

"Because if I make a big deal out of this date, I'll jinx it."

"You need someone to share this with," I said, hoping she'd tell me his name.

"I realize that."

"What are his interests?"

"Gee, I don't know. I figured I'd find out if and when he shows up for our first date."

"The next time he calls, ask him whether he likes sports or going to the theater, that way you can buy a book and study the subject before your night out on the town."

"According to Anne Marie, none of that is necessary. She said all I need to do is make the gentleman feel as though he's the most important thing in my life for that one night, and all will be fine. I'll listen to every word and show him I'm interested in him by asking lots of questions."

"Will you need help getting ready?"

"I've made an appointment to have my hair and nails done, and I've already bought a new dress so I should be fine."

"Give me a little hint. What are his initials?"

"I wish I could tell you, but I can't. If I divulge his identity, sure as we're sitting in the best-made vehicle on this planet, he'll turn tail and run."

"I give up," I said, "for now."

"You might as well because I'm not talking."

I glanced at the camera on my lap. "I hope Richard's equipment doesn't let me down again."

"The man is a genius."

"I hope you don't mean that."

"He's an expert in everything."

"Don't let Richard's know-it-all attitude fool you. He couldn't find his way out of a pillowcase open at both ends. His expertise is a figment of his imagination."

Lilly looked unconvinced. "How long should I wait before calling the police?"

"Don't call for help unless you hear my cries. This operation could take a long time. I can't leave until I have proof Bob Andrews is cheating on his wife. Richard said I should wait by the fence bordering the rear of the property. I don't intend to take any unnecessary chances, and I've worn my running shoes so I can make a quick getaway if something goes awry."

"Take as long as you need. I've brought along Anne Marie's manuals to keep me company."

According to the weatherman it was five degrees below zero with a wind chill factor of forty below. I'd worn tights, jeans, loose-fitting woolen pants covered with ski pants. Over my chest, I'd layered my bra, T-shirt, turtleneck, flannel shirt, hooded sweatshirt and thick goose down jacket. I wore a knitted stocking hat with holes for my eyes and mouth.

I was still chilled to the bone.

Shivering, I stood by the fence and tried to catch a glimpse through a window. Peering through the telephoto lens I made out a naked man and a woman.

This job would be a cinch, an easy thirteen hundred dollars.

The man had the flabbiest butt I'd ever had the displeasure of seeing. The woman's breasts sagged to her waist, and I wondered whether in time gravity would play the same cruel trick on me.

Following Richard's instructions, I removed my glove; my hand instantly went numb. I inhaled a steadying breath, positioned my finger over the button, peered through the viewfinder and saw nothing but an empty kitchen.

Figuring the duo had moved to another room, I shifted my position to the other side of the house and sat on my haunches, waiting for a glimpse of the couple. In a nearby cage I spotted glowing eyes focused on me.

The creature growled.

I moved several yards away.

The door opened and Mr. Flabby Butt shouted, "Damn mutt, shut your trap if you know what's good for ya."

The dog howled louder.

From the light over the stoop, I saw Mr. Flabby Butt was wearing a spiked dog collar, leash, and nothing else. Though I tried not to notice, the next image would be forever imbedded in my mind. His penis looked like a dried prune from which hung a colorful ribbon.

His girlfriend came outside, her nipples tightening in the cold. She wore a leather mask, long lace stockings, and a black garter belt. "Bobby, honey, what's wrong?"

"Damn fool dog got himself a whiff of somethin'."

She snapped the whip she held in her right hand against Bob's back.

"Ouch," he said with a deep laugh, turning around and running his hand over her thighs.

My stomach lurched.

The woman went inside. Bob slipped his feet into tall boots and strutted across the snow-packed yard. Before I could figure out what he had in mind, he'd released the clasp on the dog cage. "Go get 'em," he said, swinging open the gate to the chain-link fence.

The hound charged around the corner and came at me. I made a mad dash for a nearby apple tree. Hooking one leg over a low branch, I hoisted myself out of reach.

I expected to find Bob chasing me, but instead saw him disappear inside his house.

An hour later, with the dog baying at my heels, I spotted Bob and his lady friend playing tag in the kitchen. Once more

I was amazed at the size of his behind which was turned toward the window. His lady friend wrapped her fingers around his dog collar, puckered up, and planted a wet kiss on his mouth.

I raised the camera and captured for posterity a posterior better left forgotten.

Convinced Richard was trying to renege on our deal, I waved my finger at him. "What do you mean this doesn't count? You asked for a picture, and I got you one. As far as I'm concerned, we're even. I don't owe you a dime."

"My client won't pay for this photograph." Richard frowned at Bob's picture with his lady friend. "If you'd listened, you'd know we wanted to find him carousing with a white-haired woman."

"I was freezing my butt off, and you're nitpicking about the color of her hair. For all I know she's wearing a wig. What difference does it make? He's a cheating bastard."

The corded muscles on Richard's neck looked ready to snap. "Because you took a picture of Bob with his wife."

I arrived home in time to find the mail carrier leaving a notice in my mailbox.

"Got here just in the nick of time," Floyd said, handing me a registered letter.

Lilly exited my mother's duplex. "Look, I got one, too."

I signed the slip and took my mail inside. "Haven't you opened yours yet?"

"No, I didn't dare. What if it's bad news?"

"It could just as easily be good news." I glanced at the return address in the corner of the envelope. "These are from Don's Parachuting Institute. Maybe it's more junk mail, made to look like something great."

"Why would we both get a letter?" Lilly asked, looking worried.

"There's only one way to find out," I said, ripping my letter open. Lilly tore hers open, too.

Dear Ms. St. Cyr:

We rarely conduct skydiving lessons during the winter months, but at times make an exception. Anne Marie St. Cyr, a very persuasive woman, has purchased our Deluxe Parachuting program to begin the first Saturday in February. We look forward to hearing from you. Enclosed is a list of supplies not covered in our program.

Don

Lilly clasped the letter to her chest. "Wasn't that nice of Anne Marie?"

"Nice! She wants us to dangle like icicles from a parachute, risking our lives and doing her dirty work."

"What do you mean?"

I hoped my mother had forgotten. I should have known better. "This is research for her book."

"This is a humdinger of an adventure," Lilly said, her bloodshot eyes glowing.

Red eyes meant one thing—tears—man trouble. My stomach clenched. Lilly's mystery man had already broken her heart.

"What did he do to you?"

"Who?"

"The dirty dog who was supposed to go out on a date with you Saturday."

Warmth flooded her face. "Oh, him. He's doing grand."

"So your date is still on?"

"It appears so at the moment, but there's still plenty of opportunity for him to cancel."

"What time is he picking you up?" I asked, figuring I'd check him out when he arrived.

"He's supposed to show up at seven, but I'm not holding my breath."

"He'll show."

"Maybe not. I wouldn't be surprised if he skedaddled."

I gave up the fight. "Why are your eyes so red?"

"I was up half the night reading Anne Marie's manuals." Her face reddened. "Well, I never . . . in a hundred years . . ." She fanned her face.

"Those books are fiction. Thinking of them as manuals could get you into big trouble," I warned her.

"Tee hee hee, those books had me squirming in my bed last night. I doubt I'll ever be able to erase the visuals imprinted on my brain. My sister's prose is so expressive and intense I saw everything as if I were watching a movie on television. I never realized she was such a . . ."

I waited for her to finish.

"There isn't a word that does Anne Marie justice. I wonder whether she used some of those tricks in her book to snag Frank."

I covered my ears with my hands. "Let's change the subject." No daughter wanted to think of her mother doing the nasty, least of all me.

"I bet you're forever giving your mother ideas for her manuals."

Confused, I brought my hands down. "What makes you say that?"

"Simple. I remember the earrings and the outfit with the rotating tassels you wore to your birthday party."

After my aunt left, I called Richard. "Can I borrow your

night goggles for a couple of hours tomorrow?"

"Absolutely not."

"I can understand why you'd be upset about the phone . . . I will make good on it . . . as soon as I come up with the money."

"Forget about the phone. You don't owe me a thing."

Since Richard was a cheapskate, I knew something was up. "Why not?"

"I'm canceling your debt. Call me Mr. Generosity."

I thought of lots of names to call Richard, but that wasn't one of them. "Really?"

"Yes."

"Did Mrs. Andrews pay you for the picture?"

A long pause.

"She did, didn't she?"

"Well, okay, she gave me a bonus . . . not that it's any of your business."

"Why would she pay for a picture of herself?"

"She was embarrassed to see herself dressed like a dominatrix. She bought both the picture and the negatives and made me promise not to tell anyone what I'd seen."

"What did she think of Mr. Flabby Butt?"

"Strangely enough, to quote her, she thought he looked damn sexy."

"You're kidding, right?"

"No, she commented about making an enlargement to hang in their bedroom."

Gross. "Since I no longer owe you one red cent, lend me your goggles. I'll protect them with my life. If anything happens to them, I'll pay you back." Besides, how much could a pair cost?

"I no longer let my equipment out of my sight. Especially my Rigel 3200 Pro Night Vision Goggles, featuring the highest resolution that produces a crisp image in total darkness. They're brand-new, still in the box. The little beauties cost me almost seven hundred bucks, and I know you don't have that kind of dough."

I considered trying to bluff but decided against it. Sighing, I tried to think of a good argument but came up with none. "Then, are you free tomorrow night?"

"I'll come over on two conditions."

I waited a moment. "What?"

"You promise not to come on to me."

Give me a break!

"And stock your fridge with Moxie."

Chapter Twenty-two

Richard arrived at six with a duffle bag. "Remember what I said. You better not throw yourself at me."

I refrained from rolling my eyes. "I'll try to control myself."

"Touch me, and I'm outta here."

"If it'll make you feel safer, you can wait in the kitchen while I use your equipment."

"I'm not letting my stuff out of my sight."

"Suit yourself."

He ambled into the kitchen and returned with a bottle of Moxie. "This is the best brew around. Why do you need my goggles?"

"I want to spy on someone."

"It's a good thing you have me along. A surveillance operation can turn dangerous." He handed me a device with straps that crisscrossed my head and binoculars hanging off the front.

"These are much bigger than the ones we used at Cook's Seafood Restaurant."

"I've upgraded to the very best. You be careful not to drop them, and try not to get your fingerprints all over. If you set them down for even a second, I expect you to put on the lens caps."

"You worry too much. I'm not leaving the house. And

you're right here guarding them. What could happen?"

"With you, lots could go wrong."

"I love you, too." I puckered up and blew him a kiss.

"Keep that up, and I'll take my gear and leave."

"Sorry," I said, trying to sound contrite.

I set a chair in front of the living room window, flicked off the lights, and pulled back the curtains. "These are wonderful. I can see the fleas jumping off Mrs. Wilson's cat."

"Your warped sense of humor is getting on my nerves."

I mumbled under my breath. "Sorry."

"Who are you trying to catch?"

"I'm trying to solve a mystery."

"That's my specialty. Tell me the facts, and I'll crack the case."

How does a niece explain she's spying on her aunt's date? "It's top secret," I finally said, in a deep, kick-ass, investigative reporter voice.

"You coming down with a cold?"

Damn.

"Quiet," I said. "I'm trying to concentrate."

I heard a groan in the background.

"He's here." I jumped to my feet and trained Richard's night goggles on the familiar-looking minivan pulling into my yard.

"Who?" Richard was by my side, leaning so close I smelled the Moxie on his breath.

The door swung open, and the vehicle's dome light came on. "Damn, damn, double damn."

"What's wrong?" Richard asked, looking ready to bolt.

"Nothing, everything. It's my brother, Thomas."

"Is he dangerous?"

"Of course not." I rushed to the door, swinging it open. "What now?"

My nephews jumped in front of me. "Can we play, too?"

Thomas grinned and eyed my headgear and the man behind me. "Maybe I should have called first."

I pulled the night goggles off my head and was temporarily blinded by the dark. I flicked on the lights and stepped back.

My brother and his sons entered.

"What game are you playing, Auntie Monique?" my nephews asked, running curious fingers over the lenses.

Richard snatched his goggles away.

I introduced the men and watched them shake hands. Thomas sent me a curious glance.

"Richard is a P.I. He's helping me . . . on a story."

"Then you won't mind taking the boys."

I blew out a calming breath. How many times had he vowed not to show up on my doorstep without calling? "You promised . . ." I couldn't finish my sentence because I didn't want to hurt my nephews' feelings.

"Sis, I wouldn't ask, except something's come up."

"Not another . . ." *Loser.*

"I know what you're thinking, but you're wrong. This time, I know you'd approve."

"Who is she?"

"Sorry, but I can't say."

"Why not?"

"I promised her I wouldn't tell anyone."

Damn!

My curiosity skyrocketed.

Once Thomas left, I persuaded the boys to sit at my feet in the dark.

"We're bored," the oldest said a moment later.

"Just a few more minutes. While you're sitting there, tell me about your dad's new girlfriend."

I hated using the boys in this manner, but hey, it was up to

Thomas to tell me her name.

"We haven't seen her except they talk every night on the phone."

"Do you know her name?"

"Nope, Dad talks real low."

I wanted to wring my brother's neck. The nerve of him keeping secrets from his only sister.

"How much longer is this going to take?" Richard asked. "I forgot to set my VCR, and I don't want to miss the latest edition of *America's Most Wanted.*"

"What time is it now?" I asked.

"It's after seven-thirty."

"I give up," I said, standing and turning on the lamp. "Who'd like some ice cream?"

"Yippeeee!" the boys shouted, running into the kitchen, followed by Richard, who suddenly seemed in no hurry to leave.

As I scooped chocolate ice cream into bowls, sprinkling colorful jimmies on top, I knew what had happened. When my brother entered my duplex to ask me to baby-sit the boys, the mystery man had arrived, picked up Aunt Lilly, and whisked her away.

Thanks to Thomas I'd missed seeing Aunt Lilly's date.

Plus I now had a mystery woman to wonder about.

Long after Richard and the boys left, I positioned myself in a chair with a view of the window. I no longer had the night goggles so I'd switched on the outside light. Determined not to miss Lilly's return, I replaced the bulb in the socket with a 200-watt lamp that illuminated the yard like the noonday sun.

I sipped a glass of Merlot and waited, and waited, and waited. Sometime later, certain my watch was wrong, I went into the kitchen to check the time on the clock: 2:00 a.m.

Something was wrong. My naïve aunt was in trouble. She didn't know how to handle herself in today's jungle.

I called Jake's pager and left a message. I paced the living room.

"Hey, babe," he said a moment later when I picked up the phone.

"You have to send out a missing person bulletin."

"Who's missing?"

"Aunt Lilly."

"I thought she had a date."

"She should be home by now."

"Lilly's an adult. I'm sure she's fine."

"Just keep an eye out for her."

"Will do. I love you," he said, his voice warm and fuzzy, or maybe the fuzzy part was due to the wine.

"Love you, too."

"I can't wait for our wedding."

"Me neither. July will come quickly."

"Not quick enough to suit me. Call me back if you don't hear from your aunt soon."

"Thanks." I sent a half-dozen kisses over the line before hanging up.

I heard a door close, peeked outside, and saw Lilly coming out of my mother's duplex. Before she could knock, I opened the door. "When did you get home?"

"A few minutes ago."

Damn, damn, triple damn. She'd arrived while I was talking to Jake.

Looking worried, Lilly hurried into the room. "We have to call the police."

"What did that bum do to you?"

"What bum?"

"Your date."

238

"I'm not talking about my date. Father is missing. I checked his room, and he wasn't there. His car is parked outside. His favorite lasso is gone, too. I think someone tied him up and kidnapped him."

Alarmed, I reached for the phone and called Jake's pager. The phone rang a moment later.

"It's time for my break, how about I drop over for a little TLC," he said in a sexy voice. "I'll let you use my handcuffs."

Mmmmm, very tempting.

Ashamed of myself for allowing my mind to drift off course, I tightened my fingers around the receiver. "Gramps is missing. Lilly fears someone broke in and tied him up with his favorite lasso."

"So your aunt got back safely."

"Yes, but now I'm worried about Gramps."

"Maybe he went to visit a friend."

"His Olds is parked outside."

"He could have taken a taxi."

"Gramps hates taxis."

"I'll stop over and see what I can find. Meanwhile, lock your door and set the alarm."

My heart skipped a beat. "Why?"

"Just in case this isn't another figment of your imagination."

A few minutes later Jake's cruiser pulled into the driveway. Lilly and I dashed outside and joined him on the stoop.

"Wait here," he said, drawing his gun and entering my mother's duplex.

The hairs on the back of my neck stirred.

I heard Long John squawking, his voice gruff like Gramps's. "Stick 'em up, son of a bitch, drill you full of holes."

Jake motioned for us to come inside. "There's no sign of forced entry."

The bird preened in his mirror. "Let's screw. Son of a bitch. Stick 'em up."

Frowning, I covered the parrot's cage with a towel. Cobbler sniffed my furry slippers. I shoved him with the tip of my toe, but not fast enough to miss his slobbering tongue. "Gramps is home every night. I'm certain he's in grave danger. My reporter's instinct tells me we have to find him quickly. Otherwise, who knows what might happen?"

Jake rested his arm over my shoulder. I inhaled his spicy scent and felt calmer with him by my side.

"It's too soon for me to issue a report, but I'll tell the other cops on patrol to keep an eye out for your grandfather."

"Thanks."

We kissed, then I watched him climb into his cruiser and drive away.

I missed him already.

I tried to persuade Lilly to go rest in her bedroom, but she insisted on staying up with me. As I dozed off at the kitchen table, I realized I'd forgotten to lock my door or set the burglar alarm, but I was too exhausted to budge.

I was awakened by the sound of a key in the lock. I lifted my head and noticed the rays of the sun streaming through the window.

Lilly opened her eyes and stared at the door, a mixture of fear and anticipation in her eyes.

"Are you two gals waitin' up for me?" Gramps asked as he strolled into the kitchen, looking rested. He pulled the cover off Long John's cage. "Stick 'em up, partner."

The bird stretched its neck. "Stick 'em up, make my day, son of a bitch."

Gramps laughed. "Smartest bird I've ever met. Bet he

missed me while I was out."

"You should have called. We were worried," I said, the pitch of my voice frazzled.

"Goodness gracious, I was a wreck," Lilly said, locking her fingers together.

"Ain't nothin' to worry about. I took part in a li'l roundup."

He threw his jacket over a chair. Wearing a black Stetson cocked at an angle, he strutted toward the table. I heard a strange jingle and looked down at the spurs on his pointed-toe cowboy boots. In his hand he carried a lasso that he set beside the table.

I couldn't figure out what he meant. "I didn't know there was a rodeo in town."

He wiggled his shaggy eyebrows and loosened the string tie around his neck. "There was only one filly and one cowpuncher in this roundup."

Blankly, I stared at him.

Gramps threw back his head and chuckled, his tone loud enough to wake up the neighbors. "I had me a date with a dashing, high-spirited cowgal."

"A date, with a woman?"

"Of course."

I glanced at my watch. "It's almost six. You've been gone all night. Where have you been?"

"A cowboy lives by a strong code of ethics. My filly's secret is safe with me."

"What's her name?"

"I can't say."

"I'm your only granddaughter. Surely, you can tell me."

"Sorry, I swore on my honor."

Losing the last thread of control, I jumped to my feet.

Long John eyed me and blurted, "Son of a bitch."

I swung a mean look from the bird to Gramps. "That about sums it up: son of a bitch. I don't understand what's going on in this family, but there are way too many secrets around here to suit me."

That said, I stormed out of the duplex, ran into mine, and tripped over a box in my living room.

Once I'd bandaged my knee and set the burglar alarm, I took a knife from the drawer and cut the tape along the top of the cardboard carton. I opened the flaps and saw shredded book covers and ripped pages of my mother's books.

I couldn't tell Jake about the break-in without admitting I'd carelessly forgotten to lock my door or set the alarm. Even if I lied and said I'd found the box outside, he'd try to persuade me to leave the investigation to the police.

My reporter's nose twitched. I was on the scent of a story.

She'd struck again.

Elaine had paid me another visit.

She'd be sorry when I caught her and wrote a front-page story, guaranteed to ruin even a saint's reputation.

"What if it isn't Elaine?" came the small voice inside my head.

I'd deal with that when the time arrived.

I spotted a sealed envelope inside the box. Pulling it out, I ripped it open and read the warning:

Stop or you'll be sorry!

Chapter Twenty-three

"I sure hope this works," Lilly said, pursing her lips as I duct-taped another empty box shut.

"It should. I've spent a small fortune on brochures, stamps, and advertisements in the newspaper. By now everyone from here to the West Coast knows about *Anne Marie's Book Erotica Signing Extravaganza.*"

"Do you think Elaine will show?"

"I called her and said I'd give her a great deal on a book. I also mentioned I'd be alone."

"Did she say she'd come?"

She'd told me to go screw myself. "Not in so many words."

"This is exciting." Lilly wrung her hands.

A knock at the door interrupted us.

I put the tape down next to my computer. Placing my hand over the butt of my gun in my shoulder holster, I slowly swung open the door.

Gramps sauntered in carrying Long John's birdcage. "Would you two gals mind caring for my friend while I'm gone?"

Apprehension streaked through me. "I can't have that bird here swearing every time someone arrives."

"I'm fixing to be gone for a while. I don't want him feeling abandoned. And he's your parrot," Gramps said, a fact I'd deliberately forgotten.

"Oh, all right. Where are you going?"

"There's a certain filly who can't wait to hog-tie me and nuzzle my neck with her soft nose."

TMI—too much information.

I didn't bother to ask for the woman's name because I wasn't ready to hear him refuse. "When are you coming back?"

"Don't wait up."

As Gramps walked across the room toward the door, he looked over his shoulder and swung his finger at me. "Now don't go gettin' it into your head to keep that bird covered. He needs to breathe fresh air. He needs to speak his piece."

"I can't have him spouting off obscenities to the customers."

"I don't want to come into this living room and find Long John can't see out."

"There's not a chance of that happening."

"You're a good granddaughter." Gramps thumbed through one of the books I'd stacked by my computer. For a moment he was quiet, then his face reddened.

He cleared his throat. "Holy crap, and to think you're worried about Long John. It'll take a hell of a lot more than a cussing parrot to embarrass the customer who purchases this book."

After Gramps left, I covered Long John and put his cage out of sight on the kitchen table. I hadn't lied, maybe twisted what I'd said a little. He wouldn't enter the living room and find the bird covered.

"Tee hee hee, you're a sly one."

"I like to think so."

"Are you frightened?"

"No," I lied, a shiver crawling down my back. "If Elaine's responsible for the damage to my mother's books, her mind is off kilter. I want you to be very careful."

"What will I say when people arrive?"

"Have them sign this notebook with their name, address, and phone number. Explain we'll call them when the autographed bookplates arrive. Be sure to say we have over two hundred books in these boxes, plenty to go around. Plenty to bait the trap for our rat."

By eight Sunday evening we'd had a few dozen visitors interested in my mother's books. We'd taken down their names with a promise to call them back. After the last person left, Lilly and I went into the kitchen for a snack. Finding the cupboards almost bare, we settled for a bowl of ice cream. On my way out of the room, I uncovered Long John's cage.

"Son of a bitch," he squawked, giving me the evil eye.

"Don't go blabbing to Gramps that I cover you."

"You got great knockers. Stick 'em up."

I was tempted to throw the towel over him again.

Lilly and I sat on the couch and had scraped our bowls clean when there was another knock at the door.

I glanced at my watch. "It's too late for a customer. The signing was supposed to end an hour ago."

I opened the door a crack and looked down at a fragile-looking, white-haired man with a woolen cap in his hand. "Pardon my intrusion, but am I too late? My wife loves your books, and she couldn't come because she's in the hospital on a ventilator."

Before I could explain they weren't my books, Lilly dashed to my side. "Of course it's not too late, but the bookplates haven't arrived. We can take your phone number, and I'll personally deliver the book to your wife's bedside."

Sweet, generous, gullible Aunt Lilly.

This guy probably wanted the book for himself and didn't dare admit he read women's erotic fiction.

We stepped aside and the old gent caught my hand in a damp grip. "It's so good of you to give me this opportunity. I'm Marvin Jolicour."

"How long has your wife been hospitalized?" Lilly asked.

"Wife?" he asked, for a moment looking confused.

I was right about him; he read erotic fiction.

Something flashed across his face. "I don't have a wife," he said after a pause.

I patted his shoulder. The moment of truth had arrived. "There's nothing to be ashamed of. Lots of men read women's fiction."

He squeezed his eyes shut and pinched the bridge of his nose, inhaled a long, ragged breath. He reached inside his coat for what I assumed would be a handkerchief or his wallet. Instead he pulled out an ugly black gun and, stepping back, aimed it at us.

Lilly stared at the weapon in disbelief.

Unlike my aunt I was a take-charge kind of person. I needed to strike while Marvin least expected it. I reached for my gun in my holster, discharged blue paint pellets at him. Paint splattered the ceiling, the carpet, my computer monitor, and I even managed to hit Marvin's black rubber boots and one pant leg.

"Shit, you're making a royal mess. Does this stuff come off?" he asked, looking angry. "I'm a senior citizen on a fixed income. I didn't come here to have my clothes ruined."

"Put up your hands very slowly, and I won't hurt you," I said in my deepest voice.

Deep lines ridged his brow. "You're playing with a toy gun and you think I'm going to follow your orders."

"How do I know you have a real gun?" I asked, my voice quivering.

"Would you like for me to blow out your kneecaps?"

I waved my hand in surrender. "No, no, that won't be necessary."

Nervously fluttering her fingers, Lilly collapsed on the couch and covered her face with her hands. I thought she was crying so I was surprised when she hurled a pillow at the gun. The man lost his grip and the weapon hit the floor.

Unfortunately I was so shocked by Lilly's brave maneuver, I didn't react in time. Marvin stooped down and picked up his gun.

"Who are you?" he asked, waving the barrel of his gun toward Lilly.

"I'm her aunt."

"And you're the author of this smut." Disgust flooded his face.

"I wouldn't call it smut, and, no, I'm not the author."

"I've seen you lugging the books from the post office. I tried to warn you to quit your evil ways but you wouldn't listen to me."

"I didn't write the books."

"I don't believe you."

"Suit yourself."

"You should be ashamed writing such trash."

"Someone your age should be more open-minded. These books aren't bad."

He spat on the rug, already ruined with blue paint. "Pornographic filth is what it is. And you've tarnished my good name. I can't even show my face at church anymore."

I didn't know what he was ranting about, and I didn't dare ask him to explain.

His pupils narrowed to pinpricks. "I bet you were sneaking around outside my window. You watched my fashion show."

"No, I didn't."

"You're a liar, and the proof is right there on page one hundred and fifty-six. Open the book and read the scene aloud. When you're through, I'm going to kill you and torch this house."

Hoping to waste time, I picked up the book and dropped it. I fumbled to pick it up. Finally I stood on trembling legs searching for the right page.

"Hurry, or I'll shoot your aunt."

Lilly looked ready to faint.

I started reading at the top of the page.

He slipped the silk gown over his head, his penis hardened as the soft material caressed his flesh. For years he'd masqueraded as a woman, getting turned on each time he fooled his neighbors. Even the pastor at his church hadn't recognized him. But she had.

From outside his window, she'd watched him strutting around his bedroom, all decked out in silk, a feather boa, and a jeweled tiara. Soon everyone would know his secret.

"That's enough," he said, waving his gun. "Thanks to you, everyone knows what I do in the privacy of my own home."

I swallowed a gulp of air.

Lilly cleared her throat. "My sister, Anne Marie, wrote the books. She's in Europe. Monique isn't the author."

"I don't believe you, either."

I pretended to glance over Marvin's shoulder at an imaginary person. "Don't shoot him. He's a confused old man."

Marvin smirked. "Save your breath, it's not going to work. I know there's nobody behind me."

On a hunch I raised my voice. "Son of a bitch, I'm telling you the truth."

"Son of a bitch," came Long John's scratchy voice from the kitchen. "Make my day, stick'em up, drill you full of holes, let's screw, you have great knockers."

Looking frightened and bewildered, the old man dropped his gun and allowed Lilly and me to duct-tape his wrists and ankles together.

Later that night Jake stood in my living room shaking his head and frowning. "You should have told me what you intended to do."

"You'd have tried to talk me out of it. At least now I have a story. Not front-page, but writing about Marvin sure beats doing my recipe column."

Jake massaged my shoulders as I typed on my keyboard. "How about taking a break and coming to bed?" One stray hand worked its way down the front of my blouse.

I nudged it away. "I don't have time right now. Why don't you pour yourself a beer and watch a little television."

He nibbled my left earlobe. "Is this how you're going to treat me after we're married?"

I glanced at him, crooked smile, teasing eyes, his dark hair tumbling over his forehead. *Tempting.* "Probably. Are you having second thoughts?"

He kissed my cheek. "No, I'm looking forward to July and making you my wife."

"Me, too," I said, turning back to my computer and finishing a sentence.

"I've told all the guys at the precinct we're tying the knot this July."

I tried to think of the perfect word to describe Marvin: sad, dismal, weak, and settled on pathetic. "That's nice."

"You don't sound very enthusiastic."

I inhaled a calming breath for patience and smiled up at him. "I'm very excited about getting married, but I need to finish this before midnight. Otherwise my story won't be printed in tomorrow's paper."

"Okay, Grumpy, I'll leave you alone, at least until you type the last word of your article." He kissed the top of my head and disappeared into the kitchen.

The next day at work Jeannine greeted me with a smile.

"Why do you look so happy?" I asked, tucking my purse into my drawer.

"I'm taking control of my life. I've just had a long talk with Mr. Winters. I told him I was pregnant, and I needed to earn more money. He's giving me a small raise now, plus the newspaper will pay for two college courses a semester until I earn a degree."

"That's wonderful. I thought you weren't interested in becoming a journalist?"

"I'm not, but I like photography, and I'd love being a photographer for the newspaper." Her face glowed with health and happiness.

"I'm glad to hear you're feeling better."

"Me, too." She folded a letter in thirds and tucked it into an envelope before glancing up at me. "Mr. Winters said to tell you he has some good news for you."

Good news!

Horns trumpeted in my head. My heart rate reached its max. Since Mr. Winters had given Jeannine a raise, maybe he was in the mood to give me a raise, too.

Or maybe my own office.

I hurried toward my boss's office and, before I could knock on the glass panel in his door, he waved me inside.

"Come in, Ms. St. Cyr, and have a seat."

I sat across from his desk.

Mr. Winters's phone rang so I amused myself by twisting my engagement ring around my finger and trying to guess what he'd hidden in his cabinet. I wondered where he kept the keys. My imagination had no trouble conjuring the skeletons hidden behind the metal doors.

Sometime back my boss had installed a shade above the glass panel in his door, allowing him privacy whenever he wanted. Each day around lunchtime, he'd tell Doris Cote he didn't want to be disturbed. He'd pull the shade and do whatever he did. My intuition told me the shade was directly related to the metal cabinet.

What dark, dirty, little secrets lay within?

Marvin had hidden behind closed doors, too. Even though I couldn't fathom my boss prancing around with a feather boa, I knew he was hiding something. Maybe he was working undercover for the CIA or FBI. Maybe he was working on a book, an exposé, that he didn't want anyone to see until it was published. Maybe he was stark raving mad and hid the evidence of despicable crimes he committed after sunset.

I knew I was pushing the envelope but stranger things had happened. My reporter's nose twitched. That meant I was either coming into money, I'd kiss a fool, or I was on the trail of another story.

"Ms. St. Cyr," he said, raising his voice. "Have I lost you?"

"No, my mind was wandering for a moment."

"I asked you in here to tell you I'm impressed with your work. The piece you wrote about Mr. Jolicour showed great compassion. Your article read like a mystery, and I found myself holding my breath to get to the ending. Great journalism."

251

"Gee . . . gee . . . thanks." I'd wanted to come out with an eloquent reply, but gee thanks was as good as it got. *How lame.*

"Doris can't seem to say enough nice things about you."

"Doris?" I repeated in disbelief. The *Wicked Witch of the West* never said anything good about me.

"She claims you're the gutsiest woman she's ever met. Frankly, I agree."

Doris was paying me compliments, also known as *kissing butt.*

Why?

Then it came to me. I cringed.

One mystery solved. Doris was Gramps's filly, and she was earning points by trying to befriend his only granddaughter. Though it irked me to accept facts, I couldn't ignore the voice inside my head, whispering the memory I'd tried to erase.

Gramps was her *stud-muffin.*

"You did great work digging up the dirt about Walter Freedman's widow poisoning her husband. I feel bad you weren't able to write the story, but I'm going to make it up to you."

My heart almost burst from my chest. I blinked back tears of gratitude.

"The *Portland Enquirer* is hoping to expand its readership by covering stories on the overseas market."

Clenching my hands together, I pictured myself flashing my press pass and speaking to foreign diplomats.

"Where are you sending me?" I finally asked, my voice shaking despite my best effort to sound calm.

"Spain."

"Oh . . . my . . . God!" All my dreams were coming true. "I can't believe this," I said, jumping to my feet and grabbing Mr. Winters's hands, pumping them up and down. "You won't regret this. I'll make you proud."

He freed himself from my grip. "I'm sure you will. I have great confidence in you."

Gee . . . geeeeee. Fortunately, I kept my less than bright comment to myself.

"What will I be doing in Spain?"

"Covering the running of the bulls."

Gee . . . geeeee. I could hardly wait to tell my great, fantastic, fabulous news to Jeannine, my mother, and Jake. "When will I be leaving?"

"Not until summer. I figured I'd tell you now so you can make plans."

I'd log online and find out about the weather in Spain in the summertime, what to wear, what to eat, whether I could drink the water. I'd purchase a tape and learn some Spanish and acquaint myself with the local customs. I couldn't wait to start my adventure.

I twisted the gold band of my diamond ring around my finger. "When this summer?"

"I'll have to look up the exact dates, but the running of the bulls always takes place the second week in July."

His words chipped away at my euphoria.

Not July, especially not mid-July.

I needed to postpone my wedding.

Chapter Twenty-four

Lilly and I arrived at Don's Parachuting Institute around eight on Saturday morning. The entire operation consisted of a rusty flat-roofed older model trailer set up on a postage-stamp lot and a shed with a gaping hole in the roof.

Shortly after Lilly and I arrived, Don, a jovial man in his late fifties who wore thick eyeglasses, greeted us.

"Glad you could make it."

The howling wind drowned out the last part of his sentence. "Isn't it kind of cold to be jumping from a plane?" It wasn't like I was having second thoughts, more like fifth or sixth thoughts.

Don rubbed his heavy mittens together. "We Mainers are a tough lot. We don't let a little cold and a few flakes of snow slow us down."

"This is another adventure to add to my list," Lilly said, her eyes shining with excitement. Tiny icicles formed on her eyelids.

A rotund man exited the trailer. His bulky frame barely fit through the narrow door, his drooping beer belly straining the buttons on his coat. Don thumbed his hand over his shoulder. "That's Phillip, my baby brother. He's going to help you ladies get ready for the big jump."

"We aren't jumping today," I said. "My mother bought the deluxe plan."

"The only difference between the regular plan and our deluxe plan is you get a T-shirt with our logo."

"According to the registered letter we received, the course is only starting today."

Don gave me a toothless grin. I wondered if he'd lost his teeth in a rough landing.

He laughed. "The entire course takes one morning. I put that in the letter because it sounds better. The truth is the course starts and ends the same day."

"You might as well know I'm not jumping." A rush of wind pelted my face with gravel.

Acting as though he hadn't heard a word I'd said, Don nodded at his sibling. "Set up the boxes for our practice session. We have to hurry. The plane will be ready to leave in an hour or less."

Lilly clapped her gloved hands. "I can't wait."

"Let's not rush this," I said, again the voice of common sense. "What happens if the chute doesn't open?"

Don and Phillip exchanged grins. "Your next lesson's free."

We practiced leaping off boxes and rolling as we dropped onto the frozen ground. Snow caked the snowsuits that Don provided so Lilly and I wouldn't die of exposure during our expedition.

Die of exposure!

"This is a bad idea," I said as we prepared to climb into a rickety plane with a strip of duct tape running along the side.

"Hey, what's the tape holding together?"

Don laughed. "Nothing. We stuck that there as a conversation piece to get your mind off the fear of jumping."

"Are you telling me the truth?" I asked, needing some reassurance.

"If this bird doesn't bust apart," he said, glancing skyward, "then you'll know for sure."

"Look," I said, widening my stance and planting both feet onto solid ground. "I got a good deal for you guys. You already have my mother's check. Let's not waste a perfectly miserable, stormy Saturday to leap from this aircraft. Let's go out for a beer, my treat, and pretend you took us up."

Large hands circled my waist. My feet left the ground and I found myself airlifted into the belly of the plane. Phillip let go of me and shut the only visible means of escape. "If you don't go through with this, you could regret it for the rest of your life."

"Never."

"You'll thank me for this later."

"Let me out."

"There's only one way out."

"Stop the plane."

I felt the rumble of the aircraft's wheels on the snow-packed runway. Bracing myself against the back of a seat, I tried not to fall as the nose rose into the air. I blew out a breath and tried to figure a way out of my dilemma.

I was immersed deep in thought when I caught a glimpse of silver on the chute. It couldn't be. I bent closer. "Is that duct tape on the parachute?"

Don laughed again. "Nope, just a little paint we put on to cover the blood."

"Blood," I said, ready to vomit.

"I thought a little humor might help calm you down."

If I'd been able to release my grip on the chair, I'd have pounded him. "Get it into your head, I'm not jumping."

No one paid any attention.

Finally the plane stabilized, which I figured was bad news as I watched Don and Phil put on their gear.

256

I crossed my arms over my chest. "I'm not jumping."

Phil pushed the hatch open and gave me a long glance that worried me.

"I'm not jumping," I repeated, hoping he'd finally get the message.

Was he deaf? Dumb? A little of both?

Lilly came up beside me. "I'm scared, too, but I'm not missing out on this opportunity. Come on, this is going to be so much fun. And these guys are a hoot."

"They're regular clowns." I stepped back. Against my will, Phillip and Don slid my arms into straps. "You don't get it, do you? I'm not jumping. I'll meet you after the plane lands."

I watched Lilly prepare for her jump. Don hooked himself to my aunt, and they jumped tandem. I peeked out the door and watched them stretch their arms.

Phillip nudged me.

"Are you nuts?" I shouted, elbowing him in the ribs.

"There's no turning back," he informed me. "This plane is headed for Boston."

"Then I'll take a bus home."

"This isn't part of the deal. We'll be billed for your air-fare."

"Live with it," I said, glancing at the crazed look on his face, the determination in his eyes.

I watched him fasten a metal clip to the straps behind me. I pulled in one direction, and he pulled in the other. Desperate and losing ground, I searched the inside of the plane for some means of defending myself.

I saw the fire extinguisher, grabbed it, and bonked Phillip over the head. He lurched forward. Looking back, I watched his eyes roll into their sockets. I thought I was safe until he tumbled backwards out of the plane, taking me with him.

I screamed, the sound swallowed by the roar of the engine, the wind, and the wild beat of my heart.

I glanced down at the thick clouds before glancing over my shoulder at Phillip who looked about as alive as a side of beef. "Wake up," I shouted.

We fell like a boulder, his huge belly pressing into my back as we tumbled out of control.

I wished I'd paid more attention to the directions.

I wished I hadn't skipped dessert last night. I should have eaten two pieces of cheesecake and topped it off with a large Snickers candy bar.

I pictured the crater we'd make.

Imagined the impact.

Get a grip!

I sucked in a breath of icy air and fumbled in the mountainous flab behind me for the pull cord. My fingers felt a rope.

Not sure what to do but having no alternative, I yanked, hard. We whooshed upward and floated, Phillip's head bobbing on my shoulder.

"Wasn't it generous of Don to lend you another snowsuit to wear home?" Aunt Lilly said.

I groaned. He'd had little choice since I'd steered the parachute into a tree. The stiff frozen branches had ripped both my pants and Phillip's.

"I've never felt anything like that in my entire life. I'll have to call Anne Marie and thank her. I'll keep my T-shirt always as a reminder of this day."

I moaned. It would take a while for me to get over this one. Fortunately, I wouldn't be seeing my mother for a long time. My T-shirt would grace the bottom of Long John's cage, logo up, a fitting tribute.

"Wasn't it quite the coincidence that a newspaper cameraman just happened to be in the right place at the right time? The nice young man said I was going to have my picture in the newspaper."

I gritted my teeth. Philip and I swung from the lower limbs of a hemlock tree, our partially clad bodies tethered together, looking as though we'd been caught in a compromising situation. The damn cameraman had snapped our picture, too.

With time I might be able to forgive, but I'd never forget.

No more research for my mother's books.

None, zilch, zero.

No matter what argument she'd concoct, I'd say, *No way, Nohow, Absolutely, Positively, NO!*

For that matter my mother would be lucky if I ever spoke to her again.

Since I couldn't put off telling Jake about my career opportunity much longer, I knew it was time we had a serious talk.

We needed to postpone our wedding until August.

It wasn't as though I wanted to delay getting married, and I had a valid reason. Besides, we hadn't rented a hall or booked the church. What was one more month? Surely he wouldn't get upset about a few short weeks.

Plus, this was a major career move for me. I'd never covered any story outside the state of Maine. Traveling abroad as a reporter was a dream come true. I couldn't allow this opportunity to slip by. We could get married anytime, but the bulls ran on schedule.

Just thinking about the dust and the fevered crowd excited me. I could almost smell the bull dung in the streets along with spectators' sweat and fear. Jake would understand. He had to.

Would he?

259

I got a queasy feeling in the pit of my stomach.

I'd decided to try out the old adage—*the way to a man's heart is through his stomach.* As a backup, I'd purchased chocolate-flavored body paint for later that night.

Fortunately, while hiding out in Elaine's closet, I'd learned Jake's favorite dessert was chocolate cake, chocolate frosting, and mint filling.

I couldn't go wrong with steaks, grilled by Jake so, if they didn't turn out just right, he had only himself to blame. I bought a loaf of French bread and a bag of ready-made salad to which I added shredded cheddar cheese and sliced tomatoes.

I knew better than to make the dessert from scratch. I purchased an unfrosted chocolate cake from the bakery. I picked up ready-made frosting, and, since I couldn't find mint filling, decided to use crushed Junior Mints between the two cake layers.

By the time Jake arrived, I'd showered, shaved my legs, done my hair, makeup, and changed into my new silk robe with a plunging neckline. Underneath I wore a thong and matching skimpy lace bra.

"Wow," he said, running an appreciative gaze over my body.

Get it over with, tell him now, came the small nagging voice inside my head.

But I couldn't, not yet.

"Are you hungry?" I asked and saw the light in his eyes.

"Yes, but food won't quench my appetite."

Dinner was late, very late, and part of that time, I thought I should break up the fun and games and tell Jake about our wedding plans. First I couldn't because my mind and body became immersed in Jake. Afterward, I couldn't because the timing didn't seem right.

We showered together, and while Jake rubbed a thick towel over my back, I wanted to tell him then. But I couldn't bring myself to say the words.

Postpone our wedding.

Three little words. Just blurt them out. Say it, get it over with.

"You're very quiet this evening. Is something wrong?" he asked.

This was the perfect opportunity, my chance to tell him. The words stuck in my throat like a wad of cotton, making it hard to breathe, much less speak. "I'm fine."

"You look better than just fine," he said, slapping my fanny.

Later Jake cooked the steaks on the grill in my backyard. When he entered my kitchen, I'd set the table and put out our salads and dressings.

"I'm famished. If you hadn't waylaid me with your killer body, I'd have eaten long ago," he said with a teasing grin.

"I don't remember twisting your arm."

"I remember you twisting yourself around me," he pointed out with another grin.

We sat next to each other.

I poured diet dressing on my salad. Jake used the real, high-octane stuff.

"Are you dieting again?"

I couldn't go to Spain looking like a lard-butt. "I've decided to trim a few pounds."

"For July, I bet."

I nodded. Yes, only we were talking about two different events. Tell him now. "Jake . . ."

He looked up, and I continued, "The steak is really tender."

I glanced away and speared a tomato wedge.

Tell him, tell him, tell him. Like a someone beating a tom-tom, the incessant chant pounded my brain.

After dessert, I'll tell him then.

Why wait? I'm afraid of the outcome.

"Are you sure everything is all right?"

"Yeah, why do you ask?"

"You seem as though your mind is a hundred miles away." I smile reassuringly.

As we ate, I managed to keep up a conversation, talking about trivial matters, avoiding the subject that mattered the most.

Sometime later I pushed my plate away. "I made something special for dessert," I said, feeling like a jerk for trying to ply him with food in hopes of softening the blow.

I stood and removed the cake from the cupboard and watched his eyes widen in amazement.

"My favorite, how did you know?"

Why hadn't I anticipated that question?

"Would you like a slice?" I asked, avoiding the issue.

"Of course."

I slid two wedges onto plates and sat back down. Jake finished his off and started on mine.

"Aren't you going to eat your cake?"

"I'm not hungry."

"Aren't you feeling well?"

I clenched my hands, took a breath for courage and plunged ahead. "Mr. Winters chose me to cover a news story in Spain."

"That's great. I know how important your career is to you. I'm surprised you waited this long to share your good news. I'd have expected you to jump me coming through the door."

"This is a really, really, great opportunity for me. I can't turn it down. I wouldn't want to turn it down."

Confusion clouding his face, he shook his head. "I wouldn't expect you to turn it down."

Phew, maybe I'd done all this worrying for nothing. Maybe he'd understand. Maybe he wouldn't object to our postponing the wedding for a few weeks.

There's a problem, but I couldn't bring myself to say that. "I'll be covering the running of the bulls in Pamplona, Spain. I'm thinking of signing up for a Spanish course at the high school. I'm so excited."

"I don't understand why you didn't tell me right away."

I gritted my teeth. "There's a small problem. Well . . . it's not a problem really, more of an inconvenience."

He waited patiently, a storm brewing in his dark eyes, his earlier smile gone. The muscle along the side of his jaw twitched.

"The bulls run the second week of July, we need to postpone our wedding, not for long, just a few weeks, or a month at the most. I hope you understand, but then I'm sure you will because this isn't such a big deal."

Phew. I sucked in a deep breath and waited.

"Our wedding might not be a big deal to you, but it is to me."

"That came out all wrong. I didn't mean to put it that way."

"No matter how you word it, the message is the same. I'd told myself that this time would be different. But it's not." He glanced away a moment. "How about getting married sooner?" he asked after a pause.

"I've already checked. May and June are busy months. All the caterers and banquet halls are taken."

"I don't want to wait," he said, sounding like a stubborn child.

"You don't have a choice."

"I've been through all this with Elaine. First you postpone the wedding for a month, then another, then you call it off." His dark eyes focused on me for a long time before he spoke. "If you won't marry me the second week in July, then the wedding is off."

"That's not fair. You promised not to stand in the way of my career."

"And you swore you wouldn't let anything get in the way of our wedding."

"All I want to do is change the date."

"How many more times will you put us on hold for your career? Our wedding date is a symbol of the vow you made to me, and I'm holding you to it. Don't do this to us. I need you to prove I come first."

I understood his past, and I couldn't blame him for wanting proof. Elaine had hurt him deeply. But I carried excess baggage, too. This time, I couldn't turn my back on my dreams.

"Don't ask me to put my career on hold to get married. I shouldn't have to choose."

"There'll be lots of other opportunities."

"You don't know that for sure."

"No, but because of your perseverance, it's bound to happen sooner or later."

He stood, pulled me to my feet, and cradled me in his arms. I knew he was trying to turn my resolve to mush.

And I was tempted.

"Monique," he murmured into my hair. "I love you."

"I love you, too, but don't ask me to refuse this assignment."

"Not even for us?"

Tears blinded me. I stiffened, freed myself from his embrace. "Not only am I covering the running of the bulls, I might just run along with them," I said, having no idea where that moronic thought had come from.

Anger, hurt, stubborn pride, and intense disappointment flooded his face. "Monique, go chase your dreams."

I bit down hard on my lower lip.

He stepped back as though someone had shoved him. "I'm through coming in second."

Chapter Twenty-five

Two weeks later we were at a standstill. Jake wouldn't back down and neither would I. He called twice to chat, and each time I'd hoped he'd ask to come over, but he hadn't.

Meanwhile I still wore his engagement ring, hoping this would blow over, but fearing it wouldn't.

When the phone rang, I dashed across the room and lifted the receiver and was relieved to hear Jake's voice.

"Monique."

My palms grew damp. My stomach clenched. I forced air into my lungs and lowered myself onto the couch. "Hi, how've you been?"

"Good, and you?"

"Good. Well . . . not the greatest."

"I've missed you," he said.

I loved the sound of his voice. So masculine, so caring. "Same here."

"Monique, we need to decide what we're going to do."

I felt a ray of hope. "What do you mean?"

"I have the last two weeks in July off."

"You asked for the time off even after our conversation."

"I put in for my vacation before you talked about postponing the date of our wedding. I was hoping you'd changed your mind. Marry me in July?"

266

His refusal to see my side angered me. "No, I'm going to Spain."

There was a long pause, followed by muffled curses. I squeezed my eyes shut and prayed he'd see things my way, prayed he'd change his mind, prayed he'd come walking through my door and hold me in his arms all day and all night.

"I'm sorry, I'd hoped you'd had time to think about this," he said, a hollow ring to his voice.

"I've thought of nothing else." I twisted my engagement ring around my finger. "Would you like to come over so we can talk?" I finally asked in a shaky whisper, my heart torn.

"There's nothing left to discuss." Another pause. "Is there?"

"Can't we work something out?"

"I won't bend on this," he said. "This time I need to know I come first in our relationship."

I twisted my ring around my finger. "What about the ring?" I asked because I didn't want him to hang up, and I couldn't think of anything else to say.

"Keep it."

Sensing any second I'd turn into a blubbering idiot, I managed to say, "Bye." *I love you.*

Three weeks later I'd given up hope of ever seeing Jake walk through my door. Knowing I'd been right to pursue my career didn't ease the emptiness inside. My life had lost some of its meaning.

Unable to sleep, I climbed out of bed at 3:00 a.m. and went into the kitchen. I poured myself a glass of wine and grabbed the can of Pringles on my way out of the room. I sat on the couch and pulled an afghan over my lap.

Under normal circumstances, wine relaxed me. Since Jake

had left, nothing was normal anymore. Nothing eased my tense muscles. No pill could help me sleep. No joke could make me laugh.

I was sitting there drowning in self-pity when I heard a door close.

I got to my feet and pulled the shade covering my window aside. Not six feet away were Gramps and Doris Cote in a lip-lock.

I snapped my eyes shut, and pretending I hadn't seen a thing, downed my glass of wine, refilled it, and drank that, too, hoping to permanently erase the memory from my mind.

Early the next morning while still dressed in my robe and slippers, I heard a knock followed by the sound of a key in the lock.

My heart skipped a beat.

Lilly entered.

I'd hoped . . .

My stomach clenched with disappointment. *Where was Jake? Was he dating someone else?*

Elaine would eagerly console Jake. Had she taken this opportunity to ignite the flames between them? Had he fallen into her arms to get back at me?

Jake deserved better. I wasn't being fair, but I was beyond fair.

I knew he wouldn't date Elaine to get back at me. But he might go out with her because he was free, and she was there. Attractive, willing to give him what he wanted.

A wife and a mother for his children.

He'd loved her once.

Could he fall in love with her again?

"I hope you don't mind my letting myself in. I wasn't sure if you'd be up yet, so I used Anne Marie's key. I need to borrow some sugar," Lilly said, her eyes glowing, her face flushed.

"What's up with you?"

"Tee hee hee, I sure hope I don't jinx my string of good luck."

"You look happier than usual. What's going on?"

"I have another date tonight."

I'd given up asking for names. That didn't mean I wouldn't spy if given the opportunity.

"You've been out every night this week. When do I get to meet this guy?"

"An introduction isn't necessary. You already know John."

John? How maddening. I had his first name, and I still didn't know his identity. "You're sure that's the right name?"

"Of course, I know my beau's name."

"Do I know him a lot or a little?"

"You see him every day at work."

I thought hard. "There's no John at work."

Lilly's hands fluttered over her face. "You know him as Mr. Winters."

The next day was Sunday, and on Saturday night an awful thought struck. I awoke alarmed and convinced my aunt's safety depended on my ability to solve the mystery of the large filing cabinet in Mr. Winters's office.

Before Lilly became more involved with my boss, I needed to discover his deep, dark, hidden secret. Whatever he'd hidden behind the metal doors could be detrimental to my aunt's happiness.

Though until now I'd never considered the possibility that my boss might be a cross-dresser, I couldn't forget Marvin. The sweet little old man looked like a saint. Who would have thought him capable of holding women at gunpoint? Who'd have thought him capable of prancing around his bedroom in fine silk and a feather boa?

Even as I refused to accept the idea of Mr. Winters in drag, I knew there was only one way to put my mind at rest.

It wasn't as though I was snooping for my sake. I had to protect my gullible aunt who wouldn't know how to read the signs if her date showed up in heels.

So I did the only thing I could think of. I called Jeannine.

She answered on the fifth ring.

"Are you busy?"

I thought I heard a man's voice in the background. "Is someone there with you?"

"A friend, but he's leaving. Why did you call?"

He? I made a note to question her later. "I'm concerned about my aunt. She's going out with our boss."

"Mr. Winters?"

"Yup, and I need you to help me find out if he's a pervert."

On Sunday night the *Portland Enquirer* ran with a skeleton crew. Jeannine and I entered the building and avoided being seen by the maintenance man.

"I can't believe I let you talk me into this," Jeannine said. "I'm about to be a mother, and you have me sneaking into a building to break into our boss's cabinet."

"I appreciate the help, and you won't get into trouble. While I look around Mr. Winters's office, you can sit at your desk and pretend you're there finishing up some work. Once I find the key, I'll see what's inside the cabinet, and we'll leave."

"I still don't understand why you're convinced Mr. Winters is trouble."

"Haven't you noticed how he pulls down his shade every

day? What do you suppose he does behind that closed door?"

She thought a moment. "Maybe he changes into shorts and does some exercises."

"Maybe he dresses in panty hose and a tutu and practices ballet."

Jeannine giggled. "You'll never change."

She was wrong. I had changed. Without Jake, I was a hollow shell without a heart or a soul.

"Who's this friend you've been seeing?"

"He's just a guy who comes over once in a while to talk."

"You're being rather evasive."

"No, just cautious."

I would have questioned her further, but we saw Doris Cote slipping on her coat and heading toward us. I grabbed Jeannine's arm and pulled her into the storage room.

"If someone finds us in here, how are we going to explain that?" Jeannine asked.

"Don't worry, I'll think of something."

Once the way was clear, I tiptoed across the room. Jeannine sat at her desk and waited while I dashed into Mr. Winters's office with a flashlight.

Where would I hide a key?

I tried the top drawer, then all the drawers. I checked under the blotter on the desk, the paper clip holder, and the cup of pencils.

Still no key.

I heard Jeannine's voice. "Hello, Mr. Winters."

"Why are you here so late?" he asked.

Damn!

I looked for a place to hide. Except for under the desk, there was none. And he'd see me there if he sat down.

In desperation, I tried the handle on the cabinet and it twisted open. I jumped inside, which was divided into halves.

One side had hangers and barely enough room for me to stand stooped over. I shut the door, throwing me into total darkness. My flashlight slipped from my hand, and I was unable to reach it.

Since I hadn't had a chance to look, I felt around. My fingers came across a scarf or shawl, something woolen or woven. I pictured my boss traipsing about in public with his head covered, pretending to be a woman.

My worst nightmare had come true.

I heard the lights in his office click on.

"Tee hee hee."

Aunt Lilly!

My heart banged so hard against the metal walls of the cabinet, I was certain I'd be discovered.

"What do you want to show me?" Aunt Lilly asked.

"I don't want us to have any secrets from each other."

"I would never think less of you," my trusting, naïve aunt said. The poor dear didn't understand what she was up against.

"I've never told another living soul. There are some who would laugh at my hobby and think it's feminine, an inappropriate pastime for a man."

I would hardly call cross-dressing a hobby. But to each his own.

Without warning the doors flew open. There I was, crammed between a metal wall and a coat, woolen scarf over my head, confronted by the startled expressions on my aunt's and my boss's faces.

Lilly gasped. "Monique, is that you?"

"Ms. St. Cyr, what in the world are you doing in my closet?"

When I'd finally pried myself loose, I sank into the chair in Mr. Winters's office and tried to ignore the questioning glances.

"Well . . . we're waiting," came my boss's no-nonsense tone.

I thought you might be a cross-dresser.

I couldn't tell him the truth. I decided to stall. "You do lovely work," I said to Mr. Winters as I studied the afghan he'd crocheted. "The scarf is beautiful, too."

"You must swear never to tell another soul what you found out tonight," he said, his tone a stern warning.

"I was concerned for my aunt. I was afraid you might be hiding something terrible inside that cabinet. I did it for Lilly. I apologize and swear never to invade your privacy again."

For a moment I feared he'd fire me. He had ample reason, but as I looked at him closely, I wondered whether he'd heard what I'd said.

Mr. Winters and Lilly exchanged warm glances. I saw love and something else in their eyes.

Lust.

TMI—too much information. I turned away.

Who would have thought that behind the drawn shade, every day Mr. Winters crocheted to bring down his blood pressure.

"You should take up a hobby, Ms. St. Cyr. It might help keep you out of trouble."

"Yes, sir. I apologize again for interfering in your business."

Lilly wrapped a purple scarf around her neck. "Maybe you'll teach me how to crochet?"

Mr. Winters's voice dropped an octave. "I'll teach you anything you want."

I didn't like the sound of that. "Well, I'll be going. Have a good time, you two."

As I closed the door, they seemed unaware I was leaving. I sincerely hoped Mr. Winters didn't take advantage of my aunt's inexperience and gullibility.

A week later Lilly arrived at my apartment looking uneasy.

After the episode in Mr. Winters's office, I'd learned my lesson. I was through prying into other people's business. I was through quizzing people until they broke down and spilled their guts.

Instead of grilling my aunt, I smiled at her. "Would you like a cup of coffee?"

She nodded and sat at the kitchen table. "Have you heard from Jake?"

"No, and it's just as well. I've begun to sleep at night. Hearing his voice would put me back to square one."

"That's too bad. I really liked Jake," Aunt Lilly said sadly, with a faraway look in her eyes.

Man trouble. My instincts couldn't be wrong. It was too bad, but I couldn't fathom what she saw in Mr. Winters.

"Do you ever wish you'd made a different decision?" Lilly asked.

I got the feeling she was talking about herself and not me. "When Jake first left I questioned myself all the time, but I'm beyond that now. I did what I thought I had to do for myself."

"I wish I were more like you."

I poured coffee into two cups and watched Lilly stir sugar into hers. She uttered a long sigh.

What has he done to you? Silently I called Mr. Winters a string of foul names. Still, I held my tongue.

Lilly glanced down and studied the dark brew as if the answers to her problems would magically appear.

"Is anything wrong?" I finally asked, unable to stop myself.

She looked across the room and took a sip of coffee. "Could be good news, could be bad news. I guess it depends on how you look at it. I feel like such a fool."

"Damn Mr. Winters to hell," I said, no longer able to remain calm. "I don't care if he fires me, but when I see him, I'm going to tell him he's a low-down, good-for-nothing jerk."

Startled, Lilly's eyes widened. "John is a very nice man. I think I love him," she finished on a whisper.

Confused, I looked at her, tried to read between her words. "But he doesn't love you? Is that the problem?"

"If I knew the answer to that question, it would make my predicament a lot easier."

"What predicament?"

She set her cup down with a thud. Her eyes misted.

"I'm pregnant."

Chapter Twenty-six

"Pregnant! How can that be?"

A smile tugged at the corners of Lilly's mouth. "You should know. You've read Anne Marie's books."

"Are you sure you're pregnant?"

"The kit at the pharmacy gave me a positive reading."

"How does Mr. Winters feel about having a baby?"

"I haven't told him yet."

"Have you told my mother?"

"No."

Thank you, God!

"I plan to tell John this evening."

"Let's not tell my mother until she returns from her honeymoon," I suggested.

"Anne Marie and I have never had secrets between us," Lilly said, "but I don't want her to cut her honeymoon short because of me."

"Neither do I." My mother would skin me alive. She'd blame me for this entire mess, not that having a baby was a bad thing, but . . .

I'd hit bottom. My life from this point could only improve.

"I have a good idea. Why don't we go to a movie this afternoon, just the two of us to help take our minds off our troubles?"

"Yes, I'd like that."

"Good, you choose."

Lilly reached for the newspaper on my counter.

I refilled our cups and decided donuts were in order. Since I didn't have donuts I settled on Twinkies. I set the box on the table and unwrapped one. I took a bite and noticed my aunt was taking a long time deciding on a movie.

"What's playing?"

"I haven't checked yet," she said, lowering the paper and glancing at me with a strange look in her eyes.

"I have some very bad news for you," she said, her eyes flooding with tears.

My heart clenched with fear as she pushed the paper across the table and pointed toward a photograph of a pretty woman. It was one of those professional pictures which bore no resemblance to the person. I read the caption underneath and thought I'd die.

Elaine Morgan wishes to announce her nuptials to Jake Dube . . .

Chapter Twenty-seven

We never went to the movies. It was an effort for me to walk from one end of my duplex to the other. My phone rang non-stop. I didn't turn on my answering machine because I didn't want to hear the voices of Jeannine and the other people at work calling with their condolences and questions.

Jake and I had broken up. Until now, I'd refused to admit that fact. Though he was free to marry anyone he chose, in the back of my mind I'd never given up hope we'd get back together.

Marriage to another woman had done the trick. I felt as though I was drowning in reality. He would never hold me again. We'd never make love again.

I slipped his ring from my finger, my heart ripping into a million pieces.

I still loved Jake, and I probably always would. But he couldn't have cared for me much if he was able to forget me this quickly.

I ignored the repeated knocking on my door. I ignored the face peering into my window.

More pounding.

"I know you're in there. Let me inside," came Jeannine's voice.

I sniffed. "Go away. I don't want to talk to anyone."

I heard retreating footsteps, a knock on the door to the

other duplex. A couple minutes went by. I heard a key in the lock and watched the doorknob twist.

In walked Jeannine. She slammed the door shut, rushed to my side, and took me in her arms. "Your grandfather gave me the key. Why didn't you let me in?"

I hugged her, totally losing all semblance of control, bawling like a child in her arms.

"I want to be alone," I said between sniffs.

"You shouldn't be by yourself at a time like this. I never thought Jake capable of stooping this low."

"Me neither," I said, blowing my nose and adding the tissue to the growing pile on the end table. "That only shows I did the right thing by sticking to my decision to pursue my career. If he was willing to jump into Elaine's bed this quickly, he wouldn't have stuck by me later on."

Jeannine patted my back. "Would you like a glass of wine?"

"No thanks."

The phone rang and we both glanced at the caller ID.

"It's Jake again," I said, my voice hoarse. "He's been calling for the last half-hour. I'm never speaking to him again."

"I don't blame you."

I heard a car pulling into the driveway, then a knock on the door. Jeannine peeked out the window. "It's Lilly," she said, letting her in.

My aunt stomped across the room like a woman on a mission. "I just returned from giving that hooligan a piece of my mind."

For a moment I set aside my problems. "What did that worm say when you told him you're pregnant?"

Lilly shook her head. "I'm not talking about John. I confronted Jake."

My heart beat double time. "You shouldn't have."

"He's not married to Elaine. He said she put that announcement in the newspaper as a cruel hoax to hurt you."

I felt hope where there was none before. "Did he say anything else . . . about me . . . about us?"

Lilly sighed. "He won't bend. Neither will you. Unfortunately, unless someone takes matters into their own hands, I see little hope in you two getting back together."

Later that week I was babysitting my nephews and making popcorn.

"How's your dad's new girlfriend?"

Both boys shrugged. "Is the popcorn almost ready?"

I removed the bag from the microwave and gave each boy a bowl along with a glass of Coke.

"What's she look like?"

"I dunno," Mark said.

"She's kinda pretty," Matthew added.

I bet she was a real knockout, great figure, big boobs, and couldn't find her way out of a closet with the light on and the door ajar. My brother sure knew how to pick them.

But then, so didn't I.

Thomas arrived a short while later and handed me a dozen yellow carnations.

"What are these for?"

"They're for you."

"How come? What do you want from me?"

He leaned against the kitchen counter while I poured water into a vase. "There's no reason. I wanted you to know how much I appreciate your help."

"This was her idea," spitting out "her" as though the word left behind a bad taste.

He laughed. "Guilty as charged." He hesitated a moment. "Would you like to meet her?"

"When?"

"Now, she's out in the car."

I was shocked a moment later when he walked in with Jeannine by his side.

"You're Thomas's mystery woman?" I asked my friend.

"I'm dating your brother, and I'm taking things slowly."

"Why didn't you tell me?"

"I wanted to. At first, I figured I'd wait and see how things went. Then you and Jake broke off, and I never found a way to bring the subject up."

A moment later Jeannine joined the boys watching *Harry Potter* in the living room.

I eyed my brother closely. "How serious is this?"

He grinned. "Jeannine's afraid of getting hurt again. I'm ready to take another chance. If I have my way, I'll make your best friend my wife."

The next weekend started out as crappy as the rest of the week. The sun shone bright, but my mood was black. Everywhere I turned people were making out and kissing in public. It was damned depressing.

I wasn't even safe in my own home. If I looked out the window at the wrong time, I'd catch a glimpse of Gramps and Doris in a torrid embrace.

Lilly and Mr. Winters ran off and eloped. Last I heard they were heading south on their honeymoon. I'd baby-sat Cobbler in my aunt's absence, and he'd managed to destroy a pair of my favorite heels, two belts, and another purse.

I was so bitchy I could have chewed nails and spit out metal filings. Pity the person who crossed me. I looked around my disorganized duplex and decided to clean house. I started with my bedroom, tossing in the garbage can anything that reminded me of Jake. I decided to buy a new bed. This one held too many memories.

The decision added to my gloom because I'd never forget Jake. But I was mature enough to realize the pain would ease. My heart would mend and I'd be fine. I'd concentrate on building a career.

I heard a knock on the door and was surprised to see Lilly standing there.

"Why are you back so soon?"

"John and I were anxious to start out our married life around people we know." She flashed her left hand, her ring finger weighed down with a large diamond.

"You hit the mother lode," I said, admiring her ring.

"I'm not pregnant. I found out the night before we said our vows. I expected John to call off the ceremony, but he said he loved me, and wanted to go ahead with it."

"Gee, that's wonderful."

"Yes, it is." She bent down and scratched behind Cobbler's ears. "How's my good boy?"

Not so good.

"It was nice having him back home," I fibbed so Lilly wouldn't feel guilty about leaving him with me.

"That a relief to hear," she said, fidgeting with her rings.

"He wasn't any trouble at all."

"That makes me feel so much better."

At this point I started to worry.

"It's not that I don't love him . . ." she said, apprehension screaming a warning inside my brain. "But John is allergic to fur. There's no way I can keep this dog in our home, not without taking a chance of killing my husband."

Damn. I eyed the dog who looked innocent, but I knew better. It seemed we were destined to be together.

"Sure, I'll take him back," I heard myself saying.

"I'll visit him often," Lilly said, tears in her eyes. "I love this dog almost as much as I love John."

To hide my chagrin, I ducked my head and ran my hand over the dog's belly.

"Have you heard from Jake?"

I squared my shoulders. "No, and I don't care. I'm doing very well without him."

"I'm glad to hear that."

Lilly seemed nervous as though she was expecting something to happen.

"Are you feeling all right?"

She yawned. "I'm just tired. John gets pretty frisky . . ."

I waved my hands to ward off the rest of her comment. "Too much information."

"Tee hee hee. How about we go out for lunch, just the two of us?" Lilly asked.

The last thing I needed was to spend time with a happy newlywed, but I didn't want to hurt my aunt's feelings.

"All right. I'll get my coat and meet you outside in a few minutes."

Lilly left to go see Gramps, and I slipped on my jacket, hat, and mittens and dashed out the door, tripping over a sealed box on my stoop.

Once I managed to stand up, I pulled the container into my living room, eager to discover its contents.

At first I thought it might be a gift from my aunt.

The thought pleased me, almost made me happy, until I noticed my name scribbled in marker. I sliced the box open and was horrified to find several of my mother's books, the covers slashed and the pages shredded.

Elaine!

When I got my hands on that bitch, she wouldn't have one hair left on her head.

While I knelt on the floor getting angrier by the minute, I heard glass shatter. Running into the kitchen, I found a

283

broken window and a brick in my sink. I picked up the brick and freed the piece of paper held there with an elastic.

Stop or you'll be sorry!

Out of breath, Lilly dashed into my duplex. "What's all the commotion?" She eyed the brick, the note, and the box of books. I watched her run across the room and punch in the numbers on my keypad to set the alarm.

"Get your gun. I'm calling Jake."

Before I could refuse, I heard her speak into the receiver. "Jake, tell your girlfriend to leave Monique alone."

I couldn't hear his reply, but Lilly remained firm.

"Don't play innocent with me. Elaine, the little bitch, sent Monique a box of destroyed books."

Go, Lilly!

She hung up and turned around. "He'll be right over."

Jake arrived ten minutes later. Beneath his black leather jacket, he wore tight Levi's and a moss-green turtleneck. He looked even better than I remembered.

Lilly stood in the living room, leafing through a magazine as though trying to give us some privacy.

Jake examined the box. He picked up the brick and studied the note. "Elaine didn't do this."

Hearing him defend her hurt me more than I'd thought possible.

His face was shadowed with a day's growth of beard. I was tempted to run a finger along the edge of his jaw. I dropped my arms and sneered, "I'm not surprised you'd say that."

"Elaine is gone. I watched her board the plane to Hawaii yesterday. She's not coming back."

A great weight left my shoulders.

Did he miss her? Did he miss me?

Did it matter?

For a moment I lost myself in his chocolate brown eyes. When he'd teased me, they'd danced with mischief. Only now his eyes were serious. They'd lost their sparkle. They'd lost their life.

Was he as miserable as I was?

Did he wake up and think of me in the middle of the night and yearn for my touch as I did his?

"If Elaine didn't do this, then who did?"

"Beats me. I'll call the precinct and have someone else take this case."

Was he anxious to get away from me?

My throat thickened with dread. I didn't want him to leave, but he couldn't stay. No good would come of prolonging his departure. Yet I heard myself ask, "Can I get you a beer?"

"No thanks."

He'd answered quickly, much too quickly, as if he couldn't wait to escape.

My heart stilled. My hands grew slick with perspiration.

"I'll call this in and be on my way," he said, carefully avoiding my gaze.

Lilly entered the kitchen and looked sadly at both of us.

"There's no need to call the police. I threw the brick in hopes of waking you two jackasses up. You love each other. You're miserable apart, yet you're both too stubborn to bend one iota."

"You threw the brick?" I asked in disbelief.

"Bet your sweet bippy I did. I shredded the books, too. I only wish that brick had hit both of you in the head, maybe knocked some sense into you. But I can see by your faces brimming with foolish pride that I've wasted my time."

Without a backward glance she marched out, slamming the door behind her.

That left Jake and me alone, staring at each other, with no one around to run interference.

"I'm sorry if you came over here for nothing," I said, unable to take the silence any longer.

He stepped a little closer. "It wasn't for nothing. It was good seeing you again."

"Oh . . . really . . ."

"Yes, really." He glanced down at my hand. "What did you do with the ring?"

"It's in the box in my dresser."

"I thought maybe you'd sell it."

"I could never do that, never . . ." I said, fighting tears and seeing a ray of hope in his dark eyes.

"Where do we go from here?"

"Where do you want to go?"

He grinned. "I want to take you to bed, but that won't solve anything."

Mmmmm, tempting.

I reached up and rested my hand on his arm. Tiny barbs of electricity zapped my fingertips.

I feared when I was through speaking my mind, he'd leave and never return, but I owed him the truth. "I want to pursue my career. That means going to Spain in July."

He inched closer.

My heart skipped a beat.

I smelled his spicy aftershave. "I've been thinking of signing up for the Spanish course the high school is offering."

Doubting my legs could support me much longer, I braced one hand against the counter.

"What are you saying?"

"Let's go to Spain together. We'll get married there in July. You can cover your story, and I'll cover you . . . with my body," he said, his voice deep, lustful, horny.

A shiver raced up my spine.

I rushed into his arms, sinking into his embrace, feeling as though I'd finally arrived home. Jake crushed my mouth in a long kiss, his tongue delving against mine like old times.

We belonged together. We'd never stray apart again.

He bent down and slipping a hand under my knees, cradled me in his arms and carried me into the bedroom. He set me down on the bed and looked at me as though he'd never seen me until now.

"I love you," he said, before shedding his clothes and lying down beside me.

We didn't speak for some time, but what we didn't say in words, we said with our actions.

We loved each other, and we'd never allow anything to come between us again.

Later that night Jake leaned over me. "Do you really intend to run with the bulls?"

I hadn't given the matter much thought, but the idea appealed to me. "Sure, how else can I write about it if I don't experience the thrill myself?"

"Won't you be afraid of getting gored?"

"No. I'm bringing along my gun. If a bull gets too close, I'll pop him between his eyes with a blue paint pellet."

"You'll never learn," he said, kissing the tip of my nose.

"Nope." I reached for the chocolate-flavored body paint.

"Don't you dare . . ."

I tossed my head back and laughed, feeling more alive than I had in weeks. "Stick 'em up, copper," I said, squirting his chest.

He tried to wrestle the tube of paint from my hands. "Continue doing that and you'll be sorry."

I didn't stop.

Jake was wrong.

It turned out I wasn't sorry at all.

About the Author

Diane Amos lives with her husband, Dave, in a small town north of Portland, Maine. They have four grown children, a finicky Siamese named Sabrina and an energetic miniature dachshund named Molly. Diane is an established Maine artist. Her paintings are in private collections across the United States. She is a Golden Heart finalist and winner of the Maggie Award for Excellence. *Mixed Blessings* is the sequel to *Getting Personal*, Diane's debut novel. For more information about her first book, which *Romantic Times* called a definite keeper, a fun, lighthearted story that does have its more serious moments, check out her Web site at www.dianeamos.com.